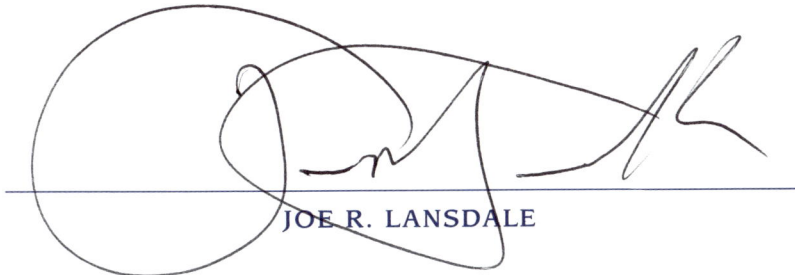

JOE R. LANSDALE

JOHN L. LANSDALE

This special signed edition is limited to 500 numbered copies and 26 lettered copies.

This is copy **490**.

SHADOWS WEST

SHADOWS WEST

JOE R. LANSDALE

JOHN L. LANSDALE

SUBTERRANEAN PRESS 2012

East Baton Rouge Parish Library
Baton Rouge, Louisiana

Shadows West Copyright © 2012
by Joe R. Lansdale and John L. Lansdale.
All rights reserved.

Dust jacket illustration Copyright © 2012
by Timothy Truman. All rights reserved.

Interior design Copyright © 2012
by Desert Isle Design, LLC. All rights reserved.

First Edition

ISBN
978-1-59606-432-4

Subterranean Press
PO Box 190106
Burton, MI 48519

www.subterraneanpress.com

TABLE OF CONTENTS

7   **RIDING WITH THE DEAD**
by Joe R. Lansdale

11   **HELL'S BOUNTY**

147   **DEADMAN'S ROAD**

277   **DEAD IN THE WEST**

RIDING WITH THE DEAD

BY JOE R. LANSDALE

These three screenplays have two things in common. None of them have been produced, and they are all about the West. The weird west.

One of them, "Dead in the West," is based on a novel I wrote years ago, the screenplay written about the same time, and another, "Hell's Bounty," is the source for a forthcoming novel written with my brother, John L. Lansdale.

"Dead in the West" was optioned a number of times as a novel and/or screenplay, and was eventually sold and never filmed. The novel, and to some extent the screenplay, have been a sizeable influence on the popularity of the weird western, which is surprising to me, but gratifying. They have done their work in small doses, over several printings with different companies, and have even spawned imitators overseas. In fact, it was a French company, Vertigo, that bought the screenplay and never produced it. Over the years, a number of American companies have tried to buy the rights, or go into some sort of partnership with the French producers, and the French owners always seem enthusiastic until it's time to close the deal, then they vaporize. Not sure what's going on there, but hey, they bought the rights. They can stick it up their butts and ride around on it if they want; but it sure seems like a loss of a good film.

The other screenplays were written for a small production company that never quite worked out. "Hell's Bounty" was the first, and it was a little too expensive for what they had in mind, and by the time we did a second, based on my short story, "Deadman's Road," the whole deal had gone south. This is often the case, and it's why I no longer write on spec, not something I ever did much of anyway.

"Deadman's Road," the screenplay, not the story, and "Hell's Bounty" were both written with my older brother, John, who has written a number of comic scripts, and is at work these days on a novel.

The screenplay for "Hell's Bounty" was written in a few days, and polished in a few more. It just jumped out of the lap top. It was written with my brother at his home, and we argued over it up and down until we got what we wanted. John is more traditional than I am, and I'm a little bit out there. What happened is, through discussion, we came up with a kind of story neither of us might have written alone. I do credit my brother with most of the characters, as he got excited and worked them out before we ever sat down to write. Which is opposite of how I work. I never know the story or the characters until I sit down. However, working on a collaboration, it's a little more necessary to have an agreement between one another on who's who in the story and where things are going, at least to some extent.

Now, having said my brother is more traditional, I have to also say that a couple of the scenes I like best in "Hell's Bounty," the odder scenes, he came up with. The tree full of the dead, for example. That's all I'll say. You'll come to it when you read the script. So, it was an interesting and fruitful collaboration, and either of these would make fine movies.

"Deadman's Road" is even more low budget in intent. And though it's based on my short story of the same name, it's vastly different from the short story. The main character, the same protagonist preacher who starred in *Dead in the West*, has changed into another character, and he's been given a partner. But I don't want to say too much about the screenplays. It's best that you discover them as you read, and on that note I should add that our screenplays are designed to be easily and happily read. We hope they are like watching a motion picture in your head, only better—you get to create with your imagination more than a movie could ever show.

So, I'm excited to have "Dead in the West," my screenplay, back in print—as it was printed some many years ago—and to have the ones my brother and I wrote together grouped with it. They all fit together nicely as a trio of six gun excitement, with a twist of weird on the side.

Put on your cowboy hats and boots and a Halloween mask, and enjoy.

Joe R. Lansdale
Nacogdoches, Texas

BY JOE R. LANSDALE
& JOHN L. LANSDALE

FADE IN ON:

FULL MOON in a velvet black sky surrounded by bright stars.

CAMERA DROPS DOWN ON

Mountainous area and a wooden sign that reads FALLING ROCK MINING COMPANY. The sign hangs askew. The CAMERA ROAMS over a boarded up mine shaft, as a DARK CLOUD blows out of the shaft, sending boards asunder. The cloud rises up in a tumbling wad, fills the night until everything is–

DARK

HOLD A BEAT

HOLD

HOLD

Then the cloud breaks apart like ripped cotton, flutters into millions of SCREECHING BATS, and the moon is visible again, the hot silver pin tips of the stars. The bats fly in all directions, then merge again, move as one, like a V Wing Fighter plane.

IN THE SKY WITH THE BATS – THEIR POV

ESTABLISHING SHOT of FALLING ROCK, a typical Western town of the late 1880s. As the bats dive down we get a glimpse of the lighted saloon, HEAR a plinking piano, and shrill laughter spills out into the street. The bats sail on. Horses tied along the route begin to snort, buck and kick.

Keep FLOWING with the bats as they rise and head straight for the belfry of a bell tower. They enter into the tower thick as flies on rot, then puff into a thick swirl of black smoke.

The smoke forms a dark pillar, and suddenly we are looking at the shadow-shape of a man silhouetted by the moonlight. We can't make out features, just the shape and some very ugly red eyes. Wings extend from the shadow's back, flap once, twice, fold against the back of the shadow and are still. The shape opens a small silver box, and out of it fly red streaks that dart to the bell, make impact, then scamper to the edge of it and crawl inside.

INT. BELL

The red streaks become living hieroglyphics that scuttle about like ants on a hot skillet. Finally they settle down, lose their glow, leaving only the vague shapes of the hieroglyphics clinging to the interior of the bell.

The shadow jumps from the bell tower, flapping wings and flying across the moonlit sky like a great bird of prey.

EXT. SALOON – THE LIGHTED DOORWAY

A MAN comes flying out through bat wings, a foot at his ass. He tumbles across the boardwalk and into the street, his hat sliding away from him.

Following him into the street is a big man holding a bottle in one hand, a crumpled hat in the other. This is TRUMBO QUILL. He's looks mean enough to eat tacks and shit horseshoes.

                    QUILL
            You don't sit on a man's hat.

The man in the street is trying to scramble to his feet, but Quill is on him with the bottle, whacks him with it a couple of times, breaking it.

Quill grabs the man by the shirt front, jerks him up and slashes his face with the bottle, tosses him back against the ground.

The man scrambles to his feet, starts running down the street. Quill drops the broken bottle, jerks his gun, shoots the man in the back of the knee. The man falls, rolling the dirt.

Quill walks up on him, stands over him.

                MAN
    Oh, Jesus, my leg. My goddamn leg. You
    ruined it, Quill.

                QUILL
    I'll fix it.

Quill puts his crumpled hat on his head with one hand, lifts the revolver, shoots the man right between the eyes.

              QUILL (CONT'D)
    All better now.

Quill drops his gun in the holster, removes his hat, straightens it as he walks back to the saloon. He stands in the light falling out of the doorway. Without looking into the saloon, still fidgeting with his hat, he yells–

              QUILL (CONT'D)
    Double Shot! Bring me a bottle.

Bursting out of the saloon, a skinny bartender, DOUBLE SHOT, in a striped shirt and a bow tie. He has a bottle in his hand, and he is really moving. He hands the bottle to Quill who takes it absently while he puts his hat on his head.

                    QUILL (CONT'D)
          Put it on my marker.

                    DOUBLE SHOT
          Yes, sir.

MOMENTS LATER

Quill is trudging up the dark street with the bottle, and we can see ahead of him tombstones and old wooden crosses. Quill passes a little marker that says: BOOT HILL.

Quill comes to a tombstone at the peak of the hill, near a big oak. A winged shadow settles in behind him on a tombstone, but we can't see it well, just a kind of bulky shape lost in the background.

Quill opens his bottle by pulling the cork loose with his teeth. He spits the cork away, takes a swig, and pours a splash on the grave. He bends down, starts pulling at a few weeds on the grave mound.

                    A VOICE
          Would you like to have her back.

Quill whirls, still hanging onto the bottle with one hand, drawing his pistol with the other.

ON TOMBSTONE

Perched there like a vulture, the shadow shape we see. We can see his eyes glowing and we can see a flash of teeth in the moonlight. But that's it. He looks like a tar baby.

                    QUILL
          What the hell are you?

                    A VOICE/SHADOW
          I'm your wish come true.

> **QUILL**
> What wish?

> **A VOICE/SHADOW**
> Your wife. You loved her, didn't you?

Quill slowly lowers his gun.

> **QUILL**
> The only thing I ever really loved... How do you know about me, about her?

> **A VOICE/SHADOW**
> A little bat told me.

> **QUILL**
> If you're telling me to pray for a miracle, or just for peace, that's what the preacher told me when she died of the pox. He's buried at the bottom of the hill.

> **A VOICE/SHADOW**
> Quite the contrary. Preachers. They're a dime a dozen. But I, on the other hand... All you have to do is sell me something.

Quill gives a lopsided grin.

> **QUILL**
> My soul? That what you're getting at? You the devil or something?

> **A VOICE/SHADOW**
> Something?

> **QUILL**
> You can bring her back, you can have my soul, my pecker, my goddamn horse and saddle.

                    A VOICE/SHADOW
          Then it's a deal?

                    QUILL
          Bring her back, it's a deal. You can't, I'm
          gonna shoot you off of that stone like a
          sparrow.

The shadow shape shows shiny, smiling teeth. It's like a Cheshire cat grin.

Then, the shape scratches it's dark right hand with a left hand talon.

CLOSE ON THAT SHADOW HAND

It appears to leak black ink.

BACK TO SCENE

The shadow extends it's dripping hand. Quill gets the idea, puts his hand out. Very quickly, the shadow cuts into Quill's open palm with his talon, causing it to bleed. And then they clasp hands. A tremor runs over Quill. When they release–

                    QUILL (CONT'D)
          You took my soul?

                    THE VOICE/SHADOW
          Not yet. Time will come.

                    QUILL
          You made me a promise.

                    THE VOICE/SHADOW
          Indeed, I did.

The shape waves a hand at the grave and the shadows on the grave began to squirm and the dirt crawls and a gap opens up. We can glimpse the coffin there.

HELL'S BOUNTY

Then the coffin cracks open, and a long fingered white hand pushes up through the wood. Quill's mouth hangs open.

Quill drops the bottle and the gun, falls to his knees, starts tearing at the wood of the coffin, causing his hands to bleed.

Through the split in the wood we see a face, a beautiful face of a woman with jet-black hair, wearing a white gown.

Quill manages to jerk the shattered lid off the cffin. The woman sits up, turns, looks at him.

Tears run down Quill's face.

A VOICE/SHADOW
She's all yours.

MOMENTS LATER

Quill is carrying the woman down the hill in his arms. She is hanging onto his neck as Quill hugs her to him tight, WHISPERING SOMETHING TO HER THAT WE CAN'T HEAR.

CLOSER ON SCENE

Her foot falls off.

Then one of her arms.

And then her whole body falls apart like a rotten marionette and crumbles to the ground.

QUILL
No! No!

Quill whirls toward the hill, drawing his gun.

QUILL (CONT'D)
You sonofabitch, you can't do that.

Quill jerks his gun and starts firing at the hill, firing in all directions, the bullets blazing at nothing. The gun clicks empty three or four times, and Quill falls to his knees amongst the remains of his wife, hanging his head.

SLOW DISSOLVE TO:

HIGH NOON

A LONE RIDER

Sitting comfortably in the saddle, riding a paint horse past a sign that reads: FALLING ROCK. The rider is weather-beaten with a black mustache, dark hair sticking out from under a wide-brimmed, sweat-stained, black hat. He's dressed all in black, except for a concho-studded vest and rawhide coat. He carries a cross-draw .44 Colt revolver. This is SMITH.

A LOGO APPEARS: 1878, WYOMING TERRITORY

FALLING ROCK

As Smith rides in, we get a look at the town, GENERAL STORE, BESSIE'S CLOTHES EMPORIUM, a tall BELL TOWER from which hangs a bright, copper bell big enough to live in, FALLING ROCK MINING ASSAY OFFICE, the livery, a few other buildings. Smith stops in front of the SUNDOWN SALOON, swings off his horse, pauses to open his saddlebag, and we go–

CLOSE ON SADDLEBAG

He opens it up. Inside, lots of sticks of dynamite.

BACK TO SCENE

He takes out one stick, pops a knife from his pocket, and snips the fuse short, sticks the dynamite in his belt.

INT. SALOON

HELL'S BOUNTY

It's not much. Clapboard walls, rough board floors with cracks wide enough to piss through. An overturned spittoon. A fly-specked mirror.

Smith comes into the saloon. Patrons look up. They are a sparse crew. A tall, slim, slick-haired BARTENDER is wiping whisky glasses with an almost clean rag. Three men are standing at the bar. TYPICAL ROWDIES.

Farther down the bar a COCKY KID. He's decked out in fancy clothes and fancy twin revolvers.

Across the way, at a table, TWO MEN wearing buckskins coated with trail dust, have buffalo guns propped nearby. A plump SALOON GIRL sits in the lap of one. The man and the saloon girl are grinning at one another.

At another table, his head lying on it, is a gray haired man, his hand clutched around an empty whisky bottle.

Smith goes to the bar.

SMITH
Whisky...in a clean glass.

The bartender, Double Shot, pours him one. Smith throws it back, turns, focuses on a table with three men playing cards.

CARD TABLE

TRUMBO QUILL. His clothes are dirty and he could grow corn under his nails. He's looking rougher than when we saw him last.

Also at the table, LESTER MCBRIDE, the undertaker, is the dealer. Weepy-eyed, red nosed, wearing a black suit and tie.

The other man is an Indian. He has a broken nose, jagged scar on his cheek. He's short-haired, wearing a derby sporting a feather. The derby is pushed back at a jaunty angle. This is BULL.

BACK TO SCENE

Cocky kid strolls over to Smith, nods at Smith's revolver.

                COCKY KID
    Nice gun.

                SMITH
    My mother gave it to me.

Cocky kid considers on this.

                COCKY KID
    Kind of an odd gift, don't you think?

                SMITH
    You don't know my mother.

                COCKY KID
    Is that a stick of dynamite?

                SMITH
    Nope.

Kid gives Smith a sour look, pushes back his coat to show his revolvers at a better angle, taps his hands on the hilts.

                COCKY KID
    You ought not to push me, Mister. These here guns were ordered special. Took six months to get here, and I don't wear 'em just for looks.

                SMITH
    No shit?

                COCKY KID
    You making fun of me?

> SMITH
>
> That's too much work.
>
> COCKY KID
>
> I'm fast, Mister. Real fast. You shouldn't mess with me.

Cocky Kid starts to bring his hand down to draw his right revolver, and when he does Smith snake-strike quick pulls the kid's other revolver and strikes him over the head with the barrel of it. The kid drops to the floor like a dead bird.

Smith casually lays the kid's revolver on the bar, points to his glass. Double Shot pours him another. Quickly. Smith carries his drink over to the card table, speaks to the occupants.

> SMITH
>
> Name's Smith... Man get a hand in this game?

Quill tosses his head toward the unconscious kid on the floor.

> QUILL
>
> Think you done bent the barrel on that special ordered gun.
>
> MCBRIDE
>
> Kind of an odd place to carry that dynamite, ain't it? Wouldn't take much for us all to go up.
>
> SMITH
>
> Can't say I'm bothered.
>
> QUILL
>
> What about the rest of us?
>
> SMITH
>
> You'll just have to be nervous.

Quill doesn't like this, but grins at Smith.

> **QUILL**
> It don't worry you none, it don't worry me none.

Smith turns his attention to Bull.

> **SMITH**
> What about you? You the nervous type?

Bull pushing his hat back even more.

> **BULL**
> Ain't no skin off my ass.

> **MCBRIDE**
> Payday! Bring another deck, this one ain't worth a chit.

ANGLE BEADED CURTAIN

As PAYDAY comes through, and as the curtain falls behind her we can see a stairway back there. Payday is a pretty, young woman wearing a fluffy white dress with blood-red flowers, knee-high black-laced boots. Her hair is the color of a brush fire, her eyes are break-your-heart blue. She's carrying cards.

TABLE

Payday puts the deck on the table. McBride, the dealer, picks it up and starts to strip it open. Payday looks at Smith.

> **PAYDAY**
> Bring you a bottle, stranger?

> **SMITH**
> Stranger. That must be me... Why not?
> Bring me anything that don't kill me, Red.

PAYDAY
People here call me Payday, not Red.

As Payday goes to the bar.

SMITH
Kind of strange name for a pretty lady.

MCBRIDE
That's because she takes everyone's payday. Either in the saloon or the bed.

Payday comes back to the table with the bottle, sets it by Smith. As she does, she notices what Smith is looking at. Quill's personal whisky bottle is placed by him and in such a way, that when he holds his cards, his hand is reflected in it. That's what Smith is looking at, and now it's what Payday is looking at. She turns and looks at Smith as he looks at her. She smiles.

PAYDAY
I got a feeling you're lucky, Mister.

Smith, glancing at Quill's whisky bottle.

SMITH
Could be.

Quill looks Payday over, puts his cards down.

QUILL
But I'm not.

Smith's face. He's disappointed. He thought he had this hand.

QUILL (CONT'D)
Fact is, way the cards are running, think I'll let Payday earn a bit of business.

> PAYDAY
> I don't like your business.

> QUILL
> You'll like it if I say you'll like it.

> PAYDAY
> Talk all day, I still won't like it.

Quill turns in his chair, glares at Payday.

SALOON GIRL

With the buffalo hunters, rises, walks toward Quill.

> SALOON GIRL
> I'll do you, Quill.

> QUILL
> (to Saloon Girl)
> I don't fuck goats.

The Saloon Girl pauses, as if hit with a mallet.

Quill looks at Payday, hard.

> QUILL (CONT'D)
> You know I run this town. You don't tell me no.

Quill stands up, takes Payday's arm.

> QUILL (CONT'D)
> I'm gonna show you what a real man's got.

> PAYDAY
> Seen what you got. You couldn't find it with tweezers and a magnifying glass.

Soon as Paydays says this, she knows she's messed up. Quill slaps her, and starts dragging her toward the curtain. She reaches for his gun, almost has it.

Quill's hand comes down on top of hers, pushes it aside.

> **QUILL**
> Oh no, I know what you can do with that.

He continues pulling her along, and then disappears through the curtain with her. We HEAR steps going up the stairs, a bit of a struggle from Payday, and–

> **QUILL (O.S.) (CONT'D)**
> No one talks to me like that, bitch.

Bull turns slightly.

> **BULL**
> (jovially)
> Seconds.

Saloon girl comes to the table.

> **SALOON GIRL**
> You, Mister. Won't you help her?

Smith shrugs.

> **SMITH**
> Leave me out of it. I learned a long time ago to mind my own business.

Ths Saloon Girl, surprised, backs off, fades away.

SCREAMING begins from upstairs, Quill CURSING. We can hear SLAPS and STRIKES.

Bull scoots back his chair, stands up.

                BULL
Guess I'll go get in line while there's some left.

                SMITH
Not today.

Bull turns and looks at Smith.

                BULL
What?

Casually, Smith opens his coat, pulls out a wanted poster. He puts it on the table, smooths it out, taps a finger on it.

INSERT POSTER

It's a drawing of Bull.

BACK TO SCENE

                SMITH
That's you.

Bull looks at it. He looks more amused than concerned.

                BULL
I'm a lot cuter than that.

                SMITH
Says dead or alive. Dead is easier.

Bull is starting to back up, throwing his coat open. He has a sawed off shotgun, the stock is sawed too. It's in a makeshift holster.

                BULL
First I got to be dead, Mister. And I'm no kid.

Bull goes for his sawed off, jerks it free. Smith, still sitting at the table, moves. It's so fast it's damn near a blur. He fires, and–

ON BULL

A small dark dot appears between his eyes. His hand drops, his gun fires into the floor as he collapses.

BACK TO SCENE

Smith looks around, just in case anyone is feeling frisky. McBride, just to make sure Smith doesn't get it wrong, raises both hands.

                MCBRIDE
     It's okay with me, Mister. I'm the undertaker.

                SMITH
     You don't get this one.

Smith folds up and puts away his wanted poster, goes around and hoists Bull's dead body up into a kind of fireman's carry. In the process, Smith's hat is knocked off.

From upstairs we HEAR–

                QUILL (O.S.)
     I'll cut your damn face off, whore.

EXT. SALOON

Smith carrying Bull's body. He looks left, then right. He sees a horse other than his own at a hitching post. He takes the body and drapes it over the horse.

As he walks back to the saloon, DOUBLE SHOT, standing at the entrance–

> DOUBLE SHOT
> (meekly)
> That's Quill horse, sir.

As Smith pushes past him.

> SMITH
> No shit.

INT. SALOON

Smith goes to where his hat fell. As he picks up his hat, the–

BEADED CURTAIN

Separates, and stumbling out of it comes Payday. She has a hand over one side of her face, covering her eye.

ON PAYDAY

She turns with her back toward us, her hand falling from her face, she looks at the patrons in the saloon. They see what we don't, and REACT to it. It's obviously a shock.

Payday's hand goes back to her eye, and she falls to the floor against the bar.

ANOTHER ANGLE

Smith watches all of this, and without so much as an expression, lights his cigar, starts outside, carrying his hat.

As Smith exits, the Saloon Girl is shaking the gray-haired man with the bottle.

> SALOON GIRL
> Doc! Wake up! Doc. Payday. Quill's done cut her up.

HELL'S BOUNTY

Doc stirs, staggers in the direction of Payday. Saloon girl reaches down, picks up his doctor bag from the floor; it's the first time we've seen it.

ANGLE QUILL

Coming through the curtain, buttoning up his pants. He goes to the bar and takes a bottle setting there and swigs. He watches Doc and Saloon Girl as they bend over the unconscious Payday.

> **QUILL**
> Hey, Doc. Fix that whore up, they'll still have to put a sack over her head and give away free beer to sell her.

> **DOUBLE SHOT**
> Uh, Mr. Quill.

> **QUILL**
> Teach that whore to make sport of me.

> **DOUBLE SHOT**
> Mr. Quill...

> **QUILL**
> What, goddamnit! What do you want? You're starting to annoy me.

> **DOUBLE SHOT**
> Your horse. The stranger done shot Bull and put him on it.

Quill, taking off his hat and slapping it against his leg.

> **QUILL**
> Sonofabitch, knew that hombre was up to something. Ain't nothing going right these days. Give me that Winchester.

Double Shot scurries away.

EXT. SALOON

Smith is still holding his hat. He takes the reins of his horse, goes to Quill's horse, is about to unleash it, raises his hat to put it on–

And Quill's horse spooks, bucks, snaps the reins loose of the hitching post and thunders off down the street in a cloud of dust.

ON SMITH

SMITH
Well, I'll be damned.

Smith climbs quickly onto his horse, starts riding hard toward Quill's disappearing mount and Bull's body.

QUILL

Steps outside the saloon with a Winchester in his hand.

SMITH

Riding hard out of town.

QUILL

Lifts the rifle and FIRES. Smith's horse buckles, goes down, dead as a doornail.

ANOTHER ANGLE

Smith is up. We see his back. We see a white puff rise up over his head from his cigar. He turns and starts walking back toward Quill, puffing the cigar, the revolver still in his hand.

A SHOT from Quill knocks Smith's hat off. Smith FIRES back, puts a hole through the flare of Quill's coat. Quill jumps back inside the saloon so furiously he knocks one of the bat wings off. He BLAZES BACK from the protection of the saloon wall.

Smith keeps walking, FIRING his revolver, ONCE, TWICE.

The shots tear at the edge of the saloon, BLOWING SPLINTERS back in Quill's face, but not doing any serious good.

Smith keeps walking straight toward Quill, not trying to be clever, not trying to avoid anything.

Quill SNAPS OFF A SHOT. This one hits. Smith turns a bit, winces. But HE KEEPS COMING. He's real close now. He pulls the stick of dynamite from his belt, lights it off his cigar.

Quill SHOOTS again. Hits Smith in the chest. Smith staggers, doesn't go down. He pulls his hand back to throw the dynamite, but–

ON FUSE

The fuse is about to go.

ON SMITH LOOKING AT FUSE

He winces.

                         SMITH (CONT'D)
    Shit. Too short.

IT BLOWS, and–

THE EXPLOSION

In SLO MO as Smith and his duds come apart in a whirl of explosives, blood and bone, and we–

                                                CUT TO:

INT. SHINY SALOON

This one is much neater than the saloon in Falling Rock. It's tricked out with a huge mirror and shiny beer taps and rows of shimmering bottles of liquor, a long bar with a silver foot-rest.

A SNAPPY-LOOKING BARTENDER

is behind the bar. His eyebrows are amazingly arched, and his hair is slicked down flat and parted in the center. He is wearing a striped shirt with elbow garters. He is polishing glasses. FAT FLIES are hovering all about him. We can HEAR THEM BUZZING LOUDLY.

WIDEN

It is a large and fine establishment, but, nifty as it looks, it is infested with these flies, fluttering here and there, landing on everything. There are people sitting at tables. They come from all eras of history.

One of them is a Roman soldier, headless and he's sitting with his helmet-wearing head on his knee, pouring a drink into the head's mouth. The drink, along with blood, runs out of the stump of his neck, onto the cowpoke's pants, but the drinking head looks satisfied, smacks its lips.

There are others at tables, women and men of different eras, gladiators, frontiersman, you name it, and most of them look like rough customers. Some have bullet holes in their heads, and in fact, BULL is sitting there, having a drink, flies on the brim of his bowler hat. One lights on the hole in his forehead.

Across the way is a–

DOOR

And it abruptly BURSTS OPEN. A wheelbarrow is taxied through, and pushing it is a MUSCULAR YOUNG BLONDE WOMAN wearing as little as possible. She is tanned and tattooed and there are pops of sweat all over what is visible of her body, and that's a lot. The tattoos crawl.

In the wheelbarrow we recognize body parts, and Smith's clothing. The contents of the wheelbarrow is steaming and it's bloody and is really scrambled with guts and brains and bone. Smith's black hat rests in the center of the pile. The flies flock to this mess, so enthusiastically, and so loud, they SOUND LIKE A BUZZ SAW.

The blonde tips the wheelbarrow, and this mess SPLATS onto the floor, runs a little, then heaps up, and SMITH, whole, stands up, brushes himself off, picks up his hat, and with flies all about him, makes his way to the bar, bellies up to it, puts a booted foot on the foot rest. He turns to look at the–

MUSCULAR YOUNG BLONDE WOMAN'S ASS

As she goes back through the door with the wheelbarrow, and is gone.

CLOSER ON SMITH

He's all put together, but you can see where there are rips and breaks in his face, and when he puts his hands on the bar top, we can see the same sort of thing going on there. His mustache is just a few, stray hairs, and he brushes at them with his hand, and they all fall away. No more mustache.

When Smith looks in the mirror...his reflection is not there. In fact, from time to time we see faces and horrible visions in the mirror that have more to do with the reflection of man's inhumanity to man than they do with direct reflection. Scenes of mayhem. Wars. Murders.

                    SMITH
  Whisky.

SNAPPY BARTENDER, without pouring, hardly moving, plants a glass in front of Smith. Smith tosses it back, grimaces.

                SMITH (CONT'D)
  That tastes more like piss than whisky.

SNAPPY holds his hand up, wobbles it.

                    SNAPPY
Fifty-fifty.

Smith makes a face, considers.

                    SMITH
Shit. Hit me again.

Snappy does just that. Smith takes the glass, turns, rests his back against the bar. Sees Bull sitting at a table, drinking, watching, flies all over him.

Smith tosses off the drink, turns back to Snappy, swats at a fly.

                    SMITH (CONT'D)
Take it this isn't Wyoming anymore.

Snappy fills Smith's glass without him asking.

                    SNAPPY
You're right, it isn't.

At that moment–

ANOTHER DOOR ACROSS THE WAY

Opposite the one through which Smith entered, springs open, and we see FLASHES OF FIRE, TWISTS OF BODIES swinging by on hooks. All manner of mayhem.

                  SNAPPY (CONT'D)
Bull.

BULL

Swallows, rises from his chair, tips his bowler back on his head and begins walking toward the open door. He pauses to look at Smith.

                    BULL
            See you there, Smith.

Smith touches the brim of his hat. Bull walks toward the fiery opening, and out comes a LARGE GOO-DRIPPING TENTACLE that grabs Bull and jerks him into the flames and the door SLAMS SHUT.

BACK TO BAR

                    SMITH
            Now I know where I am.

                    SNAPPY
            And if you want to stay out of there, at
            least for awhile, I got a little proposition
            for you. It's right down your alley.

Smith looks at the door through which Bull made his exit.

                    SMITH
            I'm all ears.

                    SNAPPY
            Some of my hired help have gotten too big
            for their britches. Gone freelance.

Snappy jerks a thumb toward the ceiling.

                    SNAPPY (CONT'D)
            Up there. Causing trouble.

                    SMITH
            Thought trouble was your business.

                    SNAPPY
            True. But what Zelzarda has done is
            disrespectful of my authority.

                    SMITH
Zelzarda?

                    SNAPPY
Demon. Couldn't handle the rules. Pretty good right hand man for awhile. Lots of power. Now he's decided he wants to run things. He's taken something belongs to me. Something even I don't mess with. I don't like that he did that. Not one little bit. That's where you come in.

                    SMITH
Could that happen? Him running things? I mean, I thought you–

Smith jerks a thumb toward the ceiling.

                    SMITH (CONT'D)
–and him run things.

                    SNAPPY
Actually, it's not that simple. And if you think the world is fucked up now, just wait until Zelzarda has his mitts on the switch.

                    SMITH
Okay. It could be bad.

                    SNAPPY
More than bad. There's a place on earth where all the configuration points of the universe unite... Am I boring you, Smith?

Smith, who is kind of wool gathering.

                    SMITH
A little over my head.

SNAPPY

Let me put it this way. It's like a gate, and on the other side of the gate are a group we like to call The Old Ones. Right timing, right spells, they could come through. Zelzarda wants to open that gate. If he brings the Old Ones through there's no more balance in heaven or hell. He'll rule the Old Ones, and he'll rule chaos. In words you'll understand, Smith, it'll be a mess up there. I want you to stop him, go up there and get him, put his candle out and stop the Old Ones. Destroy the spell.

SMITH

How do you destroy a spell?

SNAPPY

The spell is words of a sort. Hieroglyphics. Shapes and figures. Nasty little bastards. Left here by the Old Ones. Words escaped from the Necronomicon.

SMITH

The what?

SNAPPY

It's a book. Not your everyday book. But a real nasty book, and I don't mean one with drawings. The words come out of it. They're living things. I got them contained in a nice little gold box. Zelzarda took it. He's sure to let them out. It's part of the process. Long as I had that box I had them contained. But now, with them out of the box, the spell starts.

                    SMITH
            You should have been more careful with that box.

Snappy frowns.

                    SNAPPY
            And did I mention that you have two days?

                    SMITH
            Nope.

                    SNAPPY
            Yeah. Two days. Summer Solstice. June 21st. Big day for folk in my trade. Supernatural powers at their peak...that sort of thing.

                    SMITH
            It's nowhere near June 21st.

                    SNAPPY
            Time here, and time up there, they're not the same. Passes different. You've been here, oh, I don't know, six months.

                    SMITH
            Six months.

                    SNAPPY
            So far.

Smith is puzzling this out.

                    SMITH
            All right. Time flies. But why don't you go get him yourself?

Snappy doesn't like this question.

                    SNAPPY
        Demeaning to my position... You in, or–

Snappy waves his hand at the–

HELL DOOR

Causing it to fly open. Flames lick out. Bull swings into view on a hook. He's nude and tentacles are STRIPPING HIS SKIN OFF WITH A SOUND LIKE SOMEONE CRACKING A WHIP.

The door slams shut.

BACK TO BAR

                SNAPPY (CONT'D)
        –or are you out?

                    SMITH
                (swallowing)
        Count me in. I'm riding for the brand.

                    SNAPPY
        You're gonna need a little more than a
        stick of dynamite for this job.

Snappy's hands hardly move, but in the next instant, he has a .45 revolver in either hand. He places them on the bar. They are black as ebony with a tiny, red flame lick design on the butts.

Smith picks them up, examines them.

                    SMITH
        Guns made here?

                    SNAPPY
        Course not. Samuel Colt. But the ammu-
        nition is silver.

Snappy pulls a double holster gun belt out of thin air, plops it on the bar. There's only one bullet in the silver bandoleer.

> **SNAPPY (CONT'D)**
> Acts like any old bullet, except folks from down here don't cotton to silver at all. I'm an exception.

> **SMITH**
> Kind of light on ammunition, don't you think?

Snappy picks up the belt, pulls out the single bullet, and the belt fills up completely with silver ammunition.

> **SMITH (CONT'D)**
> Well, I'll be damned.

> **SNAPPY**
> You're never down to your last bullet. But that ain't all.

Snappy swings Smith's fancy saddlebags onto the bar. Again, they seem to come out of nowhere. He opens up one of the bags.

> **SNAPPY (CONT'D)**
> You still got your dynamite too. Quite a trademark, Smith. It's very fatalistic.

> **SMITH**
> Since about 1860 I've got up on the wrong side of the bed.

> **SNAPPY**
> Not complaining. You're my kind of guy. Try not to blow yourself up before you're done, though. 'Cause you're gonna be flesh and blood again... And how about a little posse.

SMITH
Well, it has been awhile...

SNAPPY
Posse, Smith. Pay attention.

Smith getting it.

SMITH
Oh. No thanks. I work alone.

SNAPPY
You didn't always.

SMITH
Yeah. That war made me the man I am today and I'm not exactly proud of it.

SNAPPY
Oh, up there, that girl. That's on your mind, isn't it, you letting that happen to her? That was pretty mean, pretty cruel. I have to tell you, I was impressed.

SMITH
That's what riding for Quantrail will do to a man.

SNAPPY
So no posse?

Smith shakes his head.

SNAPPY (CONT'D)
Suit yourself. But if you change your mind–

Snappy fans a few playing cards out of thin air. We can see that there are pictures of people on them, but we can't make them out. He shoves them in Smith's shirt pocket.

                    SNAPPY (CONT'D)
          –this is your ace in the hole.

THE BLONDE'S DOOR FLIES OPEN

And in comes the blonde poking a pitchfork at a short man wearing a cocked hat and a uniform with his hand inside his coat.

UNIFORMED MAN

PROTESTING IN FRENCH

DOOR ACROSS THE WAY

Pops open, tentacle reaches all the way across the room, grab the uniformed man and jerks him into the flames, and the door slams.

BACK TO BAR

                    SMITH
          That was quick.

                    SNAPPY
          French. No waiting. Where were we?

                    SMITH
          Me doing your dirty work.

                    SNAPPY
          Ah!

ON SMITH

We see his cracked and banged up face healing, going smooth, and we–

                                                    CUT TO:

FALLING ROCK – NIGHT

INT. SALOON – UPSTAIRS – BED

Quill is screwing the Saloon Girl he called a goat. He is really going at it. The girl looks bored, but she's making with noises, almost as if she's a recording. She's watching a moth crawl along the outside of the window of the room.

EXT. OVERHEAD THE SALOON – BATS POV AGAIN

The grouping of bats we saw before are diving straight for the saloon. Bats knot together and plunge for the roof, and just before they hit, POOF, they become a rocket of black smoke.

INT. SALOON – UPSTAIRS – BED

Quill in mid-thrust, jerks his head, looks up even as he is astride Saloon Girl. Saloon Girl sees it too. A dark funnel shape comes through the roof and darts straight into Quill's open mouth. From here on out, we know Voice/Shadow, as Voice/Zelzarda.

THE VOICE/ZELZARDA
I've come to collect.

Quill stretches his neck and raises his head, obviously in pain. His eyes flicker. We see a flash of something over his face that we can't identify. And then we–

CUT TO:

QUILL'S SHADOW ON THE WALL

Suddenly wings grow out of the shade's back, flap about. Saloon Girl SCREAMS. She wiggles out from under Quill, darts naked for the door, and is gone.

THE VOICE/ZELZARDA (CONT' D)
YOU'RE MINE.

MOMENTS LATER

Quill is walking away from the bed. We just get a glimpse of his legs. Something about the way he moves is strange, jerky. It's almost like he's trying to wear high heels for the first time. Glimpse of his wings beating once in the air; they fold onto his back to rest, and he moves out of sight through the door, never really giving us a full view.

We HOLD THIS SHOT. But from the saloon we hear a den of activity. And then a ROAR, which we can pretty much figure is coming from Quill. This is followed by YELLING AND BANGING and SCREAMING. Then, silence.

VIEW OF THE STREET

We see Double Shot and some others running like hell down the street.

INT. SALOON

Quill is perched on a table. All around him, carnage. Bodies piled like cord wood. Including Saloon Girl. Quill is eating the brain from a decapitated skull, slowly, deliciously, his long tongue flicking at the blood, teeth crunching at the gray matter.

Then the screen becomes a FALLING SHEET OF BLOOD that–

SLOW WASHES US TO:

COMPLETE REDNESS

And the Redness darkens until we have–

COMPLETE BLACKNESS

In the DARK, a dark so complete and momentarily silent, that it's as if we are in the proverbial tomb, and then WE HEAR–

                    SNAPPY V.O.
              You'll need a horse, Smith.

The darkness split by a tiny beam of light, and it's coming from above at a downward angle. As we observe the light and listen to the CLOPPING OF A HORSE.

> SNAPPY V.O. (CONT'D)
> Run all day, run all night. Shadow never tires. And another thing. You might take note of the long, dark night and the two moons. There's always the two moons. Don't ask me why. I didn't make the rules.

The CLOPPING coming nearer. There are flickers of shadows in the light.

> SNAPPY V.O. (CONT'D)
> That's how you'll recognize the gate and know the time is short, and find Zelzarda, or whatever he's calling himself.

The light is brighter and wider now, and we see a shape in the light, a shadow really, and it's the shadow of a man on a horse and it swells, and–

> SNAPPY V.O. (CONT'D)
> A word to the wise, Smith. Don't fuck this up.

EXT. FALLING ROCK MINE SHAFT – NIGHT

THUNDERING out of the shaft into the moonlight is Smith on the back of a coal-black horse. The horse, SHADOW, races up to the edge of the rise, rears up on its hind legs, frames itself against the moon, its hooves pawing at the air as COYOTES HOWL.

EXT. ROAD – NIGHT – A LITTLE LATER

Smith on horseback. He reins the horse to a stop, leans forward in the saddle, and we–

SEE WHAT SMITH SEES

The sign that reads FALLING ROCK.

BACK ON SMITH

settling back into the saddle.

                SMITH
    Well, I'll be damned.

Smith urges Shadow forward, and a he passes the Falling Rock sign, the air SHIMMERS IN BLUE WAVES. Smith pauses, turns his horse. The shimmer is gone.

Smith rides his horse back toward the sign, but the horse runs up against an invisible barrier, stumbles back a step, SNORTS.

              SMITH (CONT'D)
    Well, Shadow. Looks like we can go in, but
    we can't go out.

Smith wheels Shadow and begins to ride. After a short distance, a bit of light is visible off to the side of the road.

Smith slides off Shadow, leads him toward the light, which we can tell is a–

A CAMPFIRE

There are eight cowboys sitting around the fire. We can't see them well, just their shadowy shapes. Their horses are tied in a remuda. And now we HEAR a guitar strumming, and some COWBOY SONG being sung. It sounds kind of off. Not the best voices in the world. Sort of bullfrogs meet an asthmatic Gene Autry with a corn cob up his ass.

Smith and Shadow are coming closer, and as they do the song ends, and a CHUCKLE rises up from the cowboys.

CLOSE ON

The backs of cowboys who are sitting in a semi-circle as one of them reaches out for the coffee pot on the fire. And just as he takes hold of it, starts pulling it back—

HIS ARM FALLS OFF, dropping the pot, splattering coffee every which way.

ON THE COWBOY

Who lost his arm. THIS IS COFFEE POT COWBOY. He's a rotting ghoul, not a pretty sight. His face is part flesh and part bone. His eyes look big in his skull. His jaw is oddly long, as if it's been stretched. The rest of him isn't much either. Ragged clothes, ragged flesh.

                    COFFEE POT
    Goddamn it.

Just as he finishes speaking, his jaw swings halfway off. A tooth pops out of the jaw and flies off into the night.

The other cowboys LAUGH, really YUCKING it up, and we get a look at them. They aren't much to look at either. They all have those long jaws, and are in varying states of decay.

                COFFEE POT (CONT'D)
    (a sound that is indistinguishable, but is
    obviously not happy)

ON SMITH

He's ridden close enough that he sees what the cowboys are. He glances at their horses. They too are part flesh, part bone and odd to look at. Ears too long. Too many teeth. Shadow even studies the horses with amazement, lets out with a SNORT.

ANOTHER ANGLE

The cowboys jerk their heads toward the SNORT. They see Smith and Shadow. The cowboys spring to their feet.

SMITH
Howdy.

Suddenly one of the cowboys goes for his gun. Smith draws before the cowboy can clear leather. BLAM.

CLOSE ON COWBOY

Shot hits him in the chest. We see the dust fly up. Cowboy chuckles, looks up, laughs. Then, his expression changes. He looks down at his chest. Where the bullet hit a hole is widening. After a moment, we can see moonlight through it. It becomes wider yet; from the middle toward head and toes. The slim remains of the cowboy BLOW into a PUFF OF DUST.

ON OTHER COWBOYS

They are amazed. Coffee Pot makes a noise that his jawless mouth won't hold. It comes out in a spurt of phlegm. What he says appears in translation at the bottom of the screen.

COFFEE POT'S TRANSLATION
He's done re-killed Zeke.

SMITH

He's reining Shadow about, rushing off into the dark.

GHOULISH COWBOYS

They jump on their ghoulish horses, tear out in pursuit.

ANOTHER ANGLE

Smith is riding like the wind, Shadow easily outdistancing the ghouls and their mounts. We can see them disappearing in the background.

HELL'S BOUNTY

Smith wheels Shadow about. The horse rears, comes down at a run, tearing up ground, heading right back toward the ghouls.

CLOSE ON SHADOW

HIs eyes blaze like embers.

BACK TO SCENE

Smith and Shadow closing on ghouls. Smith puts the rein in his teeth, pulls both revolvers. Smith and the ghouls are about to collide.

SMITH FIRES. POP. POP. POP.

Two ghouls hit the dirt, their wounds widening until they no longer exist. Their horses race by Shadow, one of them reaching out to nip at Shadow with its teeth. But it's a MISS. The teeth SNAP in the air like a bear trap.

Smith has parted the cowboys like Moses through the Red Sea. He wheels to turn back. They're confused, their mounts going every which way.

One of the riderless GHOUL HORSES comes thundering back, straight at Shadow. As they meet, both horses rear up, kick at one another, and we get a FLASH OF SHADOW'S HORSESHOES. They're made of SILVER.

Shadow, his hoof comes down on the GHOUL HORSE'S HEAD with a LOUD SMACK. The horse's skull splits, and it's like a shock wave. The horse drops back down on all fours as his frame shakes and scatters apart in a POOF of dust and a RATTLE of bones.

The other riderless ghoul horse sees this, and we go–

CLOSE ON THIS GHOUL HORSE

There's an almost human look on its face. He doesn't want any part of Shadow. Not by a long shot. He breaks and runs into the darkness.

BACK TO SCENE

Coffee Pot mounted on his horse, makes a garbled noise, and then at the bottom of the scene a TRANSLATION IN SUBTITLES.

COFFEE POT TRANSLATION
(yelling to the retreating horse)
Chicken shit!

A LIGHT

It's moving fast through the darkness, across our line of vision. As it comes CLOSER, we see its a little horse drawn wagon with a man in the back, holding a set of wagon lines.

It's McBride, THE UNDERTAKER we've seen before. The wagon is packed with bottles with rag fuses sticking out of them. The flame is from a torch stuck in a receptacle at the front of his little ride.

ON COFFEE POT AND SMITH

Coffee Pot has a revolver drawn and he's firing at Smith. The bullets WHISTLE by, and one of them plucks at Smith's sleeve.

Coffee Pot's head EXPLODES.

ANGLE A WOMAN

She's wearing a black half mask, a kind of Phantom of the Opera operation without an eyehole. She's dressed in black leather from head to toe, a black hat with a red scarf tied around it. She has a black snake whip coiled around one of her shoulders. She's wearing a set of revolvers.

HELL'S BOUNTY

Long flame-red hair blows out from under her hat. She'd holding Bull's shotgun, and it's obvious she was the source of the blast that took away Coffee Pot's head. It's PAYDAY.

BACK TO COFFEE POT

Headless, he's still alive. He's waving his six gun about, firing randomly at the CREAKING OF THE LITTLE WAGON, the sound of HORSE HOOVES. His horse is wheeling wildly under him.

Payday strikes out at him with her whip, snapping off his one good arm at the shoulder, taking his pistol out of play.

> **COFFEE POT**
> (garbled)
> Translation: "Dang it."

The whip snaps again, catching Coffee Pot at the knee, and this flick of the whip takes his leg off from the knee down.

ON THE UNDERTAKER AND HIS RIG

He rides right up on Coffee pot and his horse. He has one of the bottles in his hand. He lights its fuse on the torch, tosses it onto–

COFFEE POT

Who goes up in a FLARE OF FLAME along with the horse.

UNDERTAKER riding by the blazing ghoul and his mount.

> **UNDERTAKER**
> Goodbye, asshole.

Coffee Pot and his ghoul horse collapses into a pile of smoking ashes.

ANOTHER ANGLE

There's three riders left. They turn their horses and take off running, giving their mounts the spurs.

Smith lays his revolver over his arm, fires.

Shot hits the retreating ghoul in the back. There's that quick widening of rotting flesh, then he dissolves. His ghoul horse, and the surviving riders and horses ride off into the dark.

Undertaker clatters up alongside Smith in his wagon as Payday rides up.

> **UNDERTAKER**
> Ain't never seen nothing but fire do them in before. What you shooting, boy?

> **SMITH**
> Silver bullets.

> **UNDERTAKER**
> I'll be damned. That works?

> **SMITH**
> You seen it.

> **PAYDAY**
> Silver or not, we best get to a safe place. There's a bunch of 'em around out here.

> **UNDERTAKER**
> Three hundred graves, three hundred ghouls.

> **SMITH**
> What does that mean?

> **PAYDAY**
> This isn't the place for it. Come on.

HELL'S BOUNTY

They ride off, Payday in the lead, Undertaker and his wagon bringing up the rear.

Out of the dark, riding right at them, more ghouls. Three of them.

> PAYDAY (CONT'D)
> See. I told you.

Payday puts the shotgun into its holster on her belt, draws her revolvers.

> PAYDAY (CONT'D)
> Go on ahead. I'll cover you.

Payday rides hell bent for leather, FIRING RAPIDLY, she takes off ghoul ears and eyes, kneecapping the legs out from under the horses, making them fall and send the riders tumbling.

She spins backwards in the saddle, pops off a couple more shots, taking an ankle out from under one of the ghouls, who goes down with a CRACKING SOUND.

They aren't dead, but as Payday returns to her proper position in the saddle and rides back, she runs her horse over the ankle shot ghoul. We hear ANKLE SHOT GHOUL, his face down in the dirt.

> UNKNOWN GHOUL
> (muffled)
> Dagnabit.

Payday rides up alongside Smith.

> SMITH
> I'd pay to watch you work.

> PAYDAY
> Any other time you would have to.

A WATERFALL – LATER

Shimmering in the moonlight. It tumbles THUNDEROUSLY down from overhead rocks. Smith and his companions ride into the shallow stream, and as they clop along, he looks down, sees silver shimmering in the rocks.

They ride on through the waterfall, into a cave. The waterfall puts out Undertaker's torch with a loud HISS.

INT. CAVE

Rays from the moon stick through the falls and give the interior a soft glow. All manner of odds and ends are strewn about. Rope. Saddles. Barrels. Crates. A couple of horses. Piles of hay. Living materials. A crude wheel chair.

Payday and Smith dismount as Undertaker works himself out of the wagon into the wheel chair. As Payday leads her horse to a pile of hay, Smith turns his head, watches her hips move beneath that leather. It's a nice sight. He watches how she turns her head, the way her hair frames her face. Mask or no mask, she's something. When she looks at him, he looks away, and as he does–

Something bright in the cavern wall catches his attention. He leads Shadow over to the wall, reaches out, touches a shiny bright vein of rock. He grins.

                    SMITH
Silver.

ENTERING from a smaller tunnel, looking somewhat more ragged than before is DOC.

                    DOC
Who's this?

                  PAYDAY
He's okay. He killed some ghouls.

The Undertaker has a small book, and he's wetting a pencil with his tongue.

> **UNDERTAKER**
> How many ghouls did we get tonight?

> **PAYDAY**
> I don't know. Seven...eight. In that vicinity.

Undertaker writes in his book.

> **UNDERTAKER**
> That makes two hundred or so down. Ought to be about a hundred more. Give or take a dozen or so we ain't figured.

> **SMITH**
> You know how many there are?

> **UNDERTAKER**
> Basic arithmetic. I buried near all of 'em in the graveyard. New dead, they don't come back. They aren't even being buried no more. Course, there was some buried up there before I was undertaker, and that's why I haven't got an exact count.

Doc is eyeing Smith.

> **DOC**
> Who is this man? Say he killed some ghouls?

> **UNDERTAKER**
> Silver bullets. That's what he shoots. It kills them.

SMITH
That's why you have a good hideout. The stream, the walls, they're packed with silver.

DOC
We just thought we were lucky they hadn't found us here.

SMITH
Not hardly.

DOC
How do you know about the silver?

SMITH
That's not important. I just do.

Payday is studying Smith intently.

PAYDAY
You know, you remind me of someone.

SMITH
I don't think so.

UNDERTAKER
I was thinking the same thing...can't quite place it. Someone I knew some time back...

SMITH
I don't think so.

UNDERTAKER
I'm pretty sure. You used to have a beard, maybe?

SMITH
(trying to change the subject)
How long you been here?

UNDERTAKER
A year or so, I guess. I got bad news for you stranger, you can ride in, but you can't ride out. Nobody can ride out, them things either. And being in this town ain't a good thing.

SMITH
Part of that bad thing how you lost your legs?

SLOWLY WE GO CLOSE ON UNDERTAKER

UNDERTAKER
I come out better than some.

DISSOLVE INTO FLASHBACK:

EXT. SUNDOWN SALOON – NIGHT

Trumbo Quill comes out of the saloon, stretches his arms, looks up at the night. It's our first good look at him, and we can recognize it's him, but there are changes. His face looks like leather. His ears have grown long and pointed. Horns poke out of his hat, pinning it to his head. As we watch, his face twists, and his chest swells, ripping away what's left of his shirt. He's still wearing his guns and pants and boots.

He flies into the air and sails in front of the moon, does a dipsy-doodle that causes his revolvers to fall from his holsters. A long spiked tail pops from the back of his pants and waves in the night air like a flag.

UNDERTAKER (V.O.)
Year or so back, fella named Trumbo Quill, he changed. He was bad enough before. But suddenly, he ain't really Quill no more. He's some kind of lizard, bird mix in pants. Ugly bastard.

Quill sailing down out of the sky to land in Boot Hill Cemetery.

> **UNDERTAKER (V.O.) (CONT'D)**
> He started calling up the dead from Boot Hill.

Demonic Quill with his clawed hands raised, and he's CHANTING, and out of the ground, the dead are rising. But they aren't just dead. They're those long-jawed, big toothed dead we've seen before. And they aren't slow moving. Mostly men, a few women. A child or two.

They push the dirt aside, roll back tombstones. Some of them brush themselves off. They immediately start CHATTING amongst themselves, this and that.

Quill GROWLS loud enough to SHAKE THE EARTH. The ghouls go quiet. All turn their heads to Quill who looks happier than a fly in an outhouse.

Quill takes to the sky, floating above them, letting out a SCREECH. He turns slowly and starts to beat wings back toward town, the ghouls following underneath his huge moonlit shadow.

GUN SHOP – A LITTLE LATER

The ghouls are breaking into the shop, taking guns, ammunition. The shadow of the Demon Quill flows along the street as citizens run in fear, shooting at the ghouls, who are grabbing at them, tearing at them, and finally using the guns they've stolen from the shop.

We see a woman running down the street, under the shadow of the bell tower. Ghouls are in hot pursuit. She goes down beneath a horde of ghouls ripping at her. She disappears into a huddle of dead flesh. Blood runs beneath the boots of the ghouls.

One of the ghouls turns, gnawing savagely at her arm, which has been jerked out of its socket. We see another run off with her head, like a dog protecting his meal.

UNDERTAKER (V.O.) (CONT'D)
Quill turned them loose on the town. Them ghouls ate people. Ate damn near the whole town, and didn't bother with no carrots, taters or mouth napkins. Got darn near everybody, 'cept for a few holdouts like us. Few others sprinkled here and there.

The Undertaker, ghouls running after him. He turns down an alley, sees an open window, tries to dive through. He almost makes it, but the ghouls are on him. They grab his legs and chow down. Undertaker SCREAMS.

INT. WINDOW

Undertaker screaming. Through the window we see the ghouls at work, eating pants legs and flesh together, chomping on Undertaker's boots.

HANDS REACH OUT, grab Undertaker, pulling him loose of the ghouls and inside the building. The hands belong to Payday and Doc. Payday's hair isn't as long as in the present, and she's wearing a much cruder patch over her face. They drag the undertaker toward an open door that leads outside.

A WAGON

Doc is in the seat, whipping up the HORSES, clattering down the street. Payday is in the back, trying to soothe the crippled Undertaker. Ghouls rush out into the street.

Wagon hits ghouls as it goes, trampling them under wheels and horse hooves.

As the wagon passes, the ghouls, many of which have taken awful damage, start to strain, twist, bones snap back together, and though they still look ugly and ragged, they stand...somewhat whole again.

The wagon racing off down the moonlit road.

                    UNDERTAKER V.O.
          We found out wasn't no way out of the
          town no more. That's when we took to the
          cave here.

TOWN – MAIN STREET – DAY

Undertaker is in his wagon, Payday and Doc are walking down the street. Payday's hair is longer, she has the current black leather outfit on.

                  UNDERTAKER V.O. (CONT'D)
          Discovered during the day, they weren't so
          full of beans. They weren't about much.
          Same for Quill. He was quieter than a dead
          hog in a smokehouse.

THE LIVERY DOOR

It's kicked open. There stands Payday and Doc. Behind them in his wagon, Undertaker. They all have torches. Payday her shotgun, Doc a Winchester, and Undertaker the bottles of oil.

                  UNDERTAKER V.O. (CONT'D)
          They could still hurt you, but they was kind
          of sluggish.

ANOTHER ANGLE INSIDE LIVERY

Ghouls, hanging from the rafters upside down, supported by their cowboy boots and spurs. They have their hats in their hands, arms crossed across their chests. They have their guns poked upside down in their gun belts.

GHOULS' EYES POP OPEN. They kick loose from the rafters, twist, land on their feet.

> **UNDERTAKER V.O. (CONT'D)**
> Course, they weren't all the way sluggish, and could work up some doings if they put a mind to it.

The ghouls reach down and pull their guns loose from their belts. Payday opens up with her shotgun, Doc with his Winchester.

Ghoul bodies HOP with bullet damage, and go down. Doc yells to his horse. It darts forward, pulling him and the wagon inside the barn. He starts lighting and tossing bottles.

> **UNDERTAKER V.O. (CONT'D)**
> We learned fire would keep them down for good. It didn't just cook their asses, it plumb did them in, like touching salt to a slug.

EXT. BARN – MOMENTS LATER

Undertaker is writing in his little book.

> **UNDERTAKER (V.O.)**
> I started keeping count.

MAIN STREET – LATER YET

As Payday and Doc walk along the boardwalk, Undertaker riding in the street nearby. Payday and Doc, kicking doors open, looking inside. They kick open a couple of shop doors.

The places have been rummaged. But no one's there. They continue along, look in the FALLING ROCK MINING ASSAY OffICE. It looks in order. No ghouls, and no Quill.

> **UNDERTAKER (V.O.) (CONT'D)**
> Course, we figured we got the big boy, Quill, we could put the finish on things. I don't know if he didn't like day, or just needed his rest.

Payday looks inside the building they've just kicked open. It's the–

BELL TOWER

Nothing in there. Just a great big bell tower. Payday looks up at the tower. Nothing. They go inside.

> **UNDERTAKER (V.O.)**
> Bottom dollar was, we couldn't find him. He could hide better than a seed tick in a woolly dog's coat. Kept figuring he'd come out to fight, but he left all that to his ghoul boys.

OVERLAPPING TIME DISSOLVE OF BELL TOWER SEARCH

Looking here. Looking there. Kicking doors open. Looking between and under pews. Finding nothing.

Payday and Doc leaving the place.

> **UNDERTAKER (V.O.)**
> Course, we had to be careful about supplies. Only so much oil and such. We run out of good ways to make fire, we'd be up the old shit creek without a paddle and a big old hole in our boat.

EXT. GENERAL STORE

Undertaker is sitting out front in his little rig, and there's a bigger wagon sitting out front as well, hooked to a team of horses.

We can see Payday and Doc through the window glass of the General Store, gathering up things. The store is practically empty.

They come out of the store. They load barrels of oil onto a wagon. We can see other supplies there as well. They climb on board, whip up the horses, and with Undertaker riding in his little wagon behind them, they charge down the street.

> **UNDERTAKER (V.O.) (CONT'D)**
> We packed everything there was and stored it before Quill and his walking shit sacks figured out they ought to destroy the goods.

THE CAVE

They are driving the wagon inside, and behind them comes Undertaker.

> **UNDERTAKER (V.O.) (CONT'D)**
> Course, us taking everything had to be hard on them other human stragglers, and I hope they managed to steal a few beans and crackers. But, frankly, it's ever goddamn body for themselves.

FLASHBACK ENDS AND BACK TO SCENE

> **SMITH**
> Why haven't you brought in the others, the holdouts?

> **DOC**
> They hide out just like we do. It ain't like we had a town meeting on this shit. I've seen a few of them from a distance, once or twice. But that's it. What about you? You with us?

> **SMITH**
> I work alone.

> **PAYDAY**
> Working alone wasn't going so good tonight.

                    SMITH
Actually, it was going fine.

                  UNDERTAKER
He was doing good, girl. I'll say that. He can shoot the hard-on off a mosquito with them pistols of his.

                    PAYDAY
                  (to Smith)
These aren't everyday cowboys full of whisky and bean wind.

                    SMITH
Get Quill, you don't need to keep up with the numbers. He goes down, they all go down faster than shit through a goose.

Doc looks Smith over.

                     DOC
How do you know that, boy?

                    SMITH
I'll just say a man from the South, the Deep South, hired me to bring in Quill, Dead or Alive. He told me about his... peculiarities. Besides, doesn't that make sense to you?

                     DOC
                  (nodding)
It does. We figured the same.

INT. SUNDOWN SALOON

It's lit up and full of ghoulish cowboys and dead saloon girls. They are laughing and drinking, dancing to the sound of the piano. The piano sounds awful, and the dancers are stepping on one another's feet, wobbling all over the floor.

CLOSE ON A COUPLE OF GHOULS. We'll call them Roy and Gene. They are leaning on the bar, looking at the dancers. They zero in on one woman.

> ROY
> Gene, got to tell you, all these damn Boot Hill women are so ugly they'd have to sneak up on a glass of whisky.

> GENE
> Yep. That's the truth, Roy.

Roy pointing out a woman dancing with a cowboy.

> ROY
> Except that one over there. And part of her ass fell off last night.

> GENE
> Damn, you don't say?

Roy pointing again.

> ROY
> Hell yeah. It's over there by the piano.

A GLANCE IN THAT DIRECTION

Something fleshy and fly ridden can be seen.

Into the saloon come two escaped ghoul boys from the confrontation earlier that night with Smith, Payday and Undertaker. We'll call them JIM and ELMER.

They rush to the bar, snatch up a bottle a piece, take swigs. Whisky squirts out of all kinds of holes.

                    ROY (CONT'D)
            What the hell happened to you boys?

                        JIM
            Run across a new fella who could shoot
            us dead. No fire. Just bullets. Zeke, Lem,
            Turnip, and that little short fella–

                       ELMER
            Timmy.

                        JIM
            Yeah, Timmy. They was all shot, and just
            turned to shit. Wasn't nothing left but me
            and Elmer. I think some of the other boys
            might have got it too. I heard gunfire after
            we left.

                       ELMER
            Yeah, and that new fella had a mean horse.

BAT WINGS SMASH OPEN

In comes Quill/Zelzarda. He's bigger than before. His face is full of teeth and his tail thrashes around his body like a mule skinner whipping a hard headed mule. But he still resembles Quill.

The saloon goes quiet. Looks like a still photo. Dead or not, these ghouls are as nervous as cows in line at the slaughterhouse. The piano player turns gently on his stool. One of his legs falls off. He glances down at it, but quickly looks up as Quill stalks in. Quill looks at the two surviving ghouls. When he speaks it is as if his voice is being dragged over broken glass.

                       QUILL
            Where is this Man?

Jim steps forward.

JIM
Well, sir. He was kind of tall. Dressed in black...

ELMER
Kind of nice looking in a rugged kind of way. Pretty horse. Silver hooves.

Quill roars and moves so fast it's near impossible to see. He grabs up Elmer and slams his back down across the bar, breaking it, dropping him to the floor.

QUILL
I didn't ask how cute you thought he was, Elmer. I asked where he was.

Elmer is crawling across the floor, his spine busted.

ELMER
(softly)
Sorry, sir.

And then he crawls out of scene.

QUILL

Looks madder than a hive of hornets. He pushes his face close to Jim.

QUILL
Jim. Listen. Listen carefully. I want this man done in. Now. No more whisky. No bullshitting. DO IT NOW!

Chairs clattering, bottles clinking, the ghouls are hustling like their asses are on fire. And then, except for Quill, the bar is empty.

Quill strolls behind the bar, takes a bottle of whisky, bites the neck off of it, chews on it, washes it down with whisky. His wings open wide, flutter and close again.

>   QUILL (CONT'D)
>   Ah!

EXT. SALOON

A SERIES OF SHOTS: THE GREAT SMITH HUNT

Ghouls scattering about on foot through the town.

A Ghoul peeking down an alley. A ghoul at the far end is looking back. This startles both of them. Then they are embarrassed. One clears his throat, walks off. The other follows suit, walking down the street, trying to strut, thumbs in his gun belt.

A Ghoul picking up an old washtub, looking under it. Nothing, of course.

A Ghoul walking along the boardwalk. A rat runs across the porch, out into the street. The ghoul looks at the rat, licks his lips, then breaks after it.

The rat zigs, zags. The ghoul zigs and zags, pulls his revolver, starts FIRING at the rat. Missing. The rat runs down a dark alley, and rat and ghoul disappear into the blackness. GUNFIRE IN THE DISTANCE: ONCE. TWICE. THREE TIMES.

Gene looking under a porch, his ass sticking up. He gets a quick boot in the ass, tumbles forward. He gets up on his hands and knees, wobbles to his feet.

He sees who kicked him. It's Roy. Roy points in the distance.

>   ROY
>   He ain't under the goddamn porch, you
>   maggot head. He's out there somewhere.
>   Round everybody up, and let's ride!

GHOUL RIDERS – MOMENTS LATER – GREAT SMITH HUNT CONT.

HELL'S BOUNTY

Ghouls and ghoulish horses riding off wildly into the night, melting into the darkness.

HOLD THIS EMPTY SCENE

SOUND OF CRICKETS, A FROG, AN OWL

HOLD

TIME LAPSE

A bit of SUNLIGHT on the horizon. Ghouls appear on their horses, heading back toward us. They are no longer riding hell-bent for leather. As they come CLOSER, they look defeated.

CLOSE ON ROY AND GENE RIDING

They, like the others, are starting to appear weak, as if they might slide off their horses.

> **GENE**
> You get to tell Quill we didn't find him.

> **ROY**
> I ain't telling him nothing. You can tell him.
> I don't want his boots up my ass.

> > DISSOLVE TO:

THE TOWN – LATER THAT MORNING

CAMERA MOVES THROUGH THE TOWN, SLOWLY at first, and then it GAINS SPEED, races along the street, just to the outskirts where it PAUSES ON–

A THICK STAND OF TREES

CHIRPING birds. CAMERA FLOWS through the trees and we see in the shade, the ghouls on their horses leaning against trees.

UP IN THE TREES

Draped over the limbs like rugs, are ghoul cowboys. A crow is pecking the eye out of one, who lifts his hand weakly and waves it away.

CAMERA MOVES EARTHWARD AGAIN

A sink in the land amongst the trees. It's almost like a pit. It's full of ghoul horses, cowboys, stacked like cordwood in the shade.

Someone FARTS

From the pile.

      UNKNOWN COWGHOUL
 Damn it, Homer.

      HOMER
 Sorry.

INT. CAVE – MIDDAY

Smith is saddling up Shadow. Payday and Undertaker are watching. The Doc is nearby, platting a rope. As Payday strolls over–

      PAYDAY
 A night's sleep and your gone?

      SMITH
 Like I said, I work alone.

      PAYDAY
 We could use you.

      SMITH
 You're safe here.

> **PAYDAY**
> Now I know why they never came into the
> Mining Assay Office. The silver.

As Smith swings up on Shadow.

> **SMITH**
> Could be. Good luck to you.

> **PAYDAY**
> (not happy)
> Sure.

Smith rides out through the waterfall, into–

STREAM – DAYLIGHT

Shadow and Smith riding away.

INT. CAVE

Payday is close to the falls and she can see through them, can observe the hazy form of Smith going away. She sighs, turns back into the cave.

TOWN MAIN STREET – DAY

Smith is riding slowly down the street on Shadow. Smith has a lit cigar in his mouth. As he rides, Smith reaches into a saddlebag, pulls out a stick of dynamite. He lights it off his cigar, tosses it into the open door of the General Store. It EXPLODES, knocking splinters and glass into the street right behind Smith.

> **SMITH**
> Quill. Come out, you lilly-livered sack of
> shit. The big boy sent me to bring you home.

Smith rides by another building. The sign there reads: BESSIE'S CLOTHES EMPORIUM. Smith lights a stick of dynamite, throws it up against the door.

                SMITH (CONT'D)
    Come out of your hiding place, or I'll blow
    you out.

Smith rides on, gets off his horse in front of the saloon, drops the reins loosely over the hitching post. Waits a minute. The last stick tossed goes off with an REVERBERATING BLAST, knocking pieces of the building, including women's dresses and shoes into the street.

Smith pauses, sucks on his cigar, looks at the dresses and shoes. He walks over, looks down at the clothes. Some of them are smoking. He FOCUSES on one of the dresses. Chiffon. Green.

Smith picks it up, holds it in front of him. He spies a pair of shoes. He picks those up. He takes them back to Shadow. He opens one of the saddlebags, stuffs the shoes and dress inside. He reaches under what he's just deposited, takes out a stick of dynamite, shoves it in his belt.

He goes–

INSIDE SALOON

Smith strolls around behind the bar, finds a bottle of whisky. He pulls the cork out with his teeth, drinks from the bottle. He looks at the beaded curtain–

                          FLASH BACK TO:

PAYDAY AND QUILL

Quill is dragging her through the curtain.

FLASHBACK ENDS

Smith doesn't like this memory. He quickly pours another one, downs it. Carrying the bottle, smoking his cigar, he walks to the beaded curtain, goes through, climbs the stairs.

He comes to the landing. A shadow moves across his face, causing Smith to jerk his head for a look.

It's Quill. He's half in darkness at the end of the hall. He's standing there with wings spread, crouched. He looks more and more like a demon. He moves slightly into the light. Claws are starting to poke out of his boots. His shirt is ripped, and we can see that he's covered in scales.

                QUILL
        You looking for me?

Smith grins.

                SMITH
        We've met before, you weren't quite so
        ugly then, Quill. Zelzarda, whoever you
        are.

Quill enjoys this moment. He picks at one of his long nails with another.

                QUILL
        You don't know what you're up against,
        cowboy.

                SMITH
        I know about the Old Ones. I know about
        the spell. I know what you want to do.
        That's not a good idea. I mean, really,
        pilgrim, wouldn't you rather not make
        everything so messy?

Quill steps forward one step. Smith shifts slightly.

                    QUILL
          Even your boss preferred to rule in hell
          than serve in heaven. Am I any different?

                    SMITH
          Well, you're not as snappy a dresser, and
          you're breath doesn't smell like mince
          meat pie. He has that going for him.

An ugly grin from Quill, Zelzarda, however you want to see him.

                    QUILL
          Now that you've found me, what you
          gonna do with me?

Smith drops the whisky bottle, draws quick and FIRES, hits Quill right in the teeth, knocking Quill's head back.

Quill jerks a talon to his mouth.

                    QUILL (CONT'D)
          That hurt.

Smith is disappointed.

                    SMITH
          Not enough.

Quill BELLOWS, charges down the hall. Smith opens up with the revolver. It BARKS THREE TIMES. The shots hit Quill in the chest. He staggers back, ROARS, flaps his wings which smash against the wall, knocking wood and wallpaper into a swirl of splinters. On the other side, he knocks out some of the railing.

Quill takes a deep breath, snatches a piece of railing free, throws it at Smith, hits him, sends him flying on his back to the floor, causing him to lose his cigar and his spare revolver to fall from its holster, sending it clattering to the floor below.

HELL'S BOUNTY —77

BOTTOM FLOOR OF THE SALOON

Payday comes inside. She sees Smith's revolver fall, hit the floor. HEARS A RUCKUS upstairs.

PAYDAY
Smith. Smith. You up there?

Smith sticks his face through the railing. Sees Payday poking his revolver into her belt.

SMITH
Yes. But I'm busy.

BACK TO SMITH AND QUILL

Smith scrambles backwards like a crab, still on his back. Quill pauses to pluck the silver loads from his flesh. Quill's TALONS SIZZLE. He tosses the silver away in disgust.

Smith SHOOTS again. A shot directly in Quill's chest. Then ANOTHER SHOT. And ANOTHER. Quill steps back, bends over, vomits a foul looking mess that looks like molten silver onto the landing.

This holds Quill for only a second. He wipes his mouth with the back of his scaly arm. Smith lifts his gun, pulls the trigger, and–

CLICK

CLICK... CLICK... CLICK

He reaches for his other gun... Gone.

Quill's many teeth, minus a gap from Smith's bullet, spread into a sawtooth smile.

BLAM!

A bullet whizzes up through the landing, right through Quill's pants and into the old meat and two potatoes. Quill GOES WILD. His wings beating against the wall, knocking holes in it. He flies up and slams against the ceiling, knocking himself to the floor of the landing.

Smith jerks the dynamite from his gun belt, holds it over the railing.

SMITH
Payday. Light it.

ANGLE PAYDAY

She looks up, points her pistol and fires.

THE DYNAMITE FUSE

The bullet lights it, and Smith throws it. It rolls it up against the thrashing Quill.

Quill looks at the dynamite. Makes a face.

Smith half rolls, half dives against the railing, snapping it in two. He takes a fall that lands him on a table below, collapsing it just as THE DYNAMITE BLOWS and Payday dives to the floor.

ON QUILL

Being knocked backwards in a BLAST OF FIRE and EXPLOSIVES. Boards and debris stick in him like spears. He SMACKS against a remaining fragment of floor. It breaks and he plunges through to the–

SALOON

Below as everything above Quill tumbles down on top of him in a CRASH.

SMITH

He's crawling out from under boards, fragments of ceiling, etc. He stumbles to his feet. The bar is still standing, part of the roof, the saloon's swinging doors.

Payday is up, still holding her revolver. She throws an arm around Smith's shoulder, leads him outside.

EXT. SALOON – STREET

Payday leads Smith to his horse, along the side of which is tied Payday's mount. Smith makes a couple of attempts at his stirrup before he can finally get mounted.

At that moment we hear a DEAFENING HOWL.

INT. SALOON

Coming out from under the debris, a talon. Then a wing, and then Quill stands straight up. There are holes in his wings. one of his eyes is knocked out. His body begins to repair itself immediately.

EXT. MAIN STREET

Smith and Payday riding like the proverbial wind.

INT. SALOON

QUILL, hits the bat wings so hard he sends them spinning out into the street. Then, he's airborne.

QUILLS BIRD'S EYE VIEW

The street, and the extended road... Empty. No Smith. No Payday.

EXT. THICKET

At the edge of town. Shadow and Payday's horse tied in the thicket, barely visible. Not visible at all from above.

CAMERA ROAMS and we see a large wooden trap door, partly covered in pine straw and leaves.

DARKNESS

A split of light. We're looking out of a crack, and as we look, the split widens and we see a hand pushing up the trap, and out of the crack we can see the sky. Quill flaps by.

CRACK CLOSES, and we're back into DARKNESS.

A beat.

In the dark we hear Payday.

> **PAYDAY**
> Got a match? There some candles somewhere.

The flare of a match, and we can see Smith and Payday in its light.

Payday rummages about until she finds a candle, sticks it to the match. When she does we SEE we're in a dusty–

ROOT CELLAR

Not much down there. A barrel or two. Some crude furniture, benches, a table. Two caskets on sawhorses.

> **SMITH**
> What is this place?

> **PAYDAY**
> Undertaker kept his caskets here. First place I hid after Quill turned...that way. Later Doc and Undertaker took me to the cave.

Smith gets up on one of the caskets, pushes his hat back, adjusts his gun belt.

> **SMITH**
> Silver only slowed Quill down. Dynamite just dropped junk on him. He's as good as new. Hell, I thought he was sluggish in the daylight?

> **PAYDAY**
> Well, he's turned a lot more spry lately. And he keeps changing.

Payday pulls Smith's pistol from her belt, gives it to him. Smith puts it in his holster. Now he's armed with two guns again.

> **SMITH**
> You saved my bacon back there. Why?

> **PAYDAY**
> Been asking myself the same question.

> **SMITH**
> Well for whatever reason, I'm beholdin'.

> **PAYDAY**
> I'm beginning to think you're trouble. Might have been smart to let Quill have you. But we been fighting Quill and his gang for a while now. I reckon you might can help us, you live long enough.

> **SMITH**
> That's why I'm here. Came to get Quill.

> **PAYDAY**
> You think you can do that alone?

SMITH
Not anymore.

Smith turns slightly, and when he does, he winces, rubs his shoulder.

PAYDAY
You okay?

SMITH
I been better.

PAYDAY
Take off your shirt... Let's see, I think there's some whisky down here.

SMITH
I could use a drink.

PAYDAY
That's not what I had in mind.

Smith removes his shirt. He has a nasty cut on his shoulder. Payday scrounges around, comes back with a little flat bottle of whisky. She pours a little on the cut. Smith winches. Smith takes the bottle from her, gulps a swig, hands it back. Payday gives him a long look...and it sinks in.

PAYDAY
The dynamite. You can't be him.

Payday puts the cap on the bottle, steps back, stares at Smith, touches her eye patch.

PAYDAY
You are him. I don't know how. But you're him.

She turns away from Smith.

> **PAYDAY**
> Hell. Nothing makes sense anymore.

> **SMITH**
> No it doesn't. And that fella you're thinking of, the the one you remember, that's who I used to be... Not who I am now. That fella was blown to hell.

Payday sits on a barrel, studies Smith again, her hand on her sawed off shotgun.

> **PAYDAY**
> I ought to kill you.

> **SMITH**
> Probably.

> **PAYDAY**
> You could have helped me.

> **SMITH**
> I could have. But I didn't. Now, I would.

> **PAYDAY**
> (snide)
> Because you're not who you used to be?

> **SMITH**
> That's the long and the short of it. And it's the truth.

Payday considers.

> **PAYDAY**
> I don't trust you.

SMITH
I don't blame you. But we're here now. We need each other. And each other is what we got.

Payday eases the whip off her shoulder, places it on the coffin. Smith eyes it.

SMITH (CONT'D)
How'd you learn the whip, to shoot like that? You didn't learn that in a saloon.

For a moment, it's as if Payday might not answer. Then—

PAYDAY
Learned it from my Pa. We had a traveling sharp shooter show. I was better than Pa, good as Mama used to be. Before she got sick and died. I took her place as the main shooter and trick rider. Pa, he drank too much to do much.

SMITH
Hope you don't mind me saying, but seems like you took a big jump in trades.

PAYDAY
Pa and me got bushwhacked by three hombres, I was fourteen then. They robbed and killed my pa. When they got through with me, they sold me to a whore house in Mexico. That's when I learned my new trade. It's not all a sad story. Got sold to another house, in Arizona. Three years later, one of them sold me showed. I shot his balls off, stole his horse. I meant to get in with a Wild West Show. Somehow it didn't work out. And I never found them I was looking for, and

I quit searching. I ended up where you found me.

Smith nods. He lights his dead cigar.

          SMITH
My story is a little like yours.

          PAYDAY
You was a whore?

          SMITH
          (grins)
Got left for dead on the family farm in Missouri. Five Yankee soldiers killed Ma and Pa and my two brothers. Was riding with Quantrail and the James brothers by the time I was seventeen. Always had it in the back of my mind I'd come up on them Yankees done that to my family. I didn't. Kind of spoiled me for living a civilized life... But enough reminiscing. Put out that light, will you? I need some rest.

Smith takes off his gun belt, drapes if over the table. He crushes out his cigar. He stretches out on top of the coffin. Turns on his side away from her.

Payday gently removes her shotgun, points it at Smith. She cocks back a hammer, aims it at him...and then, slowly and carefully settles the hammer down with her thumb. She puts her gun back in its little sheath.

Payday's eye is drawn to Smith's gun belt, the silver bullets. She pulls one from the belt, holds it up and examines it.

Smith stirs. She drops her hand to her side, slips the bullet into the pouch she carries on her belt.

                    SMITH (CONT'D)
                    (emphatically)
                Get that light, will you?

Payday picks up her whip, SNAPS it at the candle, flicking out the light.

DARKNESS

Out of the darkness we hear–

                    SMITH (CONT'D}
                Damn.

                                                DISSOLVE TO:

CELLAR – NIGHT

The CANDLE IS LIT by Smith. He's wearing his guns. Payday, who has stretched out on the ground, awakes, sits up.

                    SMITH
                I need to get you back to the cave. You're safer there.

Payday stands.

                    PAYDAY
                    (snide)
                We can wait till day, you know?

                    SMITH
                Day or night. Not a lot of difference with Quill. He doesn't seem to be hiding anymore... And I'm kind of on a time schedule.

EXT. EDGE OF TOWN – NIGHT

Smith and Payday are on horseback, coming out from beneath some trees, onto the road. As they do, Smith turns in his saddle and looks at the town.

CLOSE ON WHAT HE SEES

The Bell tower standing high. The bell hangs in such a way that it blocks out much of the moon. Except for the halves on either side.

BACK TO SMITH and we're still looking at the tower but from a distance.

> **SMITH**
> (mostly to self)
> Well, I'll be damned. The Two Moons. Now I know where Quill is. Now I know what we got to do.

> **PAYDAY**
> What?

> **SMITH**
> Tell you later.

THE ROAD – NIGHT

They are coming down the road. Doc on horseback, Undertaker in his little rig.

> **DOC**
> Anything happens to that girl, I'll cut off the rest of your leg.

> **UNDERTAKER**
> How the hell is it my fault? You're the goddamn planner. She's a big girl. Handle herself better than we can.

                    DOC
That's so, what the hell are we doing out here?

                    UNDERTAKER
You're the one that was so all fired worked up about looking for her. She's probably back at the cave, fixing a hot meal. Having a drink by firelight. Which is where we ought to be.

Unseen by the Doc and Undertaker, a ghoul on horseback rides up behind them. Not so close as to be in touching distance but we can see him.

CLOSE ON THE GHOUL

He's SNICKERING. He thinks he's so sneaky.

BACK TO SCENE

Doc and Undertaker and the Ghoul riding behind them.

                    UNDERTAKER (CONT'D)
Thing is, we got to stay alert.

                    DOC
I'm always alert. I was born alert. My mama used to say if there was one thing I was, it was goddamn alert.

Another ghoul boy comes out of the woods on the side of the road. Now there are two. Then another shows up. Three.

                    UNDERTAKER
Hell, wasn't for me, you'd be dead by now. You're not one for paying attention. You get your mind on something, a one-man

band in a clown suit could paint your ass
green and you'd never even notice.

At this comment, we have BEGUN TO HEAR THE HOOVES OF THE GHOULS' HORSES BEHIND THEM. And so have Undertaker and Doc.

CLOSE ON GHOULS

Six of them now. Roy and Gene among them.

BACK TO DOC AND UNDERTAKER

Without looking–

              UNDERTAKER (CONT'D)
  Shit.

              DOC
  Something's behind us, ain't it?

Undertaker looks back, then turns forward.

              UNDERTAKER
  Yep.

Doc yells to his horse, digs in his heels, and the horse takes off running. Undertaker snaps his buggy whip in the air above the head of his horse. They charge forward, trying to outrun the ghouls.

Ghouls are yelling, spurring their dead horses after the Doc and Undertaker. The Ghouls closing on the Undertaker and Doc.

ON UNDERTAKER

              UNDERTAKER (CONT'D)
  'Nuff of this shit.

Undertaker whips his rig about, starts riding straight back toward the ghouls. He snaps a match with his thumb, lights his mounted torch, grabs up a bottle, and just as he rides right through the middle of the ghouls, he lights and tosses it, hitting one of the ghouls in the head, bursting its noggin into a wafting flame that lights up the night.

Doc jerks his horse to halt, turns it, goes after Undertaker.

                    DOC
Crazy bastard!

ANOTHER ANGLE

Here comes the Doc, and he's WHOOPING IT UP, firing his revolver, hitting a ghoul in the chest three times.

ON THE SHOT GHOUL

                    SHOT GHOUL
                    (grinning)
You don't never learn, you dumb old bastard.

As Doc rides past the shot ghoul, who has pulled his pistol and is tracking Doc, the ghoul's wounds widen, and he suddenly stops smiling, starts to fall apart. And just before he dissolves–

                SHOT GHOUL (CONT'D)
Ah, horse shit.

Doc rides on, grinning.

                    DOC
Silver bullets, asshole. Made by yours truly.

UNDERTAKER

He's circled his rig and is riding back. He lights a bottle, going straight for a ghoul with it. He raises it high, just as the GHOUL FIRES; the shot hits the bottle.

When it bursts, a rain of fire falls down on the SCREAMING Undertaker. The wagon catches on fire. The horse runs wild.

The driverless rig begins to weave, and then it snaps free of the horse who continues to run away as the Undertaker's rig bounces off into a pasture and burns ferociously, taking the Undertaker with it.

                    DOC
He stops his horse, looks at the Undertaker.

                DOC (CONT'D)
        Oh, hell. No, goddamnit, no.

PULL BACK

The remaining four ghouls have gathered around Doc. Flames from the Undertaker are lighting up the scene. Doc raises his pistol, but Gene slams the gun from his hand with a quirt, knocking it into the dirt. Doc looks done for.

Roy glances over at the blazing Undertaker.

                    ROY
        (smiling big)
        Hot tonight, ain't it? Do you smell meat
        a'cookin'. I do. Kind of makin' my mouth
        drool. How about you, Gene?

Gene pushes his horse in closer.

                  GENE
        Oh yeah. It's making me hungry enough to
        eat the ass out of a menstruating mule... Or,
        we could just eat you, and your barbacued
        friend over there. That would do.

ROY
Have your horse for dessert.

Doc's face looks resigned.

One of the ghoul boys slowly raises his revolver, aims it at Doc and THEN–

–The ghoul nods forward suddenly, his hat flying off. FLAMES shoot up over his head, then his whole head is ABLAZE. His body catches on fire as he tumbles off the horse and explodes into cinders and his mount thunders panicked down the road.

ANGLE THE WOODS

On foot near the road. Their horses tied off behind them in the trees.

It's THE COCKY KID that Smith banged on the noggin. He has a bow and arrow and is notching another shaft onto the string. Beside him is the Sundown Saloon Bartender, DOUBLE SHOT. He has a torch. He lights the kid's arrow, which has a wad of tinder wrapped around the shaft near the point.

BACK TO SCENE

Doc takes advantage of the distraction, charges his horse into Gene's horse, knocking him off.

As Gene rises from the ground, an arrow hits him right between his eyes, causing him to WHIP INTO FLAMES.

ANOTHER ARROW

It whips by Roy, just missing him. If that's not enough, around a curve in the road, Smith and Payday on horseback.

ROY (CONT'D)
Shit! Run for it!

HELL'S BOUNTY —93

Roy and the remaining ghouls riding hell bent for leather down the dark road.

PAYDAY

She rides up and sees the burning Undertaker's wagon, drops off her horse, holds the reins, eases up as close to the flames as possible.

PAYDAY' S FACE

She is devastated.

BACK TO SCENE

Smith rides up, dismounts. The Doc, the Kid, and Bartender gather around.

              PAYDAY
      I shouldn't have left him.

              DOC
      Nothing you can do for him now, girl. He
      knew the chances same as me and you.

              PAYDAY
      I'm going back for that sonofabitch Quill!

              SMITH
      That's a good idea.

              DOC
      No it isn't. That ain't no good at all.

Payday starts to pull her horse around, like she's going to rush off. Smith grabs her arm.

              SMITH
      But not yet.

They exchange long looks.

CAVE – NIGHT

OUR COMPLETE GANG is riding through the waterfall, into the cave. As the others are about their business. Smith and Kid, side by side, dismount.

Double Shot comes over, grabs the horses' reins. He already has the others in his hand, pulling the horses after him.

                  DOUBLE SHOT
I'll take them.

As Double Shot goes off with the horses, Kid grabs Smith's arm.

                  COCKY KID
I know you. You're the sonofabitch hit me over the head. 1 don't know how it's you, but it's you. I don't never forget nobody tries to humiliate me.

                  SMITH
Oh, I wasn't trying that hard.

                  COCKY KID
You don't know what you're messin' with, Mister.

                  SMITH
Well, I'll give you one thing. I thought you'd be dead by now.

                  COCKY KID
There you go again.

                  SMITH
Let it go, Kid.

> COCKY KID
> I don't allow no insults, Mister.

> SMITH
> So we're gonna shoot it out? That's what
> you want?

Kid pushes around in front of Smith. He touches his guns in the holsters, loosening them.

> COCKY KID
> I ain't no kid anymore, Mister. Let's try it
> again.

Kid goes for his guns. Smith slaps the kid's hands away, draws both of the kid's revolvers.

KID'S FACE

He's incredulous.

BACK TO SCENE

Smith. A little smile. Then Smith brings both revolvers down on the kid's head. The kid drops like a towel. Smith leans over, slips the kid's guns back into his holsters.

Double Shot comes back into the scene, sees the kid lying there.

> DOUBLE SHOT
> What the hell happened to him?

> SMITH
> Sleepy.

Payday walks over.

> PAY DAY
> You might have killed him.

Smith looks down at the kid. He slowly finds a cigar, a match, lights up.

                    SMITH
        Naw. He'll come around.

Double Shot reaches in his back pocket, takes out a metal flask. He opens the bottle, takes a swig.

The Doc comes over. He looks longingly at the bottle.

                    DOC
        I'll take some of that.

DOUBLE SHOT hesitates.

                    DOUBLE SHOT
        Way you were moving about tonight, quick and ready like, I figure that ain't you no more, Doc.

                    DOC
        Tonight it is.

Double Shot reluctantly extends the bottle to Doc. Before Doc can take it–

                    SMITH
        First time I saw you Doc, you were face down on a bar table. You look pretty good with your head held up.

Doc slowly pushes Double Shot's hand back.

                    DOC
        No thanks. I ain't thirsty after all.

The Doc looks at Smith, nods and walks off into the shadows.

> SMITH
> We better get some sleep, we're gonna need it.

CAVE – LATER

Smith is rolling out his bedroll. He's by himself. We can see the others in the background, nearer the waterfall, preparing their beds.

The Kid is still conked out on the ground.

As Smith prepares his bed, Payday comes over, sits down on a rock.

> PAYDAY
> That was a good thing you did with Doc.

Smith tosses his saddle to the head of the roll, he stretches out, pulls the blanket over him, his boots sticking out at the bottom of the blanket.

> SMITH
> Wouldn't do us any good if he was drunk.

> PAYDAY
> And I guess you could have killed Jimmy.

> SMITH
> Jimmy?

> PAYDAY
> The kid...you could have killed him, but you didn't. Maybe you have changed.

> SMITH
> I said so.

She's starting to ease toward him.

> SMITH (CONT'D)
> I hope you're not just lonely.

> PAYDAY
> Does it matter?

As she comes to him, he takes her in his arms and their lips meet, and his hand touches her face, causing the mask to slide aside.

She reaches up to grab it.

> SMITH
> It doesn't matter.

He slowly reaches up, and even though she grabs his hand, she gradually lets him push the mask aside.

It's a mess under there. Her eye is closed and there are scars everywhere.

> PAYDAY
> I'm so...horrible.

> SMITH
> Trust me... You're beautiful.

He kisses her on the scar.

She melts into his arms, and we–

DISSOLVE TO:

SMITH AND PAYDAY – LATER – STILL NIGHT

They are lying together, Payday in the crook of Smith's arm. It's obvious they are nude under the blanket.

Smith eases his arm out from under Payday, slides out of the bedroll grabbing his pants, and we see his hairy legs but...he's still wearing the boots–

CUT TO:

SMITH

He's fully dressed, walking to the front of the cave. Double Shot is starting to stir. He passes the Kid who is bending down by the stream, washing his face with a handful of water. He looks up as Smith passes, rubbing his temples with his fingers. The look he gives Smith is pretty dark.

Doc is sitting on a rock near the waterfall. The moonlight is shining through the water.

As Smith comes up.

> **DOC**
> Thank you for last night.

> **SMITH**
> No need. Try this instead. I just got a couple more.

Smith hands him a cigar. Doc takes it and Smith lights it with a match from his vest pocket. He then lights one for himself.

> **DOC**
> Lost my family over drink. Too late for that, I guess... But for now, thanks. Only ones matter to me are Payday and Undertaker...McBride. And now he's gone... Stupid asshole. Getting himself killed like that.

Double Shot comes walking up, scratching his ass. He looks at Smith and Doc.

                    DOUBLE SHOT
Got to piss.

                    DOC
Well don't do it in here. May be a cave to you, but it's our home.

                    DOUBLE SHOT
I can remember when you weren't so persnickity.

                    DOC
                    (snidely)
Just great to have you back around, Double Shot.

Double Shot eases outside at the edge of the cave and waterfall, where it's relatively dry.

                    DOC (CONT'D)
He's right. I used to shit in the spittoon when I was drunk.

EXT. CAVE – THE BARTENDER – NIGHT

Double Shot pissing. He finishes, buttons up, looks up at the sky. The moon is riding high.

INT. CAVE

Double Shot entering at the edge of cave. He walks over to Doc and Smith. Double Shot looks a little bewildered.

                    DOUBLE SHOT
The moon's still high.

                    DOC
What are you babbling about?

                    DOUBLE SHOT
            The moon.

                         DOC
            You just now notice, after all this time, that
            it stays full.

                    DOUBLE SHOT
            It's not that... How long we been asleep?

Doc digs out his watch, looks at it.

                         DOC
            Well... Wait a minute.

Doc looks at the moonlight coming through the waterfall; obviously it's night. He puts his watch to his ear. Then carefully puts it away.

                    DOC (CONT'D)
            That's odd. It should have been light hours
            ago.

                    DOUBLE SHOT
            Exactly.

The Cocky Kid and Payday wander over.

                       PAYDAY
            What's going on?

EXT. CAVE – MOMENTS LATER

Smith, Doc and Double Shot are standing at the edge of the flowing water near the waterfall, looking up at the sky.

                        SMITH
            It's happening.

DOC
What's happening?

SMITH
The Old Ones. The Long Dark Night.

DOUBLE SHOT
The who?

SMITH
No time. We're ever gonna do something about Quill, now's the time, 'cause it's all the time we've got left.

DOUBLE SHOT
I don't get it.

SMITH
We don't find him, do him in, there won't be anything left to get.

DOC
We don't have nearly enough silver. I made a few bullets, but–

SMITH
Not a problem.

Smith removes a bullet from his belt, gives it to Doc.

SMITH (CONT'D)
Put that in your pocket. You'll never run out.

Doc looks perplexed, but takes the bullet.

COCKY KID
Never run out?

Smith pulls another from his belt, pokes the bullet in one of the many empty loops in the kid's gun belt. The loops fill up. Cocky Kid's mouth falls open.

> SMITH
> Long as you got one, you'll always have ammunition. Payday... You'll have to get rid of your shotgun, use your pistols.

Payday nods.

Cocky Kid grabs Smith's arm.

> SMITH (CONT'D)
> That's a bad habit you got.

> COCKY KID
> We got to get something straight.

> SMITH
> That is...?

> COCKY KID
> (serious)
> Don't hit me anymore, okay?

JUST OUTSIDE TOWN – NIGHT – LATER

OUR GANG is riding under the moonlight down the road. They look like they mean business. Smith has a stick of dynamite in his belt again.

From where they are they can see the town, the tower rising high. The moon fits right behind it, the bell blotting most of it out, showing a half on either side, giving off a hellish light.

> COCKY KID (CONT'D)
> Wasn't the moon dead high?

SMITH
Not from here it isn't.

Suddenly Smith stops. When he does it takes the others a moment to realize he has stopped. They pause and look back.

COCKY KID
Change your mind?

SMITH
We're gonna need help.

DOC
Hell yeah, we need help. But I don't think we're gonna get it. You just now putting that together?

Smith gets off his horse, walks out to the middle of the road. The others ride back to him and dismount, curious.

COCKY KID
You gonna draw a plan in the dirt?

SMITH
Deal cards.

They watch as Smith pulls the cards out of his pocket. He fans them out. We see the pictures of people on them.

SMITH (CONT'D)
I almost forgot. The posse.

The others look confused.

DOUBLE SHOT
You been in loco weed?

Smith deals one card, sailing it out into the road. As it lands we see the picture on the card. A WOMAN in a long calico dress overlapped by a gun belt. A rough looking woman. She's so ugly she could make birds fall dead from the sky. She's mounted on a pinto horse. This is BELLE STARR.

The figure grows up through the card, expanding. The next moment the woman, fully realized, mounted on the pinto, is sitting in the middle of the road. She looks over at Smith and grins. The silver bullets in her belt wink in the moonlight.

> BELLE STARR
> Howdy, Belle Starr at your service. As they say, a fella sent me.

> COCKY KID
> I heard of you. They say what you don't fuck up you shit on.

> BELLE STARR
> What would you know about fuckin'? I'm ugly as homemade sin, and I wouldn't fuck you. I don't figure your balls have dropped yet.

Cocky Kid looks as if he's been cut off at the knees.

Smith tosses another card into the dirt. Picture on the card is of a rough looking man in a Confederate uniform on a big horse. He is wearing a double bandoleer across his chest. Both are packed with silver bullets.

The rough looking man springs up from the road on his horse. He leans forward in the saddle, spits a wad of tobacco in the dust.

> BLOODY BILL
> Hell, boy, you know me. Between the two of us, we killed a regiment.

Smith nods.

SMITH
Bloody Bill.

BLOODY BILL
I'll have you know I didn't volunteer to be here. I was sent. Don't like it when I don't make my own choices.

SMITH
Just as long as you're here.

A repeat card toss from Smith. Card hits. Up pops a young man with a beard. He too has a belt full of silver bullets. He has a rifle lying across his saddle. He has a hard, hawkish look. He grins at Smith.

JESSE JAMES
You remember me don't you?

SMITH
Can't forget Jesse James.

JESSE JAMES
Right good to see you, Smith. Should have gone to Kansas with you.

SMITH
Guess it beats gettin' shot in the back of the head. Ford boy, wasn't it?

JESSE JAMES
Yeah. The dirty little coward.

SMITH
What about your brother, Frank?

JESSE JAMES
Sonofabitch surrendered. Can you believe that?

SMITH
He was always smarter than you, Jesse.

Another card dealt. Up from it springs another Confederate. This guy really looks rough. He has five pistols. Two in holsters, two in his belt. He wears a .36 Navy in a holster under his arm. Again, we can see those silver bullets in his gun belt. He's scarred and almost as ugly as Belle Starr. He grins at our team, shows teeth that would allow him to eat a water melon through a split rail fence.

QUANTRAIL
As I live and breathe, it's my old army buddy, Smith. How's it hanging?

SMITH
Low, and to the left, Quantrail.

QUANTRAIL
Was wondering if you ever found them Yankee skunks killed your family.

SMITH
Afraid not.

QUANTRAIL
See you're carrying your dynamite. You still got a death wish?

SMITH
Not so much anymore.

Quantrail shrugs.

QUANTRAIL
Long as I get to kill something.

SMITH
Gonna give you your chance. Just remember this time I'll give the orders. It

won't be like Kansas, these bastards will deserve it.

Last card. Up springs a long-haired, good looking gent on a big buckskin horse. This guy has on a low-crowned, flat-brimmed hat, two six-guns stuck in a red sash around his waist. He has a long drooping mustache.

          WILD BILL
James Butler Hickok. Better known as Wild Bill.

          SMITH
Your reputation proceeds you. I'm surprised to see you here. Never heard of you killing someone didn't need killing.

          WILD BILL
Borderline case, hoss. In limbo, as they call it. I'm here to earn my bonnet and move on to some place a might more comfortable.

Smith nods.

          SMITH
Good luck.

ANGLE TO INCLUDE AND FAVOR DOUBLE SHOT

          DOUBLE SHOT
You have friends in high places..

          SMITH
Low places. And they're not that friendly.

          DOC
          (to posse)
You excuse me and Mr. Smith for a moment.

Doc pulls Smith over to the side of the road.

> **DOC (CONT'D)**
> Don't know how you did it. Don't care. But these folks, they're murderers and scalawags.

> **SMITH**
> I figured the Ladies Temperance Movement would be the wrong kind of posse.

> **DOC**
> (not convinced)
> Hope you know what you're doing?

> **SMITH**
> None of us know what we're doing. But were kind of at die dog or eat the hatchet.

Doc nods. This is true. They join the others, mounting up.

> **WILD BILL**
> All you got to do is point us in the right direction, Old Hoss. We know what to do.

> **SMITH**
> Good. Someone should.

Smith rides out in front of the others, turns in the saddle, talks to his group.

> **SMITH (CONT'D)**
> The tower is where the bad stuff is happening. That's all you need to know. Quill will end up there. If not now, later. If we can get him before he gets there, all the better. After he gets there, we ain't got much time.

Smith points at the tower.

SMITH (CONT'D)
That piece of the moon on either side of that bell in the tower. That's the gate. The Old Ones I talked about are coming through there somehow. I wouldn't know an Old One from a retired watchmaker. But I know this. They get through, we might as well shit and go blind, 'cause it's all over 'cept for buzzards and wild dogs eatin' our asses.

BELLE STARR
Hell, fella. We gonna start shootin' or talk ourselves to death?

SMITH
(nodding)
All right, then. But it ain't gonna be no pony ride around the veranda.

Jesse lifts his rifle, rests the stock on his thigh.

JESSE JAMES
We wouldn't have it any other way.

CUT TO:

THE RIDE

This is one bad ass looking team riding in the moonlight. A heroic bunch going after the bad guys. If they were any cooler, we'd need an overcoat just to watch them ride.

Suddenly the screen is filled with other riders, galloping out to meet them. This, of course, is a LARGE outfit of Ghoul Boys, Roy in the lead.

CUT TO:

ROY AND HIS GHOUL BOYS

Roy turns to the ghoul riding next to him.

> ROY
> Quill ain't gonna like this. Them comin' into town like they're some kind of somethin'.

> GHOUL NEXT TO ROY
> Thing is, there ain't much Quill does like.

And the two groups come closer.

CLOSER.

CLOSER

AND THEN OUR TWO TEAMS COLLIDE

On the far end of MAIN STREET, and when they meet, even though our heroes are vastly outnumbered, they hit with the fury of a tornado, guns blazing, horses speeding forward, Payday's whip cracking, and we see the ghoul boys driven back toward the town proper, right into the center of Main Street.

And then things really turn ferocious. Dust from the street begins to rise and spin, and within instants we can't see anything but a cloud of dust. But within the cloud we can HEAR ACTION. SLOWLY THE DUST CLEARS. Shooting stops. Our heroes are all there, in the center of things we see them quite well, surrounded by ghouls. But, a large number of ghoul horses are empty of riders.

It's all frozen suddenly, no one moving. The ghouls just sitting on their horses, staring at our guys, who are bloody and tired and coated in dust.

Our heroes look at one another, surprised by this sudden SILENT AND UNMOVING TABLEAU.

And then Belle Star LAUGHS, loud and hardy, and Jesse swings his rifle around, POPS one of the ghoulish, riderless horses, turning it to dust.

AND NOW THE BALL IS ROLLING AGAIN. Jesse takes a SHOT in the arm from one of the ghouls that knocks him off his horse. He rolls on the ground, recovers, grabs up his rifle, starts backing down the street, firing as fast as he can cock the weapon.

There's shooting and fighting everywhere, causing our heroes to be separated by action, and from here on out we're going to pick up the pace, seeing our heroes in different locations on Main Street, making with personal fights, and we'll CUT BETWEEN THE ACTIONS AND LOCATIONS:

Belle Star, she's riding into the midst of the ghouls, blazing away, dropping them like bad habits. Then her horse takes a bullet, down she goes tumbling to the street. She starts firing, running backwards, until her back is against a building.

Some of the ghouls dismount, start walking toward her firing away. Pistol shots SPLAT all around her, knocking splinters from the wall, knocking off her hat.

Double Shot looks, sees Belle's situation. He comes riding in, shooting ghouls from behind, rides right up on the boardwalk, swings out of the saddle, puts his back against the wall by Belle.

Three ghouls on foot start moving toward them, carefully reloading their pistols as they come.

                    DOUBLE SHOT
  First time I done a truly brave thing in
  my life.

                    BELLE STARR
  Last time too.

The bullets from the ghouls start to fly, pecking at them like crows. Down they go. The ghouls rush in, tearing at them, ripping of arms, legs, eating as if it's the last buffet on earth and it's two bucks a wagon load.

SMITH

He's on horseback at the end of a long porch. He's firing at a bunch of bonnet wearing female ghouls rushing along the porch walk, under the overhang, waving rakes and farm implements. He's dropping some of them, but they are almost on him.

PAYDAY

riding hard as hell down the street toward Smith. As she passes, she snaps out with her whip, wraps it around a support post, hooks the whip on her saddle horn, jerks the porch down on top of the ghouls. We see a leg thrash, an arm thrash from under the wreckage.

Out of the alley behind Smith comes a little girl ghoul with a shovel.

Payday swings under the horse's belly, shoots, hits the girl ghoul right between the eyes, turning her to dust.

Smith throws an admiring glance in Payday's direction, but she's gone, diving back into the fray where we see Wild Bill, spinning his horse in circles, whacking at ghouls with his gun barrel as they try to tug him off his horse. Payday shoots one of the ghouls as she rides by, and Wild Bill kicks out with a boot, and frees himself of their grasp.

Near Wild Bill we see–

DOC

He's firing into the midst of swarming ghouls, but behind him, riding fast, is Roy with a two-by-four.

PAYDAY

sees what's happening. She yells to Doc. Doc turns his head toward her, but–

–it's too late. The two-by-four makes contact, smashing Doc's skull like a glass jar, dropping him to the ground as Roy rides on by CHUCKLING. On the ground, female ghouls and children dive down on Doc for a hot lunch.

ON PAYDAY

Her face falls. But there's no time for it. Ghouls are coming for her. She's back in the fight.

BLOODY BILL AND QUANTRAIL

On horseback side by side, shooting at this big wad of ghouls. Bill's revolver CLICKS empty. He looks up at the approaching ghoul boys. They seem to be coming out of the woodwork, more than we've seen before. Whatever's left of the three hundred or so, men and women, a child on a crutch.

                BLOODY BILL
Hell with this.

Quantrail, pulls the .36 Navy from under his arm, tries to hand it to Bill.

                BLOODY BILL (CONT'D)
Keep it!

Bill wheels his horse, bolts away through a gap in the ghouls. He doesn't get far.

                QUANTRAIL
You ain't no son of the Confederacy, you chicken shit.

HELL'S BOUNTY

Quantrail FIRES at Bloody Bill, hitting him in the back of the head, dropping him off his horse.

Quantrail turns back to the ghouls, LETS OUT WITH A REBEL YELL, charges them, using his knees to guide the horse, shooting as he goes. Hell, he's having a good time. And then–

A SCREECH

It's QUILL. He swoops down on Quantrail, extending one talon, hitting Quantrail's neck, cutting off his head as smooth as a hot knife sliding through cold butter. BLOOD SQUIRTS TO THE SKY. The headless corpse sits for a moment, then topples off the horse.

ANOTHER PART OF THE STREET

COCKY KID

He's on foot about to rush through an open doorway, and standing there within its frame is a grinning ghoul. The Kid skids to stop.

The ghoul glances at the cool rig Cocky Kid is wearing, grins. He drops down in a draw stance. The kid moves fast, grabs both guns from the ghoul's holsters, cracks him on the head with the barrels, causing the ghoul's skull to crack and bend in.

The ghoul blinks. The kid quickly sticks the ghoul's guns back in his holsters.

The ghoul tries to go for them. The kid outdraws him, using his own guns this time, popping off two shots, taking out both eyes and turning the ghoul to dust.

JESSE JAMES

He's still on foot. His holsters are empty of guns. He's swinging his rifle, trying to fight off a bunch of ghouls on foot. He's not killing them, but he's doing well, knocking them back with each swing of his rifle, causing teeth to fly like corn kernels, spraying blood like rain.

OPPOSITE END OF THE STREET

PAYDAY

She's at a full gallop and a shadow swoops over her. Payday sees the shadow running along the ground. She swings to the side of the horse as Quill snaps at the air with his talons.

Quill comes back. As he sweeps down, Payday lays backwards on the horse, and Quill misses again with a CRY OF DISAPPOINTMENT.

He comes a third time, hits the horse's head, even as Payday is swinging to the other side. The horse falls dead to the street and Payday hits the ground rolling.

A SCREECH

QUILL

spins in mid-air, starts back down for Payday who is running across the street in the direction of THE ASSAY OFFICE. She looks like a mouse down there, so small.

Quill drops down again.

He's almost on her.

Just as he's about to nab her, she drops to the dirt, and Quill misses his prey so close his talons cut through the back of Payday's shirt.

As Quill starts to rise, wings flapping, a ROPE LOOP flies over his head, and we–

CUT TO:

SMITH

He's on horseback, and he's wrapping his end of the rope around his saddle horn as he darts Shadow for the open door of–

THE HOTEL

Smith plunges through, causing the rope to jerk Quill toward the ground and through the doorway, catching his wings on the door frame, BREAKING THE FRAME APART and SMASHING IT TO PIECES.

Smith rides through another open door, then another, smashing Quill into the door frames as he goes, all of this happening lickity split. Quill is making more SCREECHING NOISES than a bird sanctuary.

Quill snaps out with a talon, cuts the rope.

Smith turns Shadow toward a closed door. SHADOW REARS, hits the door with his hooves, knocking it down, revealing an alley. Shadow leaps into the–

ALLEY

Smith gallops until he's in the street where there are more ghouls than quills on a porcupine. He looks across the street, sees–

ASSAY OFFICE and PAYDAY

She's right next to the door and the plate glass window. Bullets are SHATTERING the glass as the ghouls squeeze off SHOTS and miss.

Payday is firing at the ghouls, trying to bring them down. And she's not doing bad. They're dropping, but it's like trying to bail out the ocean.

SMITH

Riding in the street, blazing away. Ghouls are coming apart as his bullets find a home. He's making his way through their mass toward Payday.

Ghouls grab at him. Bullets WHIZZ by. If he weren't moving so fast on that wonderful horse, he'd be dead already. Smith lifts his feet out of the stirrups, kicks at them. He shoots. He swats with the pistols.

Finally he breaks through, rides up to the Assay Office, jumps off his horse to stand by Payday. He slaps Shadow on the ass.

Shadow bolts, running through the ghouls so hard it's like a bowling ball knocking down pins. There are a few barrels outside the Assay office, Smith and Payday push them away from the wall, climb behind them, shoot at the ghouls from between them. The ghouls fire back, tearing splinters from the barrels. It looks grim.

Payday SNAPS off her last shot.

                  PAYDAY
  I'm empty.

                  SMITH
  Reload while I hold them off.

As she starts to reload from the silver bullets in her gun belt, Smith's revolver goes empty. He draws the other.

                  PAYDAY
  I'll reload us both.

Payday snatches up Smith's empty revolver, starts to load it.

And then WE'RE STARTLED by a CRACKING SOUND. It causes Smith and Payday, even the ghouls to turn and look up at–

THE HOTEL ROOF

IT EXPLODES as Quill comes up through it, FLAPPING HIS WINGS, HOWLING. He's as mad as a eunuch in a whore house.

He takes to the sky.

HELL'S BOUNTY

We lose sight of him in the darkness, and we–

CUT TO:

JESSE JAMES

He's gotten separated from everyone else, not even near help. He's almost covered in ghouls. They have bitten chunks out of him. He's as red with blood as a slaughterhouse worker. He's looking tired. He's limping.

And then, the ghouls are all over him. One of them points his revolver, lets LOOSE WITH A SHOT.

Jesse jerks back, GRUNTS, taking it in the shoulder.

JESSE JAMES
Hot damn!

He kicks one ghoul in the chest, knocking him back. He's really swinging that rifle now, and he's banging them around. But they keep getting up. And they keep coming.

A SHADOW covers Jesse. He almost glances up but–

Too late.

It's Quill. He nabs Jesse by the shoulders, and lifts him up into the sky with a WILD, INHUMAN CRY.

The ghouls all look up. They appear to be disappointed. We see that one of them is Roy.

ROY
Now that ain't fair. He was ours.

Jesse's rifle falls, lands on Roy's head.

                              ROY
                    Ouch.

                                                CUT TO:

SMITH AND PAYDAY

They look, see Wild Bill riding on his horse on the boardwalk, twirling and twisting, firing at ghouls. Bullets are whizzing by him, slamming into the walls of buildings.

And then Wild Bill's horse goes down, throwing him into the street.

Smith steps out from behind the barrel, blazing away with both revolvers.

                              SMITH
                    Wild Bill. Over here.

Bill comes toward Smith at a limping run. And now Smith and Wild Bill and Payday are backing through the Assay Office door as the ghouls close in.

A LOUD BLAST

A ghoul in the street drops.

Our heroes turn to look at the source of the shot.

It's the Cocky Kid. He's poking his revolver out of the busted frame of the plate glass window of the Assay Office, grinning like he's at a picnic.

                            COCKY KID
                    Get your asses in here.

INT. ASSAY OFFICE

Payday locks the door. As she turns, she sees Cocky Kid standing at the big, glassless window. He grins.

                    COCKY KID
          We got more to worry about than that
          door.

                    PAYDAY
          Ever bit helps.

As our team fires at the ghouls through the glassless big window. As Smith and Cocky Kid talk they are firing away at the ghouls, not really looking at one another.

                    SMITH
          You been here all this time and didn't help
          us out?

                    COCKY KID
          Been here, been gone. Just came back in
          through the back way, blocked the back
          door so they can't come in unless they
          mean real business. Saw you folks were in
          a bit of a tussle.

Cocky Kid draws a bead on a ghoul and the SHOT goes right through and hits another behind him. They both dissolve.

                    SMITH
          We're in a tussle, all right... Thanks,

                    COCKY KID
                (grinning)
          Long as you don't try and hit me on the
          head anymore, you and me are okay.

                    SMITH
          It's not me you got to worry about.

STREET

FULL OF GHOULS. Not only those on foot, but those that are dismounting, starting to move toward the Assay Office, ready to finish the job. They look like an angry mob on its way to a hanging.

INT. ASSAY OFFICE

Our survivors have hunkered down under the windowsill, except for the grinning, Cocky Kid. He's firing both revolvers as the ghouls close in on the office.

And then the kid leaps into–

THE STREET

Firing as he goes.

      COCKY KID
 Watch this!

      SMITH
 No, Kid. Stick here.

But, it's too late. The Cocky Kid is showing how brave he is, trying to impress Smith and the others.

Cocky Kid runs up the boardwalk doing all sorts of wild things, spinning around, SNAPPING OFF SHOTS. He dives to the dirt as shots WHIZZ where he was standing. Cocky Kid is firing from the ground, coming back to his feet, he darts down an alley and out of sight. The ghouls are racing after him, leaving the street temporarily empty.

INT. ASSAY OFFICE

Smith and Wild Bill are trying to give the Cocky Kid cover by firing from the open window way.

                    WILD BILL
            And they call me Wild.

                    SMITH
                    (impressed)
            Crazy bastard. He really can shoot.

Wild Bill, suddenly practical.

                    WILD BILL
            Gives us time to reload.

As they start that process, we realize Payday is at the back of the office, picking something from an open safe. A bag from a collection of many bags.

She jerks the string on the bag, pours some of its contents into her hand. Says–

                    PAYDAY
            Silver dust.

STREET

The ghouls have recollected. There no sign of the Cocky Kid. The ghouls are moving more deliberately now. We can see that Roy is among them, at their head. He yells at the office.

                    ROY
            Might as well come on out and get eaten.

No response from the office.

                    ROY (CONT'D)
            Gonna end up the same either way.

Roy turns back to the ghouls.

ROY (CONT'D)
Okay, boys. Let's get 'em. And no holding back this time. Go!

In mass they move toward the Assay Office.

INT. ASSAY OFFICE

ON DOOR

As it is kicked in, and a wad of ghouls push inside, Rot first.

THE WINDOW

Same thing. Ghouls pushing in.

And, as the ghouls boots hit the floor in the doorway, as they drop over the windowsill and hit the floor, they FREEZE and look down.

THE FLOOR

It's covered in SILVER DUST. Empty silver dust bags are tossed here and there on the floor.

ON ROY

ROY (CONT'D)
Dagnabit.

The silver glows and dissolves Roy's boots, leaving nothing more than his skeletal feet, and then the glow climbs and Roy begins to come apart from the feet up.

Within a moment, nothing but Roy's hat.

Behind where Roy stood, more ghouls turning to dust. Same near the window.

STREET

HELL'S BOUNTY

Ghouls, seeing what's happening to their companions, fall back.

INT. ASSAY OFFICE

Smith, Payday and Wild Bill, poke their heads out from behind the furniture. They are grinning.

> **WILD BILL**
> That ought to hold them awhile.

> **SMITH**
> Yeah, but they're holding us too. We can't get to the tower. And we can't stop Quill.

CUT TO:

THE BELL TOWER

We are looking through the opening in the tower, and we can see the bell hanging there, and from this UPWARD ANGLE, it seems to be splitting the moon so that it shows on either side of the bell. But now, the moon seems to be wavering. In fact, the tower seems to waver for a moment before snapping back in line.

The sky above the tower has begun to swirl and turn dark. The night seems to be tearing open a bit. We can see something moving in that tear, a kind of talon pokes out, clutches at the edge of the night. A glow comes from the rent in the sky.

Quill flaps into view, hovers above the tower, then lights like a gargoyle on its very tip. The glow from the tear silhouettes Quill. His wings flutter once, then fold tight against his back.

INT. ASSAY OFFICE

SMITH AND THE OTHERS. They are exhausted. Sitting, leaning against furniture. We HEAR something we can't at first identify. Neither can our remaining heroes.

PAYDAY
What's that?

Now we LISTEN. It's a POUNDING SOUND. And what definitely sounds like SAWING. MORE POUNDING.

SMITH
What in the hell?

SILENCE

A BEAT

ANOTHER

And then–

THE STREET

Six ghouls with makeshift stilts. They aren't very good stilts. In fact, they are awkward, one foot rest lower than the other on one. Another looks as if it's about to break and fall over. Another ghoul has one short board to his stilts, and one tall board. He's tottering, but maintaining.

Ugly as the stilts are, they seem to work, because these ghouls are coming down the street on these damn things.

SHOT THROUGH ASSAY WINDOW

Falling in behind the stilted ghouls, walking. They all look determined.

FAVOR OUR GUYS

SMITH
Well, I'll be damned.

> **WILD BILL**
> You can say that again.

Our gang starts moving back.

At the open window one ghoul steps his stilt through, and we see it TOUCH THE FLOOR AND THE SILVER DUST. He steps through with the other stilt.

ON THIS GHOUL

He looks pretty damn happy. He starts stilting toward our heroes as the other stilted ghouls try to follow his lead.

Smith races toward a short flight of stairs calling to the others.

> **SMITH**
> This way!

Payday grabs a bag of silver dust, and she and Wild Bill race after him. As they climb the stairs, Wild Bill pauses on the bottom step, FIRES at one of the stilted ghouls, missing him, but hitting a stilt. The stilt CRACKS. The ghoul falls. Hits the silver dust on the floor, and POOF. He's gone.

Payday, she's tossing silver dust from the bag onto the stair steps, and then, our bunch are up the stairs and through a door, and into an–

UPSTAIRS ROOM

There's a big window up there, a double shutter job, and it's wide open. Another smaller window across the way. Out of that we can see a lower roof, a one story next to the Assay Office. No place else to go.

SHOT DOWN THE STAIRS

Ghouls are crowded at the bottom on stilts. One of them tries to mount the stairs, wobbles, regains his position. He looks up, sees–

PAYDAY

At the top of the stairs, standing in the doorway. She has the bag of silver in one hand. She watches the ghoul trying to come up the stairs on those stilts. He looks up at her. As she pours dust into one hand–

PAYDAY
Fairy dust... Poof, you're gone.

She throws the handful. It hits the ghoul on the steps, and, HE'S GONE. His stilts hold their position for a second, then fall over, tumbling down the stairs, hitting one of the ghouls, causing him to rock. He almost regains his balance, but...he topples. And when does, he hits all the ghouls on stilts. They start to topple like dominoes, striking the silver dust littered floor, THROWING UP BLOOMS OF SILVER...and then they are all gone.

AT THE ASSAY WINDOW

Ghouls are gathered there, looking in. One in a floppy white hat speaks.

FLOPPY HAT
That was a bad idea.

INT. UPSTAIRS ASSAY ROOM

Smith grabs a dresser, shoves it against the door.

AT THE BIG OPEN SHUTTER WINDOW

A FLAPPING SOUND. It's Quill. He lights on the sill, staring in at our heroes.

QUILL
You can't stop me. Nothing can stop me.
I don't need those dead things to do what

> needs to be done. I can do it. It's just...so...I
> don't know, messy. I hate messy.

Payday suddenly makes a wide step toward Quill, and she flicks dust from the bag, and it hits Quill right in the eye. SIZZLING SOUND as the silver dust does it work.

Quill FLAPS off the sill, hangs in the night air.

PAYDAY
> Now you know how it feels, you greasy
> sack of dog shit! Is that messy?

CLOSE ON QUILL

His eye is gone. And in fact, his scars are reminiscent of Payday's. He whips around in pain, his back is to us, and–

WILD BILL

Wild Bill is looking at the pained Quill, his back to them.

WILD BILL
> Ain't gonna be outdone by no kid.

Wild Bill races across the floor, jumps through the window and lands on Quill's back, whacking at him with the barrel of his gun.

QUILL

Makes a kind of BLEATING SOUND and takes to the sky with a BEATING OF WINGS, Wild Bill astride.

CLOSE ON QUILL'S EYE

It's healing over, the eye pushing back into place as if he has them on an assembly line inside his head.

ANOTHER VIEW

Quill begins to buck like a horse, and Wild Bill, he's holding his pistol high, slapping Quill's side, clinging to him with his other hand like Quill's a wild bronc.

WILD BILL (CONT'D)
Yeeeha, you old sonofabitch.

UPSTAIRS WINDOW

Smith and Payday rush to the window, look up. They see the shape of Quill and Wild Bill moving swiftly across the night sky. And then they see Wild Bill's shape slip and fall in the distance.

SMITH
He gave us a chance. Let's take it.

Smith speeds across the floor to the other window, looks out at the building below and across the way.

PAYDAY
A chance for what?

SMITH
To do what needs to be done. Quill has to finish up at the tower, and that's where we have to be. To make sure he doesn't do what he wants to do.

Smith grabs Payday by the arm, and they both step on the sill... and jump. Landing on the lower roof. They move across it, to the concealment of a chimney, look out at the street. It's full of ghouls. They have all given up on the Assay Office. They are gathered at the base of the bell tower, looking up, like worshipers before a shrine.

FOCUS ON THE SKY AND BELL TOWER

The sky looks funky. Full of swirls and twists of color and light. The bell tower rises toward the gap like a giant phallus about to penetrate the pulsating womb of the sky. Quill flies into view, wings his way toward the tower. He lights on the tower's tip, gargoyle style again.

BACK TO SCENE

Smith and Payday push back a bit, lay low next to the chimney. They start to slide back along the slightly sloping roof, toward the edge of it.

They look down into the–

STREET

It's about ten feet below, appears to be empty.

SMITH

Leans over the edge of the roof, looks around. He puts his fingers to his mouth, WHISTLES QUICK AND SHARP.

GHOULS

One raises his head. He's heard something. The whistle. But the scene before him is too much. He turns back to the tower, Quill, the ripping sky and the entering Old Ones.

STREET BELOW

Shadow comes trotting out of an alley into the narrow street. We can see he's been through it. There are bloody scratches on his body.

The horse stops right below where Smith and Payday are. Smith crouches, jumps, lands in the saddle.

CLOSE ON SMITH

That hurt. He makes a face, takes a breath.

BACK TO SCENE

Smith looks up at Payday. She swings down from the roof, hanging by her hands. Smith grabs her legs, pulls her down onto the horse, behind him.

They ride forward a yard, and then–

              PAYDAY
   Smith. Look.

Smith looks where Payday is pointing.

CLOSE ON WHAT THEY SEE

The Kid's hat, guns, part of his clothes, boots. A bloody shirt.

BACK TO SCENE

              SMITH
   Poor kid.

              PAYDAY
   Jerry. His name was Jerry.

Smith nods.

              SMITH
   He was all right.

Smith trots Shadow to the end of the street. They are looking out at the ghouls, and the bell tower.

Smith reaches into one of his saddlebags, takes out a stick of dynamite. He pulls a knife, cuts the fuse on the stick in half. He puts the stick in his belt.

                    PAYDAY
  Oh, hell.

Smith takes a deep breath.

                    SMITH
  All right, lady, hitch up your drawers.

With that, Smith CLUCKS to his horse, and Shadow leaps. We're talking a big leap, and it's just the beginning. Shadow is opening up full throttle, riding straight at the collection of ghouls and the bell tower.

SMASHING THROUGH THE GHOULS

Smith and Payday on Shadow dart into the main square, spilling ghouls in all directions. SHOOTING THEIR GUNS, making the ghoul boys turn to dust and goo as they plow on through. Payday runs low on ammunition, returns her guns to her holsters, goes at them with the whip, CRACKING them right and left.

The ghouls are grabbing at them, tearing their clothes, jerking off their gun belts and holsters as they claw. Payday grabs at her pouch as it is snagged by a ghoul, retains it. She loses a boot. Payday kicks the offending boot nabber in the face with her socked foot. Smith's dynamite stick rolls out on the ground, disappears beneath the ghouls' booted feet.

Smith and Payday continue fighting, mostly now by whacking at the ghouls, kicking, Payday working her whip.

They race ahead of the ghouls, come to the steps of the bell tower. Shadow gallops up them, comes to the huge double door. Shadow rears on his hind legs, WHINNIES, brings both silver shod hooves straight into the door.

INT. BELL TOWER

The wooden bar running across the two doors BREAKS, and the doors BLAST wide open.

Smith and Payday charge in on Shadow.

It's a big place with a staircase that winds its way up to the bell and the platform up there. A big rope hangs from the bell.

Smith and Payday jump off Shadow. Smith jams his revolvers into his pants, since he is beltless. We see Payday stick the bag in her pants pocket, coil her whip over her shoulder with a quick, flicking motion. Then, with effort, they shove the big doors closed as the ghouls come up the outside steps.

ON THE FLOOR

The wooden bar that Shadow busted with his hooves.

SMITH

Snatches up the broken bar, puts the fragment in so that it makes a lock of sorts. But it looks precarious.

Ghouls pounding on the outside. Making all manner of noise. The bar shakes.

Smith and Payday are back on Shadow. Smith puts his boot heels to the great horse, and Shadow goes for the stairs, climbing the damn things like a goat.

BELOW IN THE TOWER

Ghouls are rushing in.

BACK TO SHADOW

He tops the stairs, ends up on the bell tower platform. From here, out the bell shaped window, they can see Quill, who is no longer on the tower tip, but who is actually, with his talons, tearing at the opening in the sky. We see a terrible head of something poke through. And as Quill works, he CHANTS.

SMITH AND PAYDAY

They dismount Shadow at the summit of the stairs. Shadow moves to one side, Smith and Payday look around.

>PAYDAY
>What do we do?

Smith's desperate. Looking this way and that. The lip of the bell is glowing.

>SMITH
>It's the goddamn bell!

>PAYDAY
>What?

He's excited now, moving around the walkway, looking up into the bell from different angles.

INTERIOR BELL

It's full of images, figures. They are GLOWING BRIGHTLY, WORMING ABOUT.

>SMITH
>It's the words, the spell. He's hidden it in
>the bell.

>PAYDAY
>I'll say it again. What?

                    SMITH
           Trust me. Destroy the bell, we destroy the
           spell.

LOUD CRACKING SOUND

Payday moves to look down the stairs.

                    PAYDAY
           Smith. I think we have a more immediate
           problem.

STAIRCASE

The ghouls are rushing up it. Smith takes out the dynamite. He takes out one of the fuses. He cuts the fuse in half, sticks it in the dynamite. All of this is done with the precision of a surgeon. He reaches in his vest pocket, produces a Lucifer, strikes it on the side of his pants, lights the fuse, tosses the dynamite into the stair climbing ghouls.

The ghouls are close. They looks angry.

The dynamite stick HISSING, bounces along the steps, and we have an–

EXPLOSION that rocks the bell tower and knocks Smith and Payday back on their asses. The bell vibrates, RINGS.

It's worse for the ghouls, they go in all directions, in pieces. Wood spins and twists and smaller fragments float down like paper airplanes. The stairway is gone. And so are the ghouls.

QUILL TEARING AT THE SKY

He snaps his head around at the SOUND OF THE EXPLOSION. He SNARLS, but he ignores that business. He goes back to tearing at the wound he's made in the night. The head is pushing through more and more.

HELL'S BOUNTY

BELL TOWER

Smith takes the saddlebags off of Shadow. He opens them up. Full of dynamite. He reaches for his gun belt, realizes it's gone. Along with the dynamite.

> **SMITH**
> I need your bullets.

Payday shakes her head.

> **PAYDAY**
> Mine's gone too. Guns are empty... Wait a minute.

She pulls the pouch from her pocket.

> **PAYDAY (CONT'D)**
> I took one of your bullets...

She opens the pouch. It's chock full of silver bullets.

> **PAYDAY (CONT'D)**
> They multiplied.

Smith snatches it from her. He drops the pouch into the saddlebag.

> **SMITH**
> Let's just hope this is enough silver. It's sure enough dynamite.

> **PAYDAY**
> Oh.

She reaches inside her shirt, pulls out a bag of silver from the Assay office.

> **PAYDAY (CONT'D)**
> I still have this. It's half full.

Smith pokes the bag of silver into the saddlebags, slings them over his shoulder. He grabs Payday by both arms.

> **SMITH**
> You're gonna need to get out of here. At least get as far from this bell as you can.

She shakes her head.

> **PAYDAY**
> Nowhere to go. And I wouldn't go anyway.

> **SMITH**
> I can't let you stay.

> **PAYDAY**
> You're not letting me do anything.

> **SMITH**
> You could go down the bell rope.

She shakes her head violently.

> **PAYDAY**
> I'm not going.

> **SMITH**
> All right... Okay... The rope. Can you pull it, ring the bell?

> **PAYDAY**
> Why?

> **SMITH**
> He doesn't want anything to happen to this bell. But it's going to.

As he says this, he pats the saddlebags full of dynamite.

HELL'S BOUNTY 139

Payday, swallows, nods. The rope is partially coiled on the runway. She takes hold of it, gathers herself.

PAYDAY
Say when.

Smith opens one of the saddlebags, takes out one of the dynamite sticks, trims the fuse short with his knife. He puts the stick in his mouth, throws the saddlebags back over his shoulder. He finds a match, holds it in his hands.

He looks at Payday.

SMITH
Ring that sonofabitch!

QUILL TEARING AT THE SKY

THE BELL RINGS AND RINGS

Quill jerks his head around, glances at the tower. Smith is standing in the bell shaped window with the dynamite in his teeth. He holds up the match. Strikes it along the seam of his pants.

Quill dives straight back to the tower.

BELL TOWER

Smith is just about to light the dynamite, when QUILL, MOVING IMPOSSIBLY FAST, THUDS into Smith causing him to lose the dynamite, rolling him across the floor, the dynamite in the other direction, near Shadow.

Quill snatches up Smith, slings him, smashing him into the wall. It's obvious Smith is hurt. Quill STALKS TOWARD HIM, HAPPY, making the good moment last.

WHACK

Payday's whip is wrapped around Quill's neck. Quill turns, grabs the whip, jerks it away from Payday, gives her a cold stare with his one good eye.

Payday slowly waves her hand.

>**PAYDAY**
>(meek)
>Howdy.

Quill glances back at Smith, then Payday, And then, the BACK LEGS OF SHADOW SHOOT INTO THE SCENE and kick him, LAUNCH him into the bell, ringing it.

Quill falls, grabs at the edge of the hole for the bell, pulls himself up so that he's once again standing on the bell platform.

And then, SHADOW MOVES. His hooves go up, come down hard, the silver shoes flashing, striking Quill, knocking him back a stumbling step.

They collide, Shadow and Quill. Struggling. Hooves flash. Talons flash. Blood flies.

The dynamite, due to all the floor shaking, is rolling under Shadow and Quill, back and forth.

SMITH

He takes another match from his vest. He leaps for the dynamite, rolls under Shadow's hooves, comes out underneath him, grabbing up the stick, still clutching the saddlebags.

QUILL

Literally shoves Shadow back. The horse goes to one knee, hurt bad. Now Quill looks at Smith. Smith has the dynamite back in his teeth. And the match is lit and right on it.

HELL'S BOUNTY

CLOSE ON FUSE

Short.

BACK TO SCENE

                  SMITH
             (through clenched teeth)
     See you in hell, asshole!

Payday runs and jumps straight at Smith, forcing him to catch her, and in that EXACT INSTANT, Quill grabs them, and–

ALL THE DYNAMITE BLOWS

EXT. TOWER

IN SLO-MO we see the tower collapse, and as it does, the ghouls, here, there...in the street, near the tower, they collapse too, as if there was never anyone in their clothes. The rip in the sky PINCHES SHUT, snapping off a piece of an Old One's talon, or tentacle, or whatever that strange thing is. Another loses a nose.

And in that instant of final collapse.

DAYLIGHT

The sun new and red on the horizon. Birds chirping. Rubble from the tower. CAMERA ROAMS OVER TO...a piece of the bell lying in the grass. We can see the strange writing on the fragment. A rabbit hops through the grass. Hops along, nosing the ground. Hops onto the bell piece, and–

SPUT

The rabbit is gone; he's BLOWN UP. Rabbit hair floats on the wind for a moment. Birds are heard even more happily and the sun is rising higher above the trees, as we–

SLOW DISSOLVE TO:

HELL'S SALOON

The door bangs open. Out comes the MUSCULAR BLONDE pushing a wheelbarrow with Smith's hat on it, looking worse than before, filled with holes.

She dumps the wheelbarrow, dropping the goo onto the floor. As before, Smith rises up from it. And as before he walks straight away to the bar, still attended by Snappy.

Muscular Blonde is gone.

Smith puts a boot on the foot rest, leans an elbow on the bar. Snappy pushes a drink in front of him. Smith picks it up, downs it, makes a sour face.

Smith hears a LOUD FART.

He turns his back to the bar, looks out at the patrons.

BELLE STARR

She is settling her hip back into a chair. She touches her hat in a tipping manner.

> **BELLE STAR**
> Damn. That was sticky.

THE REST OF THE POSSE

They're all there. Quantrail kind of leans out of his chair, punches Bloody Bill in the arm. Bloody Bill turns, hurt, a little surprised.

> **SNAPPY**
> Boys. That's enough.

Smith turns back to the bar.

> SMITH
>
> I finished the mission. Why am I back here?

> SNAPPY
>
> You finished a job. Not the jobs.

Snappy pats a battered, scorched gold box on the bar. It's wrapped in twine with a bow tied on it.

> SMITH
>
> Shit. I should have known better than to trust you... Wait a minute. Zelzarda. Quill... He's in that box?

> SNAPPY
>
> Yep. Him and most of the spell. Some of it got away.

Smith points to the box and twine knot.

> SMITH
>
> Well, I suggest a better knot. That boy's trouble.

> SNAPPY
>
> Oh, he'll be taken care of all right.

Door flies open again, and here comes the Muscular Blonde again, pushing a wheelbarrow. We see Payday's eye patch there. She dumps the barrel, and out of it flows, PAYDAY.

She's looking good in her leathers. Her hair is full and swept back. The mask is in place.

Smith smiles at her, then–

> SMITH
>
> Wait a minute. She doesn't belong here.

SNAPPY
I couldn't agree more.

BLAM. The door flies open again. Another wheelbarrow is wheeled in by the Muscular Blonde. It's full of horse hair and two hooves with two sliver shoes. As she tips it, we–

DISSOLVE TO:

THE MINE SHAFT

Dark in there. We hear hooves clopping. We see a finger of light. It throws a shadow on the wall. A shadow of a horse bearing two riders.

CLOSE ON THE RIDERS

SMITH AND PAYDAY. She's wearing the green dress and the shoes Smith took for her.

And then the horse enters into shadow again, and we HEAR ROARING.

MOUTH OF THE MINE SHAFT – NIGHT

A crow black, 1950s topless, flame-licked roadster bearing two riders GROWLS out of the shaft. On the front fender of the roadster we see in dark, broad, theatrical lettering: SHADOW

CLOSER

Smith is at the wheel. His hair is greased and slicked back into a duck tail, and Payday's dress, though still recognizable, has transformed into a poodle skirt. Her hair is tied back in a pony tail. Her face is fresh and renewed. Smith brakes the car to a stop, grins and turns to her.

SMITH
By the way, what's your real name?

                    PAYDAY
            What do you want it to be?

                    SMITH
            I always liked Diane.

                    PAYDAY
            What's yours?

BEAT

                    SMITH
            Smith.

Smith GUNS the roadster around in a circle, then drives it to the top of a hill and brakes. Smith and Payday look out at what's in the distance, shiny in the head beams.

DOWN BELOW

A billboard: FALLING ROCK FIRST NATIONAL BANK. AUTO LOANS. On it is an Edsel Sedan, a car of the 1950's.

BACK TO SCENE

Payday looking down at the sign.

                    PAYDAY
            Well, I'll be damned.

Payday slips her arm around Smith's, and Smith HITS THE gas, guns it off the hill, sails out into the air, and–

WE FREEZE THEM THERE, PINNED AGAINST THE FULL MOON

                                            FADE OUT.

DEADMAN'S ROAD

BY JOE R. LANSDALE
& JOHN L. LANSDALE

EXT. CABIN – NIGHT – 1880'S, OREGON – NEAR MORNING

Sunlight is poking up from behind the little cabin like a rooster comb. The cabin isn't much. The only window is dark. What passes for a front yard is littered with junk, a hoe, a broken down wagon. It's *Bad Homes and Gardens,* Western style.

Suddenly. Gun shots. Three of them.

BLAM!

BLAM!

BLAM!

Red flashes show behind the window. A horrifying GROWL is heard.

Crashing through the window into the dirt yard, glass flying, comes a man. He loses his hat, staggers to his feet.

He's tall with dark hair, a spotted rawhide vest. He's holding a revolver. He is exasperated. This is JUBIL.

A HOWL from inside the cabin.

Jubil, scooping up his hat, putting it on.

JUBIL
How'd he do that? I shot him.

WIDEN

An older, ragged looking man lifts up from the wagon bed, jumps to the ground, darts over to Jubil. Jubil turns to him. This is DASH, and he's carrying a double barrel shotgun.

              JUBIL (CONT'D)
Silver bullets. I shot him with silver bullets.

              DASH
Maybe you missed.

Jubil. He's very indignant.

              JUBIL
I don't miss.

           WOMAN'S VOICE (O.S.)
Sure you do.

CAMERA JUMPS TO – A WOMAN

We get a look at her. She's climbing down from a horse. She's good to look at. Wears a hat with a blonde pony tail poking out from under it, has on a checkered shirt, jeans and boots. This is TERRY.

BACK TO SCENE

Jubil frowns.

              DASH
Who's she?

              JUBIL
A wannabe. Follows me around. I do the work, and she tries to scoop up the bounty.

As Terry comes toward them.

                    TERRY
He means I pull his bacon out of the fire.

She quickly joins them. The three of them stand looking at the cabin. As Terry and Jubil banter, Dash watches first one, then the other, like a man observing a tennis match.

Terry studies the window of the cabin. From inside they can HEAR STUFF BEING BANGED AROUND.

                 TERRY (CONT'D)
What's he doing in there?

                    JUBIL
You could go in and ask him.

                    TERRY
Way he threw you out, you'd think he'd be mad enough to come outside.

                    JUBIL
Maybe he had to tidy up a bit first.

                    DASH
Naw. He doesn't have a neat bone in his body. And now that he's like he is, he'll just go on and shit on the floor. Won't so much as hesitate or aim it in a can. Just lets it fly.

                    TERRY
That happens sometimes when they turn. Loss of bowel control.

                    DASH
No shit?

                    JUBIL
The opposite actually.

Dash studies Jubil for a moment, then gets it.

> **DASH**
> Oh. I see. You made a funny. But why doesn't he come out?

> **JUBIL**
> I fight evil bastards and such. I'm not Nostradamus.

> **TERRY**
> We could burn the cabin down. They don't like fire.

> **DASH**
> (definitely not liking this idea)
> Hell. Me neither. I live here. I don't want my cabin burned down.

> **TERRY**
> Might clean it up some.

> **DASH**
> No. No fire. I just want my dadburn brother dealt with. He's eaten half the livestock, all the chickens, and he's tried to eat me.

> **TERRY**
> That's what they do.

> **JUBIL**
> (reflective)
> They're especially bad about chasing chickens.

CABIN DOOR

It bursts open and out bounds the werewolf. He's wearing boots that his paws have torn through, showing claws. He's got on ragged jeans, a ripped shirt.

Dark wolf hair springs through the rips. His head is one hairy, greasy, toothy mess.

DASH
Hot damn. See you.

Dash exits in a hurry, gets behind a tree with his shotgun.

The werewolf steps forward, steps on the hoe. It pops up, hits him solid in the face, knocking him down. The werewolf gets up again.

Jubil jerks his revolver from the holster, fires. The shot hits the cabin.

TERRY
See. You missed.

JUBIL
He moved.

Terry darts over to the tree where Dash is trying to hide. Just before she gets there, he leans out from behind the tree, fires one barrel of the shotgun. It hits the wolf square in the chest.

WOLF

He brushes pellets out of his fur.

BACK TO DASH AND TERRY

DASH
Shit.

Terry snatches at Dash's shotgun.

                              TERRY
                    Give me that.

A brief tug of war, and Terry comes out with the gun.

JUBIL AND WOLF

The Wolf attacks Jubil. He tries to shoot, but the wolf is on him. Jubil drops the pistol, grabs the wolf, falls back, puts his foot in the critter's stomach, kicks up, flipping the werewolf into the dirt.

ON TERRY

She's pulling silver dimes from her pocket, dropping them down the charged barrel of the shotgun.

WOLF

He's up, looking at Jubil like he's a hot lunch.

ANOTHER ANGLE

Terry yells at the wolf.

                              TERRY (CONT'D)
                    Hey! Flea ass.

Wolf jerks his head to look at her, SNARLS, goes for her. She cranks down on him with the last barrel full of silver. This just as Jubil is leveling his pistol again.

BOOM!

WOLF

The shot hits the beast in the chest, knocking a large hole all the way through. You can see the distant trees through that hole.

CLOSE ON STUNNED WOLF'S FACE

Not a happy look. The snout quivers. The wolf lets out with an ANEMIC GROWL, cuts a LOUD FART. Then the critter falls over.

THE SUN IS RISING HIGHER

JUBIL, TERRY AND DASH

They congregate to look down at the wolf. He has transformed back to a man. An ugly man. Fact is, he looks like Dash.

                    TERRY (CONT'D)
    Damn. He looked better as a wolf.

                    DASH
    Mama said wouldn't nobody ever hang Zeke for a picture. Hang him maybe, but not for no picture.

Jubil looks at Dash, then at Zeke, then back to Dash.

                    JUBIL
    Ain't you two twins?

                    DASH
    He was the ugly one.

ANOTHER ANGLE

Jubil still looking at Dash.

                    JUBIL
    Now. The bounty.

Dash. He's looking nervous.

                    DASH
    Let's see. Now we said one hundred dollars, didn't we?

                    JUBIL
         We said five hundred, Dash.

                    TERRY
         Two-fifty a piece.

                    JUBIL
         What? You aren't getting spit, sister.

                    TERRY
         I'm the one killed him. I'd think that would
         be worth something.

Jubil turns back to Dash.

                    JUBIL
         Five hundred. Now would be good.

                    DASH
         I might have exaggerated about the
         amount of my poke.

Jubil and Terry look at one another, and we–

                                                    CUT TO:

MOMENTS LATER – JUBIL AND TERRY

They each have one of Dash's legs, have him lifted upside down and are shaking him. Coins are falling out of his pockets.

After a vigorous shaking, they drop Dash to the ground on his head, hard.

Terry and Jubil bend down, gather the leavings from Dash's pockets.

Standing up they sort the coins.

>   **JUBIL**
> I got eight bits.
>
>   **TERRY**
> I got four bits. Some pocket lint.

Jubil looks hard at Dash.

>   **JUBIL**
> That's a long ways from five hundred. It's a long ways from one hundred.
>
>   **DASH**
> Wait. I got something. I got something worth money.
>
>   **JUBIL**
> I ought to have let Zeke eat you.

Dash, seeming to forget the circumstances of the moment, stands brushing himself off.

>   **DASH**
> What made Zeke that way?
>
>   **JUBIL**
> Sex with the recent dead.

Dash looks concerned.

Terry is plucking and thumping the pocket lint from her collection of coins.

>   **TERRY**
> He's foolin' you. And I ought not to tell you the truth, you old goober. He's that way 'cause he got bit by a werewolf.

DASH
There are others?

JUBIL
Woods are crawling with them.

DASH
No.

TERRY
Thick as grass burrs.

JUBIL
Go get that something you're talking about, Dash. On the double.

Dash goes into the cabin.

Terry holds out the coins in her hand.

TERRY
We gonna split this?

JUBIL
You keep what you got. Me, I'm gonna use my eight bits to buy a hotel... Look, why do you keep following me around?

TERRY
Because you can find this kind of business, you got a knack. It's a goddamn gift. But, you can find them, and I can finish them. That's my knack. In other words, Jubil, we're a good team.

JUBIL
We're not a team.

> TERRY
>
> Are to.

> JUBIL
>
> No we're not.

> TERRY
>
> Sure we are. Remember the headless horseman?

> JUBIL
>
> I was doing fine.

> TERRY
>
> He was kicking your ass.

> JUBIL
>
> I slipped.

Dash is back out of the cabin with a jar. He hands the jar to Jubil. Jubil holds up the jar and looks at it.

INSERT JAR FULL OF WASHERS AND A SHINY RING ON AN AMPUTATED FINGER

BACK TO SCENE

> JUBIL (CONT'D)
>
> These are washers. And a goddamn finger.

> DASH
>
> There's a ring on it.

> JUBIL
>
> But it's a cheap ring. And it's on a finger.

> DASH
>
> I couldn't get it off Grandpa's hand. He was dead anyhow.

TERRY
You chopped his finger off.

DASH
After he was dead.

Jubil slams the jar against Dash's chest, breaking it, spilling washers and ringed finger.

JUBIL
Keep it.

DASH
Now, you didn't have to do that.

JUBIL
No, I didn't.

Dash nods toward Zeke.

DASH
What do I do with him? I mean, he's done. Right?

JUBIL
Not necessarily. But I'm not going to tell you what to do. What do you expect for eight bits and a cheap ring on a rotten finger.

TERRY
I'd burn him.

Jubil walks to his horse which is tied to a nearby tree, pulls the reins free and mounts.

Dash to Terry.

                    DASH
            I don't want to stay here by myself. Not
            with them wolfies out there.

Terry is walking toward her horse.

                    TERRY
            Suit yourself.

As she mounts we see Dash dragging Zeke toward the cabin.

LATER – FULL MORNING

Jubil riding along. Terry rides up beside him.

                    TERRY (CONT'D)
            You in a hurry?

                    JUBIL
            Trying to lose you.

                    TERRY
            You're still mad about Howard taking me
            to the barn dance?

                    JUBIL
            No I'm not.

                    TERRY
            He was a good dancer.

                    JUBIL
            Not as good as me.

                    TERRY
            He was a better kisser.

                    JUBIL
            Ass kisser.

                    TERRY
            How'd you know?

Jubil turns in the saddle and gives her a hard look.

                    TERRY (CONT'D)
            You are still mad.

A beat.

                    TERRY (CONT'D)
            Smell smoke?

They turn in their saddles, look back, see smoke rising up.

                    TERRY (CONT'D)
            I think Dash decided he didn't want his
            cabin after all.

                    JUBIL
            I think he's turned Zeke into a smoke signal.

TIME LAPSE

ESTABLISHING SHOT OF CARVER TRADING COMPANY – LATE AFTERNOON

It's a low, long, clapboard building with a sign that reads: CARVER TRADING COMPANY. A few horses are tied out front. A wagon.

Jubil and Terry ride up. They look tired. Terry looks up at the sky.

                    TERRY
            Nearly dark.

Jubil, already swinging off his horse.

JUBIL
I hope they have food. I'm so hungry I can see corn bread walking on the ground.

INT. CARVER TRADING POST

It's not much. Long table. Long benches. Shelves are spotty with supplies. A few chairs. A cook fire in the fireplace with a big pot. It's all pretty close quarters.

By the fire, a man in manacles sits on a stool. This is BILL. Nearby, a man with a deputy's badge is sitting on the end of a bench. This is DEPUTY CALEB. He's watching Bill, who is his prisoner.

There's a young, attractive woman doling out metal plates to no one in particular. She has on a long leather skirt and boots. This is CHRISTIAN.

A middle aged man is limping along the length of one of the benches. This is OLD TIMER.

The door opens. It's Jubil and Terry. They look dusty.

Jubil takes off his hat, knocks the dust off by slapping it against his leg.

CHRISTIAN
You could have done that outside.

JUBIL
Sorry.

BILL
Hell, who can tell the difference?

Bill gets glares from Christian and old Timer.

JUBIL
Was wondering we could get a meal.

                    OLD TIMER
            We serve 'em if you got the money.

                    JUBIL
            What does eight bits buy?

                    OLD TIMER
            What four bits or ten dollars buys. Beans.

                    JUBIL
            You got meat?

                    OLD TIMER
            Not unless you want to shoot a squirrel. A
            possum. Dog and cat ain't so bad you cook
            'em right... Just pay what you can afford.

Terry is taking off her hat, moving toward one of the benches.

                    TERRY
            Beans are fine.

                    OLD TIMER
            We got biscuits too. You got the teeth
            for 'em.

Jubil finds a seat at the table. He and Terry put money on the table to pay for their beans.

EXT. TRADING POST – NIGHT

Dash is riding up on a mule.

INT. TRADING POST – SHORT TIME LATER

Dash opens the door, sticks his head in.

Jubil looks at him, his face turning sour.

JUBIL
What the hell are you doing here?

DASH
Didn't think I was gonna stay back there with them wolfies, did you?

TERRY
We saw smoke.

DASH
Cabin burned down.

TERRY
Just by accident?

DASH
No. By kerosene lamp and a match. Can I come in?

JUBIL
Just don't annoy me.

Bill turns slightly, shaking the chains on his manacles.

BILL
Wolfies?

TERRY
Werewolves.

Bill looks at her like she just shit on the floor.

BILL
What in hell you talking about? Ain't no such thing.

Dash is taking his place at the table, sitting near the deputy. Christian is going around, slapping beans from a bowl onto plates with a large, not very clean looking spoon.

DASH
Tell my brother that. He was one.

BILL
You're crazy.

JUBIL
Actually, he's not. He's cheap and he's a liar, but he's not crazy.

BILL
You're crazy too.

JUBIL
I have a rule, fella. Don't speak to me in anger if I don't like you. Don't touch me with ill intent, and don't call me a liar.

BILL
I said you were crazy.

JUBIL
I've added that to the list.

OLD TIMER
(to Bill)
You don't know shit from wild honey, boy. There's all manner of business in this world you don't know a damn thing about. I've seen some things lot of so called civilized men ain't never heard of. Things I've seen would make the skin on your pecker roll back.

> **DEPUTY CALEB**
> Don't mind him none, Old Timer. He was so smart, he wouldn't be in chains.

Old Timer still looking at Bill.

> **OLD TIMER**
> I ain't never seen no werewolves, but that don't mean they ain't out there.

> **DASH**
> I've seen 'em. They ain't pretty. And they're always hungry.

> **JUBIL**
> And they'll shit on the floor.

> **DASH**
> That's right.

Christian pushes forward into the scene. She waves a hand at Old Timer.

> **CHRISTIAN**
> Old Timer here, he'll love you folks. The hubs done come off his wagon wheel. He believes a bunch of hoodoo is killing his business.

> **OLD TIMER**
> That's right. That's the truth.
> (glancing at Christian)
> Except the hub part.

Christian picks up the money Jubil and Terry put on the table, shakes it in her hand.

> **CHRISTIAN**
> Just sharing my opinion.

She moves across the room toward the far end of the big fireplace.

                OLD TIMER
    You don't know nothing child. Not a thing.

Christian is dropping the money she collected into a jar on the mantel over the fireplace.

Bill is watching her, and WE SEE WHAT HE SEES: Christian, palming a few coins.

Bill grins as she turns back around, talking.

                CHRISTIAN
    I know that road is just a road.

Jubil glances at Terry. They exchange interested looks.

                JUBIL
    What road?

                OLD TIMER
    Deadman's Road. Used to be called Pine Tree Road. Folks don't travel it no more on account of they're afraid to go there. That's hurtin' my business. Most don't want to come the long way around. It's cut what I have to trade in half. That's why I don't have no meat.

ON BILL

He's holding his plate of beans, looking at it.

                BILL
    What am I supposed to eat with?

DEPUTY CALEB

Your mouth. I ain't giving you no knife. I wouldn't give you a spoon.

BILL

I'm gonna cut your little nubbin off and mail it to the City of Portland.

Deputy speaks to the others.

DEPUTY CALEB

This worthless piece of humanity is Bill Emory. They're gonna hang him. He's killed everything that walks, flies or crawls. That's not to mention all the folks he's murdered.

BILL

He grins. He's glad to hear about his achievements. He shrugs, starts pouring the beans from his plate toward his mouth. Some of them make it.

ANOTHER ANGLE

JUBIL

I want to know about that road, Old Timer. What's the story on that?

DEPUTY CALEB

Yeah. If that's quicker to Portland, then that's the way I'll go. I'm not a believer in haints.

OLD TIMER

I believe in haints. Living out here in the thicket you see some strange things. As for haints, well, there's powers ain't got nothing to do with Jesus or Moses, any of that bunch. Nasty things out there on Deadman's Road. Old Gods. Indians talk about them. Things always a'scratchin' to get into our world. Like a dog at a door. Only they ain't friendly.

DEPUTY CALEB
I ain't afraid of no Indian gods.

OLD TIMER
(getting worked up)
They ain't Indian Gods. They're older than that. Even the Indians ain't fond of these rascals.

JUBIL
Oh yeah. Those boys, those Old Gods. They're pissy.

OLD TIMER
(to Jubil)
You funnin' me, boy?

JUBIL
(dead serious)
Not at all. I've seen plenty myself.

TERRY
Me too.

DASH
I seen one of them wolfies. My brother Zeke. That there will hold me.

BILL
Hog wash. All of it. Hog wash.

DEPUTY CALEB
What's haints got to do with the road?

DEADMAN'S ROAD

Old Timer sits on the bench, and as he begins to talk, we–

FLASHBACK

> **OLD TIMER (V.O.)**
> Gil Gimet was a beekeeper over around Schow, on the far end of what was then known as Pine Tree Road. He sold honey.

GIL GIMET riding up to a rundown store in a wagon. He's not much to look at. His face wears mean like a ski mask. The back of the wagon is packed with jars of honey. He pulls the horses up on a rise, sets the brake, gets out of the wagon.

There's a little half-Indian boy standing in the doorway of the store, maybe nine or ten.

There's an Indian woman working a little patch of garden. This is GLORY. She looks up as Gimet arrives.

> **OLD TIMER (V.O.) (CONT'D)**
> Gimet was a hot tempered man used to always getting his way.

> **GIMET**
> Hey, boy. Give old Gil Gimet a hand unloading these jars. And be careful. Them jars is worth money.

The boy hesitates.

> **GIMET (CONT'D)**
> Get out there and do it, boy. Mind your elders.

The boy looks at the woman in the patch. She nods at him.

The boy moves toward the wagon.

Gimet takes one of the jars from the back of the wagon, carries it inside.

INT. STORE – MOMENT LATER

Gimet enters. It isn't much of a store. There's a counter with a man behind it. He looks like the last bath he had was when he pissed on himself. This is TULLY.

Gimet sets the jar of honey on the counter.

> **OLD TIMER (V.O.)**
> Honey he made was in big demand. Wasn't nothing like it. It was kind of like liquor. You had a bit, you wanted some more.

Gimet looking self-congratulatory, speaking to Tully.

> **GIMET**
> I put your boy to work.

We can see Tully isn't thrilled with Gimet, but he nods.

> **GIMET (CONT'D)**
> This here is my finest yet. Sweeter than a woman's loving.

> **TULLY**
> Well, that last batch sure was sweet. There's folks come in here everyday askin' for more. How much you want?

> **GIMET**
> I want half a Yankee dollar per jar.

> **TULLY**
> Oh. That's a lot, Gil.

> **GIMET**
> Yeah. But folks want it. Ain't nobody else got it, and if they did, wouldn't be as good. You got to know your bees. Not just make them a hive and pour a little sugar water. You got to know them. Damn near each and every one of them by name.

Tully considering.

> **TULLY**
> It is mighty fine honey. But half a dollar?

Gimet grabs up his jar.

> **GIMET**
> I can take it down the road a piece. It's worth it to have someone appreciate me and my bees.

> **TULLY**
> Now no need to be hasty.

> **GIMET**
> You don't want to mess with me, Tully. I'll cut you off from any batch I make.

Gimet leans forward, close to Tully's nose.

> **GIMET (CONT'D)**
> And besides, you don't want to rile me. You know how I am when I'm riled. Insult me, insult my bees. And I don't like someone might hurt their feelings. They're the only friends I got.

Tully takes a cautious tact.

TULLY
How many jars you got?

A CRASHING SOUND

Gimet puts the jar down and rushes outside.

EXT. STORE – INSTANT LATER

The kid is standing in the back of the wagon, his hands still spread. A jar of honey is broken at his feet. The dark gold liquid is running around his boots.

Tully comes to stand in the doorway.

Gimet moving toward the wagon.

GIMET
You little bastard.

The kid panics, starts to hop out of the wagon by leaping onto the seat. As he jumps off the wagon he bumps the brake, causing it to come loose.

The boy hits the ground.

The wagon rolls backwards.

Gimet's horrified face.

The boy, frozen, watching the terrible thing unfold.

Wagon rolling down the hill, toward a tree. It slams into the tree and the jars go flying, honey shoots all over, splashing against the tree, in the wagon, on the ground.

Gimet turns and looks at the Indian boy. Tully is starting to move up behind Gimet.

> TULLY
> He's just a boy.

> GIMET
> You little bastard.

The boy breaks and runs.

Gimet draws his gun.

The Indian woman is running from the patch with her hoe in her hand.

> TULLY
> No, Gimet!

Tully tries to reach Gimet's gun hand.

CLOSE ON INDIAN BOY

He's running right at us, but the SOUND OF GUNFIRE causes him to throw up his arms and fall.

Where he filled our vision, we now see in the background–

> GIMET

He's pointing the gun.

WIDEN SHOT TO INCLUDE TULLY

Tully pushes Gimet's arm down, but it's too late. He doesn't try to hold Gimet. He runs toward his boy.

> GIMET
> Months of work. Months of work. All of
> it ruined.

ANOTHER ANGLE

Tully runs up to the boy, slowly rolls him over, looks down at the boy's dead face.

> **TULLY**
> You done killed him, Gimet. You killed my boy.

> **GIMET**
> Course I did. Dirty little half-breed.

The woman has arrived at the body, she drops the hoe, she puts the boy's head in her lap. She turns and looks at Gimet. Her face is destroyed.

Tully, slowly rising from the ground.

> **TULLY**
> Over jars of honey.

Gimet slipping his gun back into its holster.

> **GIMET**
> My goddamn honey. My money. The work of my bees.

Tully picks up the hoe, starts to charge Gimet.

> **GIMET (CONT'D)**
> Wouldn't do that, less you want to stretch out beside him... You know I won't hesitate.

Tully has made a few steps. Gimet draws his gun, cocks it, Tully weakly drops the hoe with a cry. He's defeated.

The woman, glaring at Gimet.

> **INDIAN WOMAN**
> My baby. You killed my baby.

GIMET
He had it coming. Stick him in a hole out back.

INDIAN WOMAN
You'll pay for this. I swear by the Old Ones. You'll wander in the dark forever.

GIMET
Glory, you old squaw. You ain't gonna do nothing but shit and fall back in it.

Gimet starts walking toward his wagon, turns as he passes Tully and the woman.

GIMET (CONT'D)
I think that will conclude our business.

EXT. PINE TREE ROAD (DEADMAN'S ROAD) – SOME TIME LATER – NIGHT

The Moon rolling in the heavens.

Glory in the middle of the road, down on her knees with a bone, scratching something in the dirt.

OLD TIMER (V.O.)
No one knows for sure how she did it. But ain't no one doubts she did something.

She's bent over, scratching in the road, but we can't see exactly what she's doing.

GLORY

CHANTING. (It's not a language we understand, or anyone else for that matter.)

OLD TIMER (V.O.)
There was plenty said she had powers. Powers like her ancestors. That she could heal. And if she could do something to the light side, ain't no doubt in my mind she could do something to the dark side, she got worked up enough.

ON THE CIRCLE

It has a crude drawing of a bee in the center. Arrows going out from the bee pointing forward down the road, and another pointing backwards. In front of both arrows are little shields.

GIMET'S CABIN IN THE WOODS – SIMULTANEOUS

Gimet is in his cabin. He sitting in a rocking chair, and he's doing needle work. He's very serious about it, taking his time doing it right. We can hear a buzzing sound. His bees. They're all around in the cabin. There's a cracked window and the bees are going in and out of it.

BACK TO GLORY

Glory draws a knife across one of her wrists, slowly.

GIMET

GLORY'S CHANTING abruptly fills the cabin. Gimet jumps, sticks himself accidently with the needle. He looks around. He drops his work. He pulls his gun from a scabbard on the table.

GIMET
What in the hell?

He lets out a yell as a strip of flesh is ripped off his face, ripped as if an unseen hand has grabbed at it, torn it like paper. Gimet's face is ripping, popping. It looks like gophers are running under the flesh on his face.

DEADMAN'S ROAD

GLORY

She swaps the knife, cuts her other wrist, slowly. Her blood drips onto the pattern she's drawn in the dirt.

GIMET

An eyeball leaps from his head. Gimet SCREAMS. He falls against his table, turns with his back against it.

The front of his shirt is ripped away, and his intestines, his organs leap from his body, splattering against the wall, knocking the window glass out.

GLORY

She's squatting, her head down in the circle, and the circle is full of blood, and not a drop is outside of it.

> **OLD TIMER (V.O.)**
> Tully realized Glory was missing, he put together a little posse. I was part of it.

A LITTLE LATER – THE ROAD, STILL NIGHT

Tully and four other men are riding down the road. Among them is Old Timer. They pause when they see Glory, her face down in the circle of patterns.

> **OLD TIMER (V.O.) (CONT'D)**
> When we found Glory, she was lying dead over some kind of scratchin' she had done. Cut her own goddamn wrists, she did. Bled out like a hog.

Tully looking down from his horse.

> **TULLY**
> (weakly)
> Figured she'd be out here.

Tully dismounts. The others remain on horseback. Tully turns Glory over gently.

> **TULLY (CONT'D)**
> (distraught)
> She's done killed herself.

Old Timer leans forward in the saddle.

> **OLD TIMER**
> It's HIS fault. Let's go get him.

Tully gently lowers Glory to the ground.

> **TULLY**
> She's gone after him in her own way. Ain't nothing we can do she ain't already done.

> **OLD TIMER**
> No offense, Tully, but I ain't a believer in magic. I'm one for doing it the old fashioned way. With a rope.

Agreement from the other riders, and we–

CUT TO:

INT. GIMET'S CABIN – SHORT TIME LATER, STILL NIGHT

The door is kicked open. Tully and the others fill the doorway. They look appalled.

WHAT THEY SEE

DEADMAN'S ROAD

Gimet is lying on his back. His skin is peeled off. His chest is ripped wide open, and inside his chest, is a busy beehive. Bees are everywhere.

>   **OLD TIMER (CONT'D)**
> Jesus.
>
>   **TULLY**
> You believe now?

BACK TO PRESENT – CARVER'S TRADING COMPANY

OUR GROUP LISTENING TO THE STORY

>   **OLD TIMER**
> That made a believer of me.
>
>   **BILL**
> Bullshit. Someone cut him up. Wasn't no magic.
>
>   **OLD TIMER**
> Believe what you want, punk. And that wasn't the end of it.

FLASHBACK CONTINUES

Tully riding on horseback down the dark road with Old Timer at his side.

>   **OLD TIMER (V.O.) (CONT'D)**
> Word got around that Gimet was alive, and on that road. Some people saw him. But a lot of others turned up missing. Me and Tully went out there to see, to finish Gimet off if need be.

We see shadows. We hear SOUNDS.

OLD TIMER (V.O.) (CONT'D)
But we didn't have no idea what we was up against.

Tully and Old Timer looking this way and that, nervous as pigs in a slaughterhouse line.

A Shadow LEAPS.

It hits Tully, knocking him off the horse.

Old Timer wheels to follow the action. He's drawn his gun.

OLD TIMER (CONT'D)
Tully! Tully!

Tully's boots being pulled into the thicket. That's all we see of him, but we can hear him yelling.

TULLY (O.S.)
Help me! God, help me!

CRUNCHING NOISE. CHEWING NOISE. BREAKING NOISE. A SLURPING SOUND.

OLD TIMER (V.O.)
I didn't prove to be much help..

CUT TO:

COMING TOWARD US

Old Timer on his horse, leaning forward, thundering away down the road–

AND WE CHANGE ANGLES, GET THE REAR VIEW, watch until Old Timer is swallowed by shadow in the distance.

END OF FLASHBACK

INT. CARVER'S TRADING COMPANY – NIGHT

Jubil, Terry, the others sitting around the table.

          BILL
          (laughing)
So, you run like a badger with turpentined balls, didn't you?

          OLD TIMER
          (snappy)
I did. I ain't proud of it. But if that ain't bad enough, to add insult to goddamn injury, ain't nobody takes that road no more. And it's the short cut.

          JUBIL
And that's rainin' on your business.

          OLD TIMER
That's right. Whatever Glory did, it killed him, but he come back.

          BILL
You don't know that. Thing dragged that friend of yours off was most likely a cougar.

          OLD TIMER
Wasn't no cougar. Maybe that's the curse on Gimet. Being dead, but not good and dead.

          TERRY
And you need him good and dead. As in not moving?

Old Timer nods.

OLD TIMER

What I need is someone to clear that road for me. That's it in a nutshell.

TERRY

You're talking to the right people. Me and Jubil, we kill haints and such. For money, that is.

JUBIL

What's this we stuff? Since when is it we?

TERRY

Don't pay him any mind. He's just cranky because Dash here didn't pay us. And I went to the dance with someone else.

Jubil gives her a cold look.

OLD TIMER

I'll pay you good to clear the road.

JUBIL

How much?

OLD TIMER

A lot.

TERRY

That's our price. Done.

DEPUTY CALEB

I don't believe in any haints, but me and Bill here will ride along with you. It'll get him to the hangman quicker, haint or no haint, and I'm for that.

CHRISTIAN
I'll go to.

OLD TIMER
I need you here.

Christian takes off her apron, tosses it on the table.

CHRISTIAN
I'm quittin'. I'm off to see the big city.

JUBIL
We don't need an entourage.

CHRISTIAN
Road don't belong to you. We can go anywhere, anytime we want.

DASH
I'm goin' too.

TERRY
But you're a chicken shit.

DASH
I'm a safer chicken shit when I'm with you two.

JUBIL
Is there a place we can put up for the night.

Old Timer nods.

OLD TIMER
The barn.

JUBIL
How far to this road you're talking about?

OLD TIMER
You start in the morning, you'll get there by night. Time he's out and about.

JUBIL
He's always on the road?

OLD TIMER
Or near the road. Ain't that many come back to tell much.

TERRY
It's a binding spell.

DEPUTY CALEB
What?

JUBIL
The magic used to put him there is limited to one spot. That road. It's not uncommon.

TERRY
Typical black magic spell.

CHRISTIAN
So this should be a snap for you two. Mostly the easy part will be taking Old Timer's money for being a fool.

OLD TIMER
Watch your mouth, girl.

JUBIL
We do our business, he won't show again. We can promise you that, Old Timer.

OLD TIMER
I believe you young fella.

DEPUTY CALEB
I don't know about haints, but I could use some help to watch Bill here. Least for awhile. I could use a night's rest, start tomorrow morning fresh.

Old Timer grins at this, goes away.

JUBIL
I'll spell you. All I need is three or four hours and I'm as good as ever.

TERRY
You could rest all week and your aim wouldn't be any better.

Jubil looks hurt.

JUBIL
You don't know everything, you know.

Old Timer comes back with a shotgun.

OLD TIMER
You can all sleep. He causes any trouble I'll blow a hole in him and tell God he died. Go on out to the barn. Me and him will stay in here.

Old Timer looks at Bill, cocks back the hammers on the shotgun.

Bill, looks nervous.

DEPUTY CALEB
You sure.

OLD TIMER
Hell, I don't sleep worth a damn anyway.

DEPUTY CALEB
I'll spell you in a couple hours or so. I can wake up to the minute, I set my mind to it.

OLD TIMER
Suit yourself.

The others start to file out toward the barn.

When they're gone–

OLD TIMER
Bill. Late at night, I sometimes like to go get me a goat, put his back feet in my boots, and then have a romantic moment. You know, satisfy some manly urges.

BILL
I don't doubt that, you old corn holer.

OLD TIMER
But ain't no goat here. If you get my meaning.

Old Timer grinning wide.

Bill looking as nervous as one of those goats might look.

DISSOLVE TO:

A ROAD – NEXT DAY – LATE AFTERNOON

Jubil and Terry are riding along on horseback. After a moment, Terry turns and looks behind her.

TERRY
They look kind of sad back there.

Jubil turns on his horse and looks back. We see what he sees:

The Deputy, Bill, Christian riding on horseback somewhat in the background. Dash on his mule.

BACK TO SCENE

          JUBIL
Until you came long, Terry. Everything went right.

          TERRY
I've never known anything you've done to go right. I'm your good luck charm, Jubil.

          JUBIL
That's depressing.

          TERRY
Who was smart enough to ask for half the money up front?

Jubil doesn't say anything.

          TERRY (CONT'D)
Who?

Nothing.

          TERRY (CONT'D)
          (louder)
Who?

          JUBIL
You.

          TERRY
Thank you.

                                  CUT TO:

THE REST OF OUR RIDERS

Deputy Caleb. Bill. Christian. Dash.

They are plodding along. We can see Jubil and Terry up ahead of them.

> **BILL**
> (to Deputy Caleb)
> Next time you want to leave me with that Old Timer, just go on and hang me yourself. I reckoned all night long he was gonna diddle me.

Deputy Caleb grinning.

> **DEPUTY CALEB**
> So he told me. Said he just loves a little joke.

> **BILL**
> I think he'd have really done it, if I'd had a fresh shave and some smell pretty on.

> **DEPUTY CALEB**
> Thing to remember, Bill. There ain't gonna be a next time with Old Timer. They're gonna hang you, and I'm gonna be in the crowd with a big bag of parched peanuts. Enjoying myself. Watching you kick.

LATER – NIGHT

Jubil and Terry come to a turn off, and there's a sign there. It sags and reads: PINE TREE ROAD.

SHOT OF THE ROAD

Dark. Limbs hang way out and low over the road; the wind wags the limbs, shadows twist and leaves crackle as they tumble across.

Jubil turns and looks behind them. The nearby shadowy shapes of the entourage.

> **JUBIL**
> Here comes the rag tag.

The others ride up.

> **DEPUTY CALEB**
> Wouldn't it just be easier for us to ride together?

> **JUBIL**
> Might as well. Not like it makes a lot of difference. Besides, we might need something to put between Gimet and ourselves.

Terry points at Bill.

> **TERRY**
> That would be you.

Bill holds up his shackled hands.

> **BILL**
> I might be more help without these.

> **DEPUTY CALEB**
> Not likely. Besides, in spite of what our companions think, I don't believe we have anything to fear, outside of maybe a pissed off raccoon.

Bill drops his hands.

> **BILL**
> You aren't quite as stupid as you look, Deputy.

                    DASH
          After them wolfies, nothing would surprise
          me.

                    BILL
          Wolfies, my ass.

                    DASH
          You're smart, you'll stay close to them two.

                    JUBIL
          Not too close. I don't like a crowd. Terry's
          bad enough.

Dash leans out from his mule toward Bill.

                    DASH
                    (confidential)
          And just as a little side note. Did you
          know that when they hang you, you mess
          yourself?

Jubil reins his horse toward the road, starts down it. He and Terry putting some paces between them and the others. They have only gone a short distance when:

                    BILL
          Hey. This horse is favoring his left back leg.

Everyone stops. Jubil rides back to join the deputy who has got off his horse.

Deputy has hold of Bill's horse's reins.

                    DEPUTY CALEB
                    (to Jubil)
          You mind taking a look, fella?
                    (to Bill)
          You better not be funnin' me, Bill. Not

unless you want me to pistol whip you
until you think you're someone else.

Jubil swings off his horse, moves toward the horse's back left leg, which it is obviously favoring.

          JUBIL
    Call me Jubil. Goes down better than fella.

          BILL
Or shit ass.

Jubil punches the horse a little. It bucks, Bill flies off and lands in the dirt.

          JUBIL
        (Not meaning it)
    Sorry.

The others are climbing off their horses. As Jubil picks up the leg, looks it over.

          CHRISTIAN
    You don't look like you know what you're doing.

          JUBIL
    I don't fix them. I just ride them.

Jubil drops the horse's leg down.

          CHRISTIAN
    My daddy was a blacksmith. Here, let me look.

          JUBIL
    Be my guest. Catch up when you get finished.

Jubil gets on his horse. He and Terry and Dash ride on. Christian takes the leg, lifts it.

CHRISTIAN
I need some light.

Bill is getting up, angrily brushing himself off.

DEPUTY CALEB
Make yourself useful, Bill.

The Deputy takes a match from his pocket.

DEPUTY CALEB (CONT'D)
Hold some light for her.

Bill takes the match, but not happily. He strolls over to Christian, strikes it on his pants, holds it close to the hoof.

CHRISTIAN
About to throw a shoe. Needs the nails hammered in better.

BILL
(quietly to Christian)
I seen you take that money back at the trading post.

Christian looks at him, but turns to the Deputy standing nearby.

CHRISTIAN
Give me your pistol, Deputy. I need a hammer.

Deputy pulls his rifle from the scabbard on his horse, cocks it. He then holds it with one hand, reaches his revolver free with the other. He tucks the Winchester under his arm, empties the shells into his hand, puts them in his pocket. He hands Christian his empty revolver, then steps back a pace.

                    DEPUTY CALEB
    Go ahead.

Christian positions the hoof over her knee. Bill leans forward as the match burns low.

                         BILL
                (whispering to Christian)
        Get me a gun with bullets, it could be
        worth a lot of money to you.

                       CHRISTIAN
                       (whispering)
        Where would you get any money?

                         BILL
                       (whispering)
        Money I stole from Wells Fargo. It's in the
        deputy's saddlebags.

She gives him a look. It could mean anything. She turns back to her work, the match goes out as Christian hammers the nails in.

                      BILL (CONT'D)
                       (whispering)
        Keep me in mind, honey.

                    DEPUTY CALEB
        Bill. If you can't speak loud enough for us
        all to enjoy, keep shut.

DEADMAN'S ROAD – A SHORT TIME LATER

Jubil and Terry and Dash on the road. They are joined by Deputy Caleb and Bill and Christian.

ON JUBIL

He sniffs.

                    JUBIL
            Smell that?

BACK TO SCENE

Dash, quietly lifts his arm and smells his pit. Just checking.

                    TERRY
            Smell what?

                    DEPUTY CALEB
            Something dead.

                    JUBIL
            Long dead... Terry, what about the goods?

Terry knows immediately what this means. She reaches in the saddlebag and pulls out a little bottle of clear liquid, holds it up.

                    TERRY
            Holy water.

                    JUBIL
            Good.

Terry digs some more, comes up with a silver crucifix, holds it up.

                    JUBIL (CONT'D)
            All right. That's good.

As she replaces the crucifix, she brings out a leather bag, unties it, pours some of the contents into her hand.

CLOSE ON HER HAND

She's holding silver bullets.

> JUBIL (CONT'D)
> Good. What about the Bible? You got the Bible?

As Terry puts the silver bullets back in the bag and into the saddlebags.

> TERRY
> Why would I have the Bible?

> JUBIL
> You're the one said we were a team.

> TERRY
> This is my ditty bag, not yours. I'm just being helpful. I don't have a Bible. No one told me to bring a Bible.

> JUBIL
> The Bible. It's a religious symbol. A barrier against otherwordly evil, so on and so on.

> TERRY
> Maybe you have a Bible.

> JUBIL
> I don't have a Bible.

> TERRY
> Then I guess we don't have one.

While they're arguing, cut to Bill. A bee flies into his nose. He lets out with–

> BILL
> Goddamnit! A bee.

He snorts the bee out. Now he is swatting at another bee that hits his ear.

> **DASH**
> (to Bill)
> Quit being such a sissy.

> **BILL**
> I'm not a sissy.

> **DASH**
> Are to.

> **BILL**
> I'm not the one afraid of wolfies.

Dash gives Bill a contemptuous look.

> **DEPUTY CALEB**
> All right, you two. That's enough.

> **DASH**
> He started it.

They continue to ride along again.

As they go, we have SHOTS OF THE WOODS

We see something, but we can't quite make it out.

A shadow flicking from tree trunk to tree trunk.

A SNAPPING stick.

Less of a shadow now. A shape. White as the bottom of a fish belly. Just a glimpse. Nothing to write home about.

They ride along a little more, looking left and right.

The wind has picked up.

Dry leaves tumble.

Thunder rumbles.

A BURST OF LIGHTNING and the sky grows darker. LIGHTNING FLASHES again and it strikes a tree beside the road, causing it to burst into flames.

And in its brief glow:

VIEW DOWN THE ROAD

Something runs across the road, almost on all fours. What we see is something white and stooped, scuttling along. When it moves, it's as if sections of its motion have been removed. Little specks of darkness whirl all around the figure.

Everyone pulls their horses to a stop.

                BILL
What was that?

              DEPUTY CALEB
What was what?

Bill is pointing at a dark spot in the road.

                BILL
That.

VIEW DOWN THE ROAD.

Nothing. Just the tree burning.

BACK TO SCENE

              DEPUTY CALEB
There's nothing there.

> **DASH**
> (smug)
> Who's the sissy now?

> **BILL**
> (agitated)
> It's gone now. But it was there. A man...or something like a man. I think. It ran across the road.

> **DEPUTY CALEB**
> I thought you weren't a believer.

> **BILL**
> I'm converted. Give me a gun. Give me a knife. Hell, give me a pointed stick. A rock to throw. Anything.

> **DEPUTY CALEB**
> What are you trying to pull, Bill? You think you're gonna do some kind of trick, then–

> **TERRY**
> Be quiet.

She says this softly, and we look at her, and she is looking straight ahead, talking without looking back at them.

> **TERRY (CONT'D)**
> He did see something. It was white and man-like and short in the trouser department.

> **CHRISTIAN**
> I think I saw something too.

THE DARK EMPTY ROAD

The tree has burned out. Smoke is floating against the darkness and it's silver in the moonlight, and then it is a wisp, and finally, it's gone.

A LIGHTNING FLASH. The road is briefly lit up again.

Still nothing.

> DEPUTY CALEB
> There isn't anything out there but bad weather. Is there Jubil?

Jubil doesn't answer.

Deputy Caleb rides up beside him. They ride along now, slowly.

> DEPUTY CALEB (CONT'D)
> Is there?

> JUBIL
> You don't want to know.

> DEPUTY CALEB
> Yes. I do.

> JUBIL
> Gimet.

ON TERRY

Unseen by the others, she eases a small bottle of whisky from her saddlebag, unscrews it quickly, and takes a snort. She closes it up and drops it back in the bag.

BACK TO ALL

> CHRISTIAN
> The sky is clearing. Moon is out.

DEPUTY CALEB
One odd lightning storm, that's for sure.

THE ROAD

Cloud shadows roll across it and then go away. Moonlight lays against the road. And then above the road, BUZZING ALONG, are bees.

BILL
See. Bees. He had bees with him. Remember. They said he was a beekeeper.

DEPUTY CALEB
Bees don't mean nothing.

BILL
They don't come out at night like this. These bees ain't right.

DEPUTY CALEB
(to Bill)
You are gettin' spooked.

JUBIL
(to Deputy Caleb)
He's right.

TERRY
They're familiars. Witches have them. Sometimes they're cats. Gimet's familiars are bees.

CHRISTIAN
What's a familiar do?

TERRY
Serves its master.

> **DEPUTY CALEB**
> I feel like I'm knee deep in bullshit.

As they ride we see something they don't. Movement along the left side of the road. The brush is starting to thin, and this movement we see is rapid, and it's the white shape we saw before, only we're getting a little better look this time. Not much better, but some. We can see a white skull, almost blue in the moonlight.

LOUDER SOUNDS as the thing moves through the brush. They glance over at the sounds.

> **JUBIL**
> That's him.

> **DEPUTY CALEB**
> God Almighty.

Bill clucks to his horse and rides ahead of the others.

> **DEPUTY CALEB (CONT'D)**
> Come back here.

Our gang picks up their pace, and pretty soon the horses are really moving. Bill is still up ahead.

The thing in the brush is rushing along now, moving ahead of our riders, almost loping on all fours. And soon it breaks way ahead of them and is gone.

OUR RIDERS

They have caught up with Bill. Deputy Caleb reaches out and grabs Bill's reins.

> **DEPUTY CALEB (CONT'D)**
> Slow up, or I'll shoot you out of the saddle.

BILL
Glad to. That thing has done gone on ahead.

They all slow down as they come together. Gradually they stop, sit astride their horses.

DASH
I don't know about you folks, but that about does it for me. He's up there, and I think we should go back the way we come.

CHRISTIAN
He'd just catch up with you, you old fart.

DASH
I'd make him work for it, at least.

JUBIL
Rest of you can do what you want. Me and Terry, we got a job to do.

Terry, surprised, gives Jubil a look.

TERRY
Now we're a team? What changed your mind?

JUBIL
That thing. And money.

DEPUTY CALEB
We're better if we stick together. We do that, we got a chance. But I'll tell you monster hunters. I get clear of that thing, I'm gonna keep on riding and take Bill with me.

DEADMAN'S ROAD

                        BILL
            I'm for that.

They began to ride along at a trot. Soon they come to a place where off to the left is a clearing, and in the clearing are what looks to be a series of white waves. But we go–

CLOSER

It's not waves. It's tombstones rising up in the moonlight. Crosses.

Then across the moonlit field of stones and crosses, comes Gimet. He's moving ape-like, and very fast. The clearing rises up and there's a hill, and on the hill is one big white tombstone, and nearby is the only mausoleum. A large white tomb with a marble door and a marble slab in front of it.

With an effortless leap, the beast jumps up on the tombstone, sits there like a king on a throne.

                    BILL (CONT'D)
            Look at that sonofabitch.

CLOSER ON GIMET

A black cloud forms around Gimet's head. It's the bees, buzzing around his skull like a crown.

REAL CLOSE ON GIMET

We get a good look. And it's nasty. His head appears to be mostly skull. A slice of flesh spots it here and there. There are a few sprigs of hair sprouting out from the top of his noggin. The skull is split in places and the moonlight shines through the splits and pokes out in our direction like rays. The eyes are empty as well, and the holes in the back of his head have plugged them with moonlight.

Gimet is bare chested, and in fact wears only the ragged remains of a pair of pants; he's almost naked. Fact is, bare chested is a literal description. This is the first time we've got this full frontal. The chest is split open, and there's a bee's nest in there, and it throbs like a heart, and when it does, it glows honey-gold and we can see bees moving around it like planets orbiting a sun.

ANGLE ON OUR CROWD

They are looking out at the thing.

> **TERRY**
> This one. It's a little different than what we're used to, huh?

> **JUBIL**
> A little.

> **DASH**
> I think I like the wolfies better.

CLOSE ON TERRY

She has pulled the bag of silver bullets out of the saddlebag, is furiously loading her pistol.

> **JUBIL**
> Give me that.

She quickly hands the bag to Jubil and he starts loading his pistol.

> **DEPUTY CALEB**
> What's that? What you got there?

> **TERRY**
> Silver bullets.

> **DEPUTY CALEB**
> I want some.

> **CHRISTIAN**
> He's gone.

Everyone looks toward–

THE TOMBSTONE

Gimet isn't there.

BACK TO SCENE

> **CHRISTIAN (CONT'D)**
> He was there. I blinked and he was gone.

> **DASH**
> Yeah. And that's what I'm fixin' to be.

The brush beside the road explodes and out of it comes Gimet, moving fast. He leaps. One of his feet hits the back of Jubil's horse.

Jubil lets out with a YELL.

Gimet bounces off the back of Jubil's horse, onto Bill's horse, grabs Bill by the head and slings him off the animal and into the road.

Gimet. Moving. Fast.

He jumps off the horse, grabs Bill by the handcuff chain and drags him kicking and SCREAMING into the brush on the side of the road with the graveyard.

> **BILL**
> Don't let him have me! Don't let him! For godsakes, shoot my ass dead.

Bill is out of sight now.

WE HEAR ALL MANNER OF RUSTLING AND BRUSH BREAKING

                    BILL (CONT'D)
                    (from a distance)
               Come get me deputy. I'm supposed to hang.

Horrible SCREAMS from BILL.

                    CHRISTIAN
               You two are supposed to be the experts.
               Do something.

                    TERRY
                    (matter of fact)
               He's fucked.

ON JUBIL

Jubil swings off his mount, pulls his rifle free as he does.

                    JUBIL
               All right. We'll go in.

                    TERRY
               We will?

                    JUBIL
               Yes, we will.

Terry dismounting more slowly, pulling her saddlebags off, throwing them over her shoulder.

No one else has dismounted.

                    DEPUTY CALEB
               Are you out of your mind? Bill ain't no one
               to nobody.

                    CHRISTIAN
               I know I didn't like him.

DEPUTY CALEB
Let him go.

JUBIL
Do what you will.

Jubil starts moving in the direction that Gimet dragged Bill away.

Terry. She takes a deep breath and follows. She grabs Jubil by the arm.

TERRY
Winchester isn't loaded with silver.

She pulls the bullet bag from the saddlebag, opens it, shakes out a few shells into Jubil's hand.

He gives her a look. It's the only time he's actually looked sweet on her.

JUBIL
Thanks.

He quickly cocks out the shells in the rifle, starts loading the Winchester with silver bullets.

TERRY
Don't miss.

JUBIL
I never miss.

TERRY
You always say that, then you always miss.

Jubil doesn't look so friendly now.

JUBIL
Coming?

He pushes into the brush and Terry, after a short pause, follows.

They disappear.

BACK TO THE ROAD

                DASH
Well, I'm just as shit scared as before, but I'm going with them. They got the silver bullets.

Dash swings off his mule and goes through the spot where Jubil and Terry vanished. The bushes shake.

Deputy Caleb and Christian look at one another. They quickly dismount. Deputy Caleb goes into the brush.

Christian pauses. She's all alone.

She turns, looks at the saddlebags on Deputy Caleb's horse.

She slides over to them, jerks one open.

OUR VIEW OF CONTENTS

Money.

BACK TO CHRISTIAN

She grins like a Christian with Four Aces and a mistress.

She mounts Deputy Caleb's horse, and thunders off down the road as fast as she can go.

MOMENTS LATER – IN THE WOODS – IN THE MOONLIGHT

Limbs are moved apart by hands, and then we realize it's Jubil. He pushes into view. Terry comes up behind him.

DEADMAN'S ROAD

A beat later, Dash, and then Deputy Caleb.

Dash looks back.

> **DASH (CONT'D)**
> Where's Christian?

> **DEPUTY CALEB**
> I heard her ride off. She chickened out. I wish I had.

> **DASH**
> Someone better go get her.

Jubil looks at Dash.

> **JUBIL**
> Go ahead.

Dash considers this. Nope. He ain't going nowhere.

> **TERRY**
> There. There's Bill!

SHOT OF BILL'S HANDCUFFED HANDS

They are poking through a mass of brush.

The Deputy moves there quickly, grabs the handcuff chain, tugs.

> **DEPUTY CALEB**
> Got ya.

He tugs so hard he falls backwards. There's no Bill attached to the arms and handcuffs. The arms appear to have been chewed off at the shoulders.

Deputy Caleb, scrambling to his feet, tossing the handcuffed arms.

> **DEPUTY CALEB (CONT'D)**
> My God!

> **TERRY**
> Like I said. He's fucked.

Deputy Caleb leans over Bill's handcuffed arms.

> **DEPUTY CALEB**
> He's been chewed on.

Deputy Caleb looks around.

> **DEPUTY CALEB (CONT'D)**
> Look. There's blood.

A nasty swipe of blood on the ground. It leads off into the woods like a dark drag mark.

> **JUBIL**
> That's the way the rest of Bill went. Come on.

They're going along the path made by the blood.

CLOSE ON DASH

As they go through a shadowed place, what appear to be vines hang down from the trees, draping over Dash's head and shoulders.

Dash starts pushing the vines aside. And then he pauses.

Where the vines fell against his face are dark wet marks.

Dash reaches up and touches his cheek, rubs it, pulls his finger back. He holds it out in front of him. He has a look on his face that wouldn't pass for pleasant.

He slowly reaches up and touches the vines.

He recoils.

                        DASH
            Hot damn!

The others, who are nearby, pause.

                        JUBIL
            What?

Dash has moved out from under the shadow of the tree and into a more moonlit area.

                        DASH
            Those aren't vines.

Jubil strides over, takes hold of one of the vines, pulls at it as he backs away, pulling it out into the moonlight.

CLOSE ON THE "VINE"

It's a bloody strand of gut.

                        JUBIL
            Intestines.

                        DASH
            And look there.

THEY LOOK

Stuck on a broken limb, the sharp point having penetrated the back of the head so that it pokes out the eye, is Bill's noggin, still adorned with his hat. The head looks like it has been used for a few rounds of soccer. His spinal cord dangles like a bell rope.

Underneath the limb is Bill's headless, armless body. It's sitting on the ground, as if it stopped to rest. The chest is ripped open. A few bees are buzzing around the corpse.

Behind Bill, not too far away, we can see the gravestones.

BACK TO OUR GANG

Jubil steps on something, pauses. He lifts his foot for a look.

WE SEE

A heart. A chunk has been bitten out of it.

BACK TO JUBIL

He reaches down, picks it up.

Jubil tosses it into the brush. He goes over to the remains of Bill, bends down and wipes his hand on Bill's pants leg.

          DASH (CONT'D)
That is just nasty. I been known to pick my nose after digging in my ass, but that... that's...nasty.

Terry looks at Dash.

          TERRY
That was something I didn't need to know.

          DASH
Well, I guess we can go back now.

          JUBIL
Not likely. I come to find and kill Gimet, and collect a reward.

          DEPUTY CALEB
          (to Terry)
What about you, girl?

> TERRY
>
> What he said.

> DEPUTY CALEB
>
> You, old man?

> DASH
>
> I'm sticking with them.

> DEPUTY CALEB
>
> Well, I didn't sign on for that.

> JUBIL
>
> Told you. You can leave at anytime. I won't think the worse of you, because truth is I didn't think that much of you to begin with.

Jubil moves forward. Terry falls in beside him. Dash hastens to catch up.

For a moment Deputy Caleb hesitates, then sighs and starts after them.

> DEPUTY CALEB
>
> All right. All right. I'm gonna stay, I ought to have some of those silver bullets.

Terry stops, opens up the saddlebag, takes out the small bullet sack. It's nearly empty. She pours the last three bullets into Deputy Caleb's hand.

> DEPUTY CALEB (CONT'D)
>
> That's it?

She opens the other saddlebag, squats down on the ground.

She removes a bandoleer of silver bullets, drops it on the ground.

She takes out her whisky bottle, sets it on the ground.

She takes out a roll of cloth. Beneath it is a large pile of silver bullets.

As she moves the cloth, a Bible falls out of it and lands on the ground.

Jubil looking at the Bible.

Terry looks up at him.

          TERRY
          (sheepisly)
I forgot.

          JUBIL
And the whisky?

          TERRY
Well, I need something to keep me warm.

Dash picks up the cloth that the Bible was wrapped around, holds it up. It's a fancy set of bloomers.

          DASH
These sure won't keep you warm.

Terry snatches them away from him.

          TERRY
Give me that.

Deputy Caleb empties the chamber of his revolver on the ground, bends down and takes a handful of silver bullets from the saddlebag, stuffs them in his pockets. He loads his six gun then.

While he's doing this, Dash is emptying his revolver. He reaches over to get shells.

          JUBIL
There he is.

They all look up.

THE GRAVEYARD

Gimet is moving between the stones like a wind-blown wraith. He lets out with a sound that's somewhere between a CACKLE and a WHINE. He disappears over the hill between some leaning stones, and is gone.

                    JUBIL (CONT'D)
Let's go.

Snatching up their goods, they head out.

THE GRAVEYARD HILL

They arrive at the top and look down. Terry is wearing the bandoleer. Jubil has the saddlebags thrown over his shoulder. They see a cabin below the rise.

                    JUBIL (CONT'D)
That must be Gimet's place.

                    DASH
I bet he ain't in no mood for company.

                    JUBIL
We'll find out.

                    DASH
Before we do... Terry, you feeling cold?

                    TERRY
A mite.

She takes the bottle out, takes a swig, passes it around. They all take a jolt.

They start down the hill toward the cabin.

EXT. GIMET'S CABIN

They stop at the front door. When they speak, they speak softly.

              JUBIL
    I'm going to kick it in, and then we'll rush
    in shooting.

              DASH
    That's not much of a plan.

              TERRY
    It's the only plan he ever has. Wait here.

Terry eases around to the window, which is knocked out with dried blood crusted all around the sill. This is from Gimet having been exploded by Glory's curse.

Terry looks in.

WHAT SHE SEES:

INT. GIMET'S CABIN

There's a lot of dust and there are skeins of spider- and cobwebs. There's all manner of crochet and knitting supplies on the table.

BACK TO TERRY

She goes around to the other side of the cabin. She looks in the larger window there. It too is devoid of glass.

INT. GIMET'S CABIN

We get another look. Same scene, different angle.

JUBIL AND THE BOYS

Terry comes around the opposite side of the cabin she started from.

Jubil lifts his shoulders in question as she joins them.

> **TERRY**
> No one inside.

> **JUBIL**
> We'll check it out anyway. Dash. You and the deputy wait here a moment.

> **DASH**
> Gladly.

Jubil prepares to kick the door.

Terry steps in his way, takes hold of the door knob.

The door opens easily when she turns it.

Terry gives Jubil a shit eating grin. Jubil scowls back at her.

Terry and Jubil peek inside.

INT. GIMET'S CABIN

Slowly, Terry and Jubil enter.

A SCREECH TO RAISE THE DEAD.

Jubil lifts his foot as a raccoon darts out the door.

EXT. GIMET'S CABIN

DASH

The speeding raccoon runs up Dash like he's a tree.

Dash SCREECHES and falls back and the raccoon leaps off of him and heads off in the dark.

ANOTHER ANGLE

Deputy Caleb. He has his gun drawn.

                DEPUTY CALEB
        So much for sneaking.

INT. GIMET'S CABIN

Dash and Deputy Caleb enter behind Jubil and Terry. We can see that Dash is scratched up.

                JUBIL
        I stepped on its tail.

                DASH
        I damn near shit myself.

                DEPUTY CALEB
        From this position, you smell like you did.

                DASH
        Find you another position.

                TERRY
        He always smells that way.

Dash takes this as a defense, gives a big affirmative nod.

                DEPUTY CALEB
        What now?

                JUBIL
        We set a trap.

                DEPUTY CALEB
        Looks to me, we're the ones trapped.

JUBIL
We can control things better here. One door, two windows. And we have our defenses.

DEPUTY CALEB
The silver bullets?

JUBIL
That's one.

DASH
There's a two?

Jubil nods. He slams the saddlebags down on the table and reaches in one of them and pulls out the Bible.

DASH
I hope you aren't counting on the power of prayer.

Jubil opens it, rips out a handful of pages.

DASH
Hey, ain't that a bad thing? Won't devils stick a fork up your ass for that?

Jubil wads the pages and begins placing them in a circle on the floor, each wad a few feet apart.

DASH
Gimet's afraid of paper wads?

No one answers.

Jubil completes the circle.

JUBIL
Grab that bench.

There's a bench at the table. Jubil gets one end, Deputy Caleb the other. They place it in the middle of the circle.

JUBIL
Now. Everyone in the circle.

They comply.

JUBIL
Two of us can face the rear window, the other two will be facing in the direction of the other window and the door. He can't sneak up on us that way.

DASH
So we're gonna offer him his dinner on a bench?

JUBIL
He'll come for us. But we're not offering him anything but a hard time.

DEPUTY CALEB
You don't know he'll come back.

TERRY
Actually, he does. His shooting, most of his thinking, isn't that good. But about the supernatural, he knows his business. And believe me, it pains me to admit it.

JUBIL
Why, thank you, Terry. I know that must have hurt.

TERRY
To the bone.

                    JUBIL
        There's no guarantees, but my figure is
        he's chosen us as his next meal. We are in
        his domain, and have been since we got
        on Deadman's Road.

Jubil lights a lantern on the table and turns its flame down low.

They take seats on the bench. Jubil and Deputy Caleb facing one way, Terry and Dash the other. Jubil places the Bible on the bench between Deputy Caleb and himself.

Jubil pulls his pistol and lays it on his leg. Without looking back, he talks, and when the others talk, they do so without changing their position.

                    JUBIL (CONT'D)
        Courage. Don't start banging away. We let
        him come in.

                    DASH
        We do?

                    JUBIL
        We do. We let him come in, and we are
        protected in the circle for as long as it lasts.

                    DASH
        What's that mean? How long does it last?

                    JUBIL
        You'll find out. Thing is, keep calm. And
        when I say, and not before, we unload on
        him with our silver bullets.

                    DASH
        They'll kill him. Like the werewolf?

                    JUBIL
I'm not sure.

                    DEPUTY CALEB
You're not sure? What kind of master monster killer are you?

                    JUBIL
One that's not sure. But this should work. Up to a point, anyway.

                    DEPUTY CALEB
Oh, that's inspiring.

TIME LAPSE

They are still sitting. No one is making a sound.

TERRY AND DASH'S POV

The door.

A slight noise. Nothing serious, but a bit of a flutter.

                    DASH
                    (To Terry, soft as a mouse farting
                    in cotton)
We didn't lock it.

                    TERRY
                    (soft)
There's no lock.

                    JUBIL
Shhhhhhh. We want him to come in.

ON DASH'S FACE

It's obvious he doesn't want him to come in.

DEADMAN'S ROAD

BACK TO SCENE

ANGLE DOOR

It CREAKS, moves slightly.

ON TERRY AND DASH

Dash swallows. Terry picks up her revolver and carefully cocks it.

JUBIL AND DEPUTY CALEB

Deputy Caleb turns his head to look over his shoulder.

Jubil grabs his elbow.

JUBIL
Watch your post.

Deputy Caleb reluctantly turns back to face in the proper direction.

THE DOOR

Fingers appear at the door, white and crab like.

The door opens a bit more, creaking as it does. A shadow falls into the room.

SERIES OF CAMERA SHOTS

Dash and Terry. They are sweating.

The door creaks more. The shadow moves slightly.

Dash raises his gun, points it at the door, using his other hand to support it. His hands shake.

A bee buzzes into the room, flies about, circles back and exits the way it entered.

The shadow pulls back suddenly, and is gone.

JUBIL AND DEPUTY CALEB

They sit looking at the window. Nothing there but a moonlit square.

A beat.

A shadow.

And then, silently, Gimet leaps up and lands squatting on the window sill, his head ducked to poke inside. Sitting there, he looks almost like a bird of prey with a halo of bees circling about his head and buzzing about the glowing hive in his chest. The sound of the bees BUZZING is very LOUD.

Deputy Caleb lifts his gun.

Jubil puts his hand on Deputy Caleb's arm, leans toward the deputy's ear, and we're close on this shot, Jubil's lips close to Deputy Caleb's ear.

                JUBIL (CONT'D)
                (soft)
     Courage.

Gimet climbs into the room with catlike grace. He scuttles under the table like a spider.

We can't see him now.

Bees come out from under the table and float up along the edge of the circle made from the Bible pages.

The bees dart back under the table.

SCUTTLING SOUND AGAIN

DASH AND TERRY

                    DASH
                    (soft)
            It's behind us, isn't it?

                    TERRY
                    (equally as silent)
        Hush.

ANGLE THE TABLE

Gimet's hand appears, clutches the floor. Then his other hand. He's pulling himself slowly out from under the table.

His head appears. He lifts it, looks right at Jubil and Deputy Caleb.

Gimet SCREECHES like an alley cat and–

HE SPRINGS, but as he leaps, he hits an invisible wall formed by the pages, and the pages burst into flames, and the flames whip up and all around, protecting our four monster hunters.

Singed, Gimet falls back with a HOARSE CRY. He lands on his knees, and moving backwards, he scuttles beneath the table again, and out of sight.

Bees attack our heroes. They hit the wall of flame and are scorched. They fall to the floor and...disappear.

The flames from the pages die suddenly.

WE HEAR A SCRATCHING NOISE

Jubil stands up, steps forward, puts his revolver on the table, grabs the lantern, turns it up and lifts it.

Moving along the wall, high up, like a pale cockroach is Gimet. It's his long nails we heard, SCRATCHING against the wall. He turns his head toward them and lets out with–

A HISSING NOISE.

Jubil grabs up his pistol and FIRES.

Wood from the wall two feet below Gimet PUFFS AND EXPLODES.

Now Deputy Caleb is standing beside him. He fires twice.

Both shots hit Gimet. One in the head; it throws a fragment of skull spinning. The other hits the torso.

Gimet hurries along the wall to the window.

Jubil slings the lantern and hits Gimet in the back.

A BURST OF FLAMES.

Gimet heads out the window on fire, black smoke churning. The fire is licking at the bees around him and they are falling to the floor like burned-out comets.

Now all four of the monster hunters are facing the window.

Gimet, charred and smoking, leaps back on the sill, crouches there. He GROWLS AT THEM.

Bullets fly. We don't know who's shooting they are coming so fast and furious.

Gimet abandons his post, leaving only a black trail of smoke where he had squatted.

A last shot from Dash hits the bottom of the windowsill.

                JUBIL
Save the bullets.

            DEPUTY CALEB
It's not like they stopped him.

> JUBIL
>
> He's strong magic, that's for sure.

> DEPUTY CALEB
>
> Way you shoot, it really doesn't matter. The girl's right. You can't hit an elephant in the ass with a cannon.

> TERRY
>
> But he chunks a lantern pretty good.

> DASH
>
> It's over?

> JUBIL
>
> I don't know.

> DEPUTY CALEB
>
> Sure it is. We kicked his ass.

> JUBIL
>
> I'm not so certain. The bullets hurt him, but he can take a lot.

Jubil eases over to the window, leans on the sill, pokes his head out.

Nothing but moonlight and gravestones can be seen on a little rise of hill.

> DASH
>
> What do we do now?

Jubil pulls his head back inside.

> JUBIL
>
> We wait.

TIME LAPSE

Terry is tearing pages from the Bible, handing a clutch to each of the guys. They take them, and:

Jubil is wadding up his pages, placing them on the windowsill.

Dash is wadding up others, putting them on the other windowsill.

Deputy Caleb is wadding up a few and is placing them along the closed door.

Deputy Caleb finishes. He has a few Bible pages still in his hand. He runs his thumb and fingers over them.

He looks at the others.

He starts to say something.

Pauses.

Obviously something is on his mind.

Finally.

      DEPUTY CALEB
 I need to go.

      JUBIL
 What?

      DEPUTY CALEB
 You know. Can you turn your heads.

      JUBIL
 Go in here?

      TERRY
 Which is it?

DEPUTY CALEB
What?

TERRY
Little boy number one, or little boy number two.

DEPUTY CALEB
Number two.

DASH
A big two?

DEPUTY CALEB
Pretty big.

TERRY
I don't even want a number one.

DEPUTY CALEB
I'll go out.

DASH
That thing is out there.

DEPUTY CALEB
We scared him good. He's not so bad. I hit him twice. He shows up, I can hit him while I'm still squatting.

JUBIL
Suit yourself. Dash. Why don't you go with him?

DASH
Ha! I got safer things to do than watch him shit. I'm not spreading out. I'm sticking.

                    DEPUTY CALEB
          I'll be fine.

Deputy Caleb opens the door. The balls of bible pages are fluttered aside. The pages in his hand flutter as well.

                DEPUTY CALEB (CONT'D)
          You'll have to replace them.

                         TERRY
          Where you going with those pages.

                    DEPUTY CALEB
          You know.

                         TERRY
          Oh no, you don't. You're not wiping your
          ass on those. We might need them.

                    DEPUTY CALEB
          I can't just–

He's interrupted by–

                         DASH
          Here.

Dash picks a long scarf of crochet off the table. He tosses it to Deputy Caleb, who catches it.

                     DASH (CONT'D)
          Compliments of Gimet.

Deputy Caleb throws the crocheted scarf over his shoulder.

Terry comes over and holds out her hand.

He gives her the Bible pages.

Deputy Caleb goes out and closes the door. Terry moves to replace the wadded pages along the door line. As she does, we go–

CLOSE ON DASH

> **DASH (CONT'D)**
> There goes the dumbest sonofabitch ever squatted to shit over a pair of boots.

EXT. NIGHT – MOMENTS LATER

CLOSE ON A BUNCH OF BEES

They are buzzing furiously in the moonlight.

WIDEN THE SHOT

We see their source. Gimet. He's got his mouth wide open and bees are flowing from it, and they are flying out of his chest in a thick wad as well.

CAMERA FOLLOWS as the bees come together and rise up high in the night sky and look like rotten acne on the face of the moon.

AND THEN THEY DIVE until they puncture the grave mounds. They hit the dirt so hard dust puffs up.

Gimet perches on a grave stone with an effortless leap.

BACK TO THE GRAVES.

The dirt moves a little.

A little more.

A hand comes out of one grave.

A head lifts from another, dirt falling off it like a waterfall.

More graves are giving up their dead. Here. There. A hand. An arm. A head.

Now we get a good look at one of the ghouls coming totally free. It stumbles. It staggers. It's stiff. It does a deep knee bend.

CLOSE ON THIS DEAD GUY

He comes out of that deep knee bend, opens his mouth, and out come a swarm of bees.

More dead are pushing out of graves. All of them are stretching, causing bones to crack and shift, like tired old folks about to go out and get the Sunday paper. They are in various stages of decay.

Bees are leaving the dead bodies from every available orifice. And on some of these corpses there are a lot of orifices.

INT. GIMET'S CABIN

Terry is stretched out on the bench. Jubil is by the window. Dash is up walking around.

          DASH
How long does it take to drop a turd?

          TERRY
You're worried about the deputy? I thought you said he was a dumb sonofabitch.

          DASH
That's why I'm worried about him. Maybe we should all go out and get him.

Terry sits up on the bench.

          TERRY
You're the one didn't want to go with him.

> DASH
>
> I like to work in large numbers.

Jubil leaves the window. He walks over to the bench, stands beside it.

> JUBIL
>
> I think we should all stay here. He should have took his dump on the backside of the house.

> TERRY
>
> He was feeling brave.

> JUBIL
>
> People who can shoot well think they're always safe.

> TERRY
>
> Sour grapes.

> JUBIL
>
> What?

And now, while they talk, the camera gives a view out the window. We see:

The top of the hill, a few gravestones. Suddenly Deputy Caleb darts over the hill, something dangling from his boot. We are seeing him from a distance, but he is really hauling ass.

> TERRY
>
> Sour grapes. You're just mad because you can't shoot worth a damn.

> JUBIL
>
> No, I'm not. I'm just stating a fact.

TERRY
An opinion.

DASH
What about the shitter?

TERRY
He's a big boy.

JUBIL
Wait a minute. You still haven't answered that. What do you mean, sour grapes?

EXT. DEPUTY CALEB

We are close on him running. We can see that he's dragging the crocheted scarf on the heel of his boot like a run of toilet paper.

BACK TO:

INT. GIMET'S CABIN

CAMERA takes in the room, but we can still see through that window. Deputy Caleb has his gun drawn and he is starting to YELL.

Our folks in the cabin don't hear him at first, because it is distant and they are talking.

DASH
I guess I ought not care what happens to that big head sonofabitch, but I hate to think a man might get et while he's doing his business.

TERRY
Enough with the shitting already.

BLAM! BLAM!

Gunshots.

STILL VIEWING THROUGH THE WINDOW

We can see that Deputy Caleb has turned to fire at something. And now we see that something.

The dead. They are coming over the hill. And they are not shuffling. They are sprinting.

Our gang has turned toward the gunfire, rushed to the window, are looking out the window, and now they see Caleb moving some freight, the dead galloping behind him.

                DASH
    Run! Run, you dumb sonofabitch!

EXT. DEPUTY CALEB

He is running all out. So are the dead. One of the dead abruptly has a leg snap out from under him, and down he goes, tumbling over and over as he falls down the hill.

He rolls right past Deputy Caleb, and then sort of rolls in front of him.

As Deputy Caleb leaps over him, the dead man reaches up, just missing the deputy's boots, but managing to snatch loose the crocheted scarf.

The scarf falls over the dead guy's face like a fishnet.

INT. GIMET'S CABIN

Our Trio at the window.

                DASH
    He sure can run.

And Deputy Caleb can certainly do that. He has left the dead far behind. He is heading straight toward them.

Closing on the cabin...closing.

>> JUBIL
> He's coming through the window.

They step aside, and like an Olympic diver, Deputy Caleb leaps through, crashes into the table. He staggers to his feet.

>> DEPUTY CALEB
> Goddamnit, didn't you hear me yelling?

Dash looks out the window. He slaps Deputy Caleb's arm with the back of his palm. Points.

SHOT OUT THE WINDOW

Lots of dead folk. The one that broke his leg is crawling toward them, and at a very nice clip.

BACK TO SCENE

>> DASH
> See what you brought back.

EXT. THE HILL

Coming over the hill are the zombies. And among them we see–

CHRISTIAN

>> CHRISTIAN
> She's naked, and walking downhill with
> the zombies.

INT. GIMET'S CABIN

Dash is still looking out the window.

> **DASH**
> Ain't that Christian without her drawers?

Everyone goes to the window.

> **JUBIL**
> Yeah it's her.

> **TERRY**
> She's one of them.

> **DASH**
> And she ain't got no drawers.

> **TERRY**
> You said that.

EXT. HILL

Christian turns slightly as she comes down the hill. Her back half is black as night.

INT. GIMET'S CABIN

VIEW FROM WINDOW

We can see Christian wandering down toward them.

> **DEPUTY CALEB**
> Why is part of her dark like that?

EXT. BOTTOM OF THE HILL

She's near the cabin now, and then her whole back half seems to explode and take to the sky. It's the bees. All that remains of Christian is a head to foot slice. And it just keeps coming.

JUBIL
(to Deputy Caleb)
Now you know why. Grab the table, push it up against the window.

They grab the table, turn it over against the window.

Jubil grabs the bench, turns it long ways and sticks one end under the latch on the door.

DASH
Those ought to hold just about long enough for us to scratch our privates and kiss our asses goodbye.

DEPUTY CALEB
We still got an open window.

JUBIL
We'll have to deal with it.

Terry goes over to the potbelly stove. There's a hatchet stuck in a log. She pulls the hatchet out. She brings it over to Jubil.

TERRY
We'll shoot. You chop.

Jubil has the saddlebags.

JUBIL
Great... All right. We'll get down and put our backs against the table. The door might hold for awhile, and if they come through the window across the way, some of you very fine shots can show us how it's done.

As they are following Jubil's orders–

> DASH
>
> What happens if they get in?
>
> JUBIL
>
> Then it's assholes and elbows.

THUMP! THUMP!

Something is banging at the table from the other side.

The door is banged, the bench slides back a notch, then the back end of it fits into a gap in the flooring, and holds.

A face at the open window across the way.

Terry's hand flies up and her pistol is in it. She fires. The head splits open and falls apart.

And now it begins, and everything is fast and THE CAMERA is like a wild animal moving around the room. We have:

The table being pushed.

More faces at the window.

Terry, Deputy Caleb, and Dash are blazing away.

The bench at the door is wobbling.

Our team is starting to shoot through the door, and when they do we BECOME THE BULLETS, and away we fly, and–

EXT. GIMET'S CABIN

The silver bullets, punch holes in the door and they hit the zombies outside and the bullets sizzle like bacon in a pan when they STRIKE the meat. Down go the zombies, smoking.

ANOTHER ANGLE

A dead guy at the open window near the door, and he's going for it, his boots scuttling against the wall beneath the window as he puts his arms in and the Bible pages explode and run up his arms. He staggers back, on fire, wanders into a couple of other dry meat and bones dead folk, and when he bumps them, they too burst into flames.

INT. GIMET'S CABIN

The blazing dead guy is visible, staggering back. We can see the others on fire, wandering about like soccer moms at a mall sale.

                    TERRY
        Put some more pages up there.

                    DASH
        You put them up there.

No one moves to do that. And the CAMERA SHOWS US THAT:

The bullets our gang fired have knocked pretty big holes in the door, and we can see through the holes and we can see the things moving out there.

We go–

CLOSE ON ONE OF THE BULLET HOLES IN DOOR

A zombie eye is looking in through one of them. It's nothing more than a hollow space, that eye, a tunnel to nowhere.

ON TERRY

She lifts her revolver and fires, and as the bullet exits her gun, we go–

SLOW MO

DEADMAN'S ROAD

Silver load spinning in the air and it goes right for the hole, and it's a perfect shot. It enters the empty eye socket, and for a moment we've got the bullet load in darkness, spinning like a silver missile in the blackness of space, and BLAM!

EXT. GIMET'S CABIN

Out the back of the dead guy's head, and–

SPEED UP

Bullet whistles as it cuts the air.

INT. GIMET'S CABIN

Tearing at the walls. Boards creaking.

DASH
They're pulling the goddamn lumber off.

A LOUD CRACK

It makes them look up. A zombie is on the roof, pulling back the lumber shingles. It pokes its face through a hole. Grins.

Deputy Caleb fires, hits him in the teeth.

The table they have their backs against is starting to move them forward.

EXT. GIMET'S CABIN

At the window with the table, the Bible pages are burning and there are burning dead folk wandering around the yard, falling apart.

INT. CABIN

The bench. It's moving again, starting to slip out from under the door handle.

The door flies open, and, of course, the balled up Bible pages are knocked back.

TERRY
(surprised)
Damn! I didn't think of that.

The table they have their backs against is moving more and moving faster, sliding them across the floor.

The door is wide open and the dead are coming in.

ANGLE THE WINDOW BEHIND THE TABLE

The Bible fire has burned out. The dead are climbing in between the gap they've made between the window and the table. Hands reach over the table. One of them grabs Dash.

Dash, as if he's electrified, leaps up, only to find himself facing the dead folk coming through the door. He gives one of them a kick in the groin.

It just looks at him.

Then he remembers the gun in his hand. He jerks it up and fires, knocking a hole through the thing's chest.

Terry leaps up.

TERRY (CONT'D)
Jubil. The table won't hold.

Terry is spinning, shooting left and right.

Jubil up, swinging his axe.

Deputy Caleb rolls across the floor, grabs a balled up Bible page, comes to his feet, stuffs it in the open mouth of an attacking dead folk. The thing's head bursts into flames.

Deputy Caleb likes this. He starts grabbing at the other wads of paper on the floor. He's throwing them at the dead folk. They are starting to run from him as he chases them around the little cabin like a kid playing tag.

A dead guy falls through he roof, lands on the floor, face down.

Jubil chops off his head with the axe.

Close quarters now. It's that assholes and elbows business Jubil talked about. The dead buggers are pushing our defenders into a circle.

Jubil goes crazy. He leaps out of the tight little wad and starts swinging the axe. Heads fly. Limbs fall off. He hits one on top of the head and the axe splits the monster's skull down the middle, all the way to the thorax. It falls.

Some of the dead folk they have knocked to the ground are crawling on the floor, grabbing at the defender's ankles.

Terry's revolver clicks empty. She will use it to pisol whip the dead from now on.

Jubil chops down on the floor crawlers. He leaps back, grabs the saddlebag of ammunition as dead folk climb over the table.

He fights his way to the other defenders, who are down to gun butts, fist and feet and harsh language.

Dash butts one of the dead so hard the guy's face caves in.

Dash grabs his forehead.

DASH
Shit. That hurt.

Deputy Caleb drops his pistol and jerks a leg off the upended table. It snaps free. He starts to swing it like the classic vision of Davy Crockett at the Alamo.

DEPUTY CALEB
Go back to hell!

EXT. GIMET'S CABIN – BIRD'S EYE VIEW

The dead are coming from everywhere, surrounding the cabin. It is a frightening scene. There are so many it looks as if all the ants in the world have left their colony to swarm on the cabin like a piece of gingerbread.

INT. GIMET'S CABIN

Dead are dropping through the roof.

They are tearing out the walls.

They are coming through all the windows.

Jubil has the saddlebags slung over his shoulder. Terry holsters her revolver and plunders Jubil's saddlebag, the half hanging over his back.

She jerks out the Bible. She tears pages, wads them, throws them.

More dead burst into flames. They fall. The cabin is beginning to catch fire.

Jubil swings the axe and stars cutting a path through the dead, moving as he does toward the wall, his fellow defenders following him.

JUBIL
Come on! We got to make a run for it.

Jubil comes to a piece of the wall still intact. The rest of the place is thick with dead folk.

JUBIL (CONT'D)
Watch my back!

The others continue to fight.

Jubil starts chopping at the wall.

It takes several blows, but the planking splits, and Jubil tears it free, and there's Christian.

She's just standing there looking in at him.

JUBIL

can't help himself. He takes a moment to admire her breasts. Then with a scream lunges forward.

EXT. CABIN

Jubil swinging the axe sideways, slicing into Christian's neck, bringing her down, nearly chopping her head off.

The others are flowing out behind him, and they break for it.

Just flat ass take off running, pushing the dead folk around like a right winger bitch slapping the Constitution.

They are breaking free, hauling some serious ass. It looks good. They are in this order: Jubil, Terry, Dash, and Deputy Caleb, who is the slowest of the bunch, as he's stopped to kick a zombie to the ground.

And then one of the dead leaps off the roof and lands on Deputy Caleb's back. He hits the dirt as he comes to one knee–

DEPUTY CALEB'S POV

Crawling on the ground toward him. The near headless body of Christian. Her head hangs on a strand of flesh and her eyes are looking at him.

DEPUTY CALEB

We see he is holding a crumpled Bible page. He reaches out and stuffs it in the mouth of Christian's near-decapitated head. Flames lick out of her mouth and through her eyes, spurt from her nostrils. She stops crawling. Stops moving.

And then before Caleb can get to his feet, more dead are on him. They bite into him. They tear at him. One of them begins to twist his arm off. Deputy Caleb lets loose with the MOST BLOOD CURDLING YELL IN THE HISTORY OF CINEMA.

OUR GANG

They stop. Look back.

All the dead have stopped chasing them. They are making a lunchable out of Deputy Caleb.

All our team can see of Deputy Caleb is his miserable, blood-splattered face, his mouth wide open in a scream that will no longer come.

Jubil runs forward a few feet, toward Deputy Caleb, lets fly with the axe.

It's on target.

It hits Deputy Caleb in the forehead and splits it wide open. It's a merciful killing.

Although there are dead still tearing at Deputy Caleb, working his brains out of the crack made by the axe, the dead are now taking notice of the others again. A few of them rise up and start after them.

JUBIL (CONT'D)
Get to the wood line.

Our remaining gang bolts.

AMONGST THE TREES – SECONDS LATER

They are running through the woods.

Shadows here and there.

Dead are coming along fast.

Jubil goes around a swathe of trees.

Terry goes the opposite direction.

And Dash, he's just running as fast as he can go in a straight line.

CUT TO:

TERRY'S PERSONAL BATTLE

She's running between a row of trees. She is being pursued by a couple of female ghouls and a guy.

She pulls her gun and starts plucking silver bullets from her bandoleer and loading her gun as she runs.

When it's loaded, she spins and drops to one knee and fires off two shots in rapid succession.

She hits one of the women and the man, both in the chest, and they both puff and dissolve on the run.

The last ghoul, a woman, keeps coming.

Terry leaps sideways, kicks out in a roundhouse motion, catches the woman in the belly with the toe of her boot.

But, the female ghoul grabs her boot and flips Terry backwards, causing her to lose her gun.

Terry comes to her feet instantly.

The ghoul charges.

The two women collide.

Terry and the ghoul roll around on the forest floor, punching and kicking and pulling hair, the ghoul's teeth flashing close to Terry's face.

TERRY
Let go of my hair, you harpy.

Rolling over and over.

Terry comes up on top, and she's got her John Wayne on. Starts swinging. And man is she pounding this ghoul. It's fist of fury time.

The ghoul finally grabs the sides of Terry's arms, and pulls her forward, throws her tumbling over her head.

Terry rolls up. A glint of moonlight on something in the leaves.

The revolver.

Terry leaps for it. Grabs the gun, rolls over and comes up and fires just as the dead ghoul bounds to stand over her, is starting to bend over and grab her.

The shot is right up between the dead ghoul's legs. It's a clear highway shot; the top of the ghoul's head leaps off like a tossed cap.

And then, it's dust time.

Terry sighs. That was tough.

CUT TO:

ANOTHER LOCATION IN THE WOODS – MOMENTS LATER

Dead are stalking through the woods.

We follow one dead guy wearing a rotting suit as he breaks off from the others. He's very carefully looking from tree to tree, like he's playing Hide and Go Seek.

He looks around a tree, and finds–

Nothing.

He goes to another tree.

Nothing.

ANOTHER ANGLE

Dash is leaning up against a tree, his arms by his side. He looks terrified.

And he should.

The dead guy in the suit is moving his way, looking behind every tree in his path.

He's getting closer to Dash.

One tree.

Two trees.

The third tree is Dash's.

As Mr. Dead Guy in a Suit moves toward Dash's tree.

CLOSE ON DASH

He looks pretty darn worried.

BACK TO SCENE

We see where we expect the dead guy to be, but–

No dead guy.

Where did he go?

Dash turns right, peeks around the tree.

There's nothing there.

He turns back to peek the other way.

Nothing.

He lets out a sigh.

He turns to his right again.

It's Mr. Dead Guy in a Suit.

Dash lets out with a scream.

The dead guy grabs him.

Dash struggles, boxes the dead guy's head like a speed bag. Dust flies. The dead guy's head moves. But if he's bothered, there's no sign of it. Mr. Dead Guy in a Suit doesn't let go.

ANOTHER ANGLE

Terry steps into the scene. She has a silver bullet in her hand.

CLOSE AS

Terry stabs the bullet into Mr. Dead Guy in a Suit's ear, and slams her palm against it.

Mr. Dead Guy in a Suit now has an expression like someone who has just felt the first workings of a dose of laxative.

His head explodes like a rotten pumpkin. Flies in all directions.

Terry grabs Dash by the elbow and jerks him forward. Dash looks as if he's been stunned with a mallet.

>   **TERRY**
>   Will you quit fucking around.

>   CUT TO:

JUBIL'S ORDEAL

Jubil has a limb pulled way back and he's hiding behind a tree, holding this limb. He's holding it tight, and it's all he can do to maintain it.

We hear someone coming.

Jubil grins.

He's glancing in the direction of the path, looking down at the ground.

JUBIL'S POV

The toe of a boot becomes visible.

BACK TO JUBIL

He lets go. The limb makes contact, and the contact is with–

DASH

He's on the ground, rubbing his head.

                    DASH
            Dagnabit.

WIDEN

Terry is right behind him.

Terry shoots a look at Jubil as she steps out from behind the tree.

                    JUBIL
            Sorry.

                    TERRY
            You better be glad that wasn't me, Buster.

Jubil helps Dash up.

                    JUBIL
            You okay?

                    DASH
            Peachy.

                    JUBIL
            I didn't know I had lost them.

Terry wheels, looks back.

OUR HEROES SEE

A bunch of the dead folk coming their way.

BACK TO SCENE

                    TERRY
            You didn't.

EXT. BOTTOM OF HILL, JUST AT THE TREE LINE – MOMENTS LATER

DEADMAN'S ROAD

Jubil, Terry and Dash. They are running. The dead are pursuing, threading their way between the trees.

Heroes break out into a kind of clearing.

More gravestones.

And something unique. And we'll go–

CLOSE ON THIS

A large mausoleum. It has an upright white marble stone that makes a kind of door. Seven feet tall. And in front of it, lying flat, is a slab of white marble the same size.

BACK TO SCENE

Our trio is stumbling toward the stone. They are exhausted, have had, to put it mildly, a rough night.

And behind them–

The dead...well, they're dead tired, of course, and in this case, it means nothing. They are spry and they are coming on strong.

Our trio reaches the big slab monument. They step up on the ground slab. Dash looks like he's about to fall over.

CLOSE ON MARBLE DOOR

Written on it is: EMMALEENA FRIZZELL.

Dash goes to one knee.

                    DASH
    You'll have to go on with out me. I'm too
    weak. Shit...what am I saying? Help me up.

Jubil is helping Dash up.

Terry turns, looks back.

The dead scampering toward them.

> **TERRY**
> Wait a minute.

> **JUBIL**
> What?

> **TERRY**
> Give me the saddlebags.

Jubil jerks the saddlebags off his shoulder, tosses them to Terry. He looks back at the charging dead.

> **JUBIL**
> This better be a really good idea.

Terry reaches into one of the saddlebags. She takes out the bottle of holy water. She tosses the bags back to Jubil.

She starts sprinkling the holy water around the edges of the stone. She sprinkles it against the sides of the stone doorway.

And just in time.

The dead arrive.

One of them, a big guy, steps on the stone.

WHOOOOOSSSSSH

The dead foot on the slab goes up in a puff of smoke, and then the owner of the foot goes with it.

The others pause, stand back.

JUBIL
Lady. You are one smart huckleberry.

TERRY
I know.

DASH
I thought I was done et. Maybe we ought to take a swig of that stuff.

Terry is screwing the lid on the holy water bottle, when–

A CREAKING SOUND, like a stone grating against another stone.

ANGLE SHOT so that we see the stone door starting to topple. Dash turns quickly, looks back.

DASH'S POV

The stone growing larger. It's falling toward him.

ANOTHER ANGLE

Terry leaps to one side off the slab, Jubil the other.

Dash. He's screwed.

The stone SLAMS down on him so hard that parts of him shoot out from under it, and the marble shatters in all directions.

The dead scramble about, collecting Dash's squeezed out juicy parts.

TERRY

She's in the midst of the dead. They look happy, like seals that have been thrown a fish. They are starting to gather around her, closing...closing.

JUBIL

He's on the opposite side of the slab from Terry. He has his own admirers.

THE MAUSOLEUM DOORWAY

Standing in the doorway is Gimet, bees buzzing around him. He starts to move toward the exit, pauses. He glances toward the sky.

THE SKY

It's growing light.

BACK TO GIMET

Gimet turns and darts back into the mausoleum.

JUBIL

He's fighting for his life, kicking this one, punching another, pulling his gun to whack them with.

Out of the corner of his eye, he sees Gimet retreating into the tomb.

He glances toward Terry. She's rolling on the ground with one of them, and two others are trying to come to their dead comrade's aid. Others are pushing in to partake of the buffet.

Jubil starts in Terry's direction, but two of the ghouls grab him. He stomps out with his right foot and snaps one of the dead thing's kneecaps. It sags to the ground Now Jubil is wrestling with another.

They are closing in on him. He is starting to disappear from view.

TERRY

She has the holy water bottle in her hand. She smashes it against the head of the one holding her on the ground.

Her attacker lets out with a KIND OF NOISE that could only come from a dead throat.

WE CAN HEAR a rumbling sound in the background that we can't identify.

Terry has fought her way to her feet.

JUBIL

He's pushed up against the side of the mausoleum. He jams the pistol back in its holster, jerks the saddlebags off his shoulder, swings it with all his might, knocks one of his attackers back. A silver bullet flies out of the bag when he swings back to clock another.

Jubil sees the bullet.

A light goes on.

He kicks the closest dead guy back.

He quickly snaps open the bag, takes out a handful of silver bullets and throws them right into the face of the nearest dead guy.

The bullets strike like flying parasites, dissolving the attacker instantly.

Jubil's grabbing the bullets one or two at a time. He's throwing them. This way and that. And he's accurate.

TERRY

Two of them are coming at her. She throws her gun, hits one in the head. The other one reaches out, grabs her.

THE RUMBLE, LOUDER NOW

A WHISTLING SOUND

It's a rope, and it flips over the head of one of the dead guys. The rope swings out, goes tight.

ANGLE ON OLD TIMER

He's in a wagon drawn by two horses. He's bumping over some rough terrain. We can see the rope is attached to the wagon he's driving.

He makes a turn and the rope tightens even more, and the dead thing is snapped away.

The dead thing on the rope bouncing along behind him.

Old timer starts to turn the wagon in a big circle, heads back toward the mausoleum.

TERRY

She's kicking and punching dead things.

A HAND

It reaches out and grabs Terry by the back of her shirt, snatches her up.

ANOTHER ANGLE

Terry is pulled onto the seat of the wagon by Old Timer.

ON JUBIL

He has managed to move away from the mausoleum wall, toward the door of the mausoleum. It's not so much a choice, as a response against the growing tide of the dead.

With a jerk of his head, he sees Old Timer and Terry in the wagon, going away from him. A little smile fits onto his lips.

He turns toward the mausoleum door, darts inside, slinging the saddlebag over his shoulder.

A couple of the dead come in after him. He jerks the crucifix from the saddlebag, leaps forward, sticks one of them between the eyes with it, causing him to turn into dust. Jubil kicks out at the same time at the other, clipping a leg out from under him. He bends forward and stabs this one with the crucifix.

SHOT THROUGH THE DOORWAY

The dead. Lots of them. And then–

A RAY OF SUNLIGHT

It broadens and falls over the marble slab on the ground and fills the doorway.

The dead turn and look at the sky.

ON ONE OF THE DEAD, A WOMAN

When she speaks, dust puffs from her mouth.

>   **ONE OF THE DEAD**
>   (through dead dusty vocal cords)
> Damn.

              CUT TO:

THE WAGON

>   **OLD TIMER**
> I had a feeling you might need help. And I
> didn't like being a coward.

                    TERRY
Jubil. He's still back there.

                  OLD TIMER
I didn't plan on being that brave.

                    TERRY
Turn back. You have to.

The wagon thundering across the ground. It passes over the hill out of sight of the mausoleum.

CLOSE ON OLD TIMER AND TERRY

                  OLD TIMER
One more brave act, and I consider myself caught up.

                    TERRY
One will do it.

DEAD THINGS AT THE MAUSOLEUM

They are looking at the sky.

A bleed of sunlight flowing through the clouds. Brighter even than before.

They start to scamper away, in all directions.

The wagon with Old Timer at the reins is turning back. It hits a bump, Old Timer goes sailing and the wagon turns over and bounces across the ground, tossing Terry about like a rag doll. The axle line snaps free, the horses run off.

OLD TIMER

He's on the ground and his neck is turned in a really bad way. His eyes are glassy. This will not be healed by a neck brace and a week in bed. He's gone.

TERRY

She's flat out on the ground too. Limp. Not moving.

GRAVEYARD

Living dead. They are everywhere. Panicked. They are rushing back to their graves.

They are tearing at the ground, trying to find a hole to hide in.

THE SUN

Bright and gold. We hold on it a moment.

BACK TO SCENE

The dead weaken. They cease to dig.

They start to fall over or fall apart.

The rays of the sun, rich as butter, lying on the corpses.

They slowly all fall down and turn to dust.

Dust motes float in the sunlight.

                                                               CUT TO:

INT. MAUSOLEUM

Toward the rear of it.

Dark in there.

Shadow shape of Jubil.

>   JUBIL
> Come to Papa, Gimet. Come take your medicine, you sonofabitch.

A BURST OF LIGHT

It's Jubil striking a match.

A BUZZ. A bee hits him on the neck. He slaps at it.

THE BUZZING GROWS

Jubil holds the match in that direction.

He sees bees moving down a small hole at the back of the mausoleum.

>   JUBIL (CONT'D)
> Gimet. You weasel.

Jubil starts over that way. Steps in some water.

He pauses, looks down.

Bees buzz him. He swats at them, causing the match to go out.

ANOTHER MATCH FLARES

Jubil bends down and rubs his hand in the water, comes up with a muddy palm. He slaps the mud on his face, starts rubbing it all around.

CLOSE ON A BEE

It's buzzing around Jubil's cheek. It gets close to the mud. Backs off.

INT. GIMET'S HIDDEN SHAFT

The light of a match. We can see Jubil too. He's on his belly and he's coming head on toward us, wiggling his way through the passage.

Jubil drops into a larger portion of the shaft.

The match goes out.

Darkness.

A beat.

ANOTHER MATCH FLARES

And Jubil is looking at a dead woman. She is looking right at him, teeth bared. She looks like she was dragged through a briar patch by a runaway horse.

> **JUBIL**
> Emmaleena, I presume.

She grabs at him.

They tumble backwards.

SHOT OF THE MATCH

It flies out of his hand and tumbles in SLOW MO through the air, and we follow it as the flame goes down and then when it hits the earth–

It goes out.

SPEED AGAIN

Some really rough action noises.

A grunt.

JUBIL (CONT'D)
Goddamn hell bitch.

Silence.

A long dark moment.

FIRE

Another MATCH HAS BEEN LIT.

The passage way is ILLUMINATED.

We can see Jubil is breathing heavy, sitting on his ass. He's lost his hat.

We can see beside him Emmaleena. The silver crucifix from the saddlebag is sticking between her eyes.

Jubil digs into the saddlebag, pulls out the damaged Bible.

He puts the Bible between his knees, tears pages from it with his free hand, drops the Bible back in the saddlebag.

He lights the top of the pages, and before they can flame up good, he twists the pages to make a kind of huge wick.

He puts the bottom of the wick in his mouth. He pull his revolver, pulls the saddlebags which have fallen off his shoulder toward him, opens them.

INSERT INTERIOR Saddlebags

All that's left are four silver bullets and that piece of the Bible he's just dropped back inside.

BACK TO SCENE

DEADMAN'S ROAD

Jubil loads the four shells into his revolver, slips it back into his holster. He puts the Bible inside his shirt, tosses the saddlebags aside.

He takes the wick from his mouth and holds it up.

Light jumps around in the darkness and makes shadows scramble. Something is moving around down there.

Jubil holds the wick up higher.

The light isn't good. We can only see about six inches around him.

A NOISE

Jubil wheels. The little light shows nothing.

SCUTTLES, CRACKLES, SLIDING SOUNDS

SOMETHING IS OUT THERE

Jubil glances at the corpse of Emmaleena. He puts the wick against the nightshirt on her rotted corpse. It jumps ablaze, lights up the whole room as the body catches fire along with the shirt.

We SEE JUBIL'S MUD COVERED FACE

It looks eerie.

He turns to a NOISE.

GIMET

He's looking right at Jubil, no more than a foot away. He looks far more eerie.

Gimet dives for Jubil. Jubil drops the wick and falls back and away, just missing the burning corpse.

AND THIS SCENE IS FIRELIT BY EMMALEENA'S HUMAN TORCH

Gimet is on top of him.

VIEW OF GIMET'S JAWS

They are coming very close to Jubil. Gimet's teeth are wet and sharp and long. They snap like a rabid dog. Spittle flies. Bees are buzzing all around.

Jubil is just able to hold the teeth at bay. Bees are stinging at his hands. Jubil is CRYING OUT.

Gimet is pushing through Jubil's defenses. Jubil's arms are tiring and Gimet is almost to Jubil's face.

Jubil, holding Gimet with one arm, draws his revolver with the other.

But it's too late to fire.

He slams the gun sideways into Gimet's mouth as Gimet bites down ferociously. Teeth burst and fly like seeds from an overripe pomegranate.

Gimet spits the gun out, and snaps at Jubil's face.

Jubil grabs the saddlebags at the same time and shoves them into Girnet's face. Gimet bites them with his snaggle toothed mouth.

The teeth, even the busted ones, tear through the saddlebags. Gimet's head shakes doglike and rips the rest of the saddlebag from Jubil's grip.

Gimet really comes down on Jubil, and Jubil, just barely, slips sideways, and Gimet gets a mouthful of dirt.

Jubil coils his legs and puts both feet in Gimet's stomach, kicks out with all his might.

Gimet flies back against the wall, bounces forward, rolls into the burning corpse. Gimet lets out with a horrid growl as the flames lick at him. From a squatting position he does a kind of squatting dance, flames whipping all around him.

> JUBIL (CONT'D)
> Dosey do, you weasel bastard!

Jubil grabs his gun up from the ground. In that moment he wheels away, we wheel with him, lose sight of Gimet, and then–

GIMET, BLAZING LIKE THE OLYMPIC TORCH, comes down on Jubil and now they're rolling and twisting, and Jubil's jacket picks up a flame or two, and along the ground they tumble. Now Gimet is on top, and the flames are gone, but Gimet's back smokes like a French lounge singer.

Gimet is hammering Jubil with his fist.

Jubil sticks the revolver under Gimet's chin, pulls the trigger. Top of Gimet's head flies off like a tossed cap at a pep rally.

Gimet twists like an eel, hustles off into the shadows like an outhouse rat.

Jubil, still on his knees slides over and grabs the arm of the burning torso of Emmaleena's corpse, twists it off, sticks it into the flames.

The arm catches fire. Jubil, working forward on his knees, holding the arm torch in one hand, the revolver in the other, follows the path Gimet took.

The passageway becomes larger. Jubil can stand. He moves forward waving the human arm torch.

As he moves along, he sees on the underground walls great hives, pulsing with dark bounty.

A CRACKING SOUND

It makes Jubil jump.

It's one of the hives. It has broken open.

Jubil holds the torch toward the hive. In the light of the torch we see that honey, mixed with something that could only be blood, is running out of it, dripping down the cavern wall.

Jubil moves forward. And is brought up short.

JUBIL'S POV

Lying over a rock on his back, his exposed chest pulsing violently, is Gimet. Bees are circling over Gimet's body like fighter planes.

JUBIL

He moves forward, toward Gimet, cautious as he goes.

He looks down on the monster.

Gimet's eyeless sockets glow with a red flame of menace.

          JUBIL
   You've done run out your string, Gimet.

Gimet kicks up with a leg, hitting Jubil in the balls.

Jubil staggers back, bent over. When he regains his composure:

          JUBIL
   It's like that, is it?

Jubil moves quickly to Gimet, pokes the barrel of his revolver right on the throbbing hive in Gimet's chest, pulls the trigger.

The honey and blood in the hive in Gimet's chest spurt up like a little geyser, coating Jubil's already mud and blood splattered face.

Gimet writhes a little, but not much. He's as weak as a kitten.

DEADMAN'S ROAD

Jubil holsters his gun, reaches inside his shirt, brings out the remains of the Bible. He drops the Bible piece into Gimet's chest. The pages pop into flames and the flames lick up big, and Gimet catches on fire from head to toe. The fire grows bigger and bigger.

Jubil, wiping his face with his sleeve, backs away, watches until he sees that Gimet is completely consumed, then turns and darts back the way he came as the fire spreads and fills the room and the hives on the walls catch fire, pop and burst with blood-laced honey.

INT. MAUSOLEUM

The hole at the back of the place.

We see a light there.

Jubil pokes the human arm torch through, wiggles up after it.

When he's out of there, he drops the torch in the puddle of water, staggers toward the door.

EXT. MAUSOLEUM – MORNING

Jubil steps outside.

The sun is bright.

In the distance, something.

Jubil starts in that direction. He's walking at first. As he gets closer to the object, we realize it is Old Timer. Flies are buzzing on his eyes.

Jubil bends down to check for life.

He looks up, sees something else in the distance.

The look on his face: Not good.

Jubil swallows, jumps to his feet and starts to walk, faster as he goes. Then he starts to run.

He reaches the inert form of Terry, drops down beside her.

He lifts up her head. She doesn't move. Blood is dripping from her lips.

              JUBIL
   Oh, no.

He cradles her head, looks defeated.

Beat.

              TERRY
   Are you crying?

Jubil sees she has opened her eyes. He stands up, dropping her head on the ground. Hard.

            TERRY (CONT'D)
   Ouch.

              JUBIL
   No. The sunlight is making my eyes water.

Terry sits up, rubbing her head.

              TERRY
   You were crying...and that hurt, jackass.

              JUBIL
   I wasn't crying. And it was supposed to hurt.

              TERRY
   Where's Old Timer?

Jubil points.

Terry looks.

Old Timer lying dead in the grass.

                                                                        CUT TO:

EXT. THE HILL – MIDDAY

Jubil and Terry placing a rock on a mound of rocks.

                    TERRY
          Think Old Timer will like being here?

                    JUBIL
          If he doesn't, I guess he's shit out of luck, huh.

                    TERRY
          There's that.

DEADMAN'S ROAD – LATE DAY

Jubil and Terry are walking down the road.

                    JUBIL
          Another job we got took on.

                    TERRY
          We got half of it.

                    JUBIL
          You mean you got my half.

                    TERRY
          I'll share. You want to come get it?

She turns to face him, walks backwards, sticks her hand in the front of her jeans, jumps it up and down inside her pants.

JUBIL
You can't keep it there forever.

She smiles, turns and continues to walk by his side.

TERRY
Too bad about the guys. Except Christian. And Bill.

JUBIL
We told them not to come along.

TERRY
Just the same. I was getting used to Dash and the deputy. Old Timer was all right.

JUBIL
Hey! Look.

Jubil points.

DEPUTY CALEB'S HORSE

It's grazing beside the road.

BACK TO SCENE

Jubil creeps up on the horse, takes the bridle.

JUBIL
Easy there.

Terry comes up.

TERRY
I ride front end.

> JUBIL
>
> I'm the one who caught him.
>
> TERRY
>
> Caught him? You walked up on him.
>
> JUBIL
>
> It was me done it, though.

LATER

They are riding off on the horse. Terry is in the front, and Jubil is riding double.

> TERRY
>
> Well, partner. This didn't turn out too pretty, did it?
>
> JUBIL
>
> Look at it this way, at least we get to work outdoors.
>
> TERRY
>
> There's that.

FOCUS ON

A bee. It is buzzing through the air and it lands on the horse's butt. The horse jumps as the bee obviously stings and flies off.

> TERRY (CONT'D)
>
> Whoa there.

CLOSE ON LEFT SIDE OF HORSE'S SADDLEBAGS.

The bag has come unfastened. And there is something hanging out of it.

It's a greenback.

A little wind picks up and plucks at the dollar and carries it skyward and we watch it float and we go–

TO BLACK

DEAD IN THE WEST

(A Weird Western)

BY JOE R. LANSDALE

Based on his novel, *Dead in the West*

FADE IN:

LOGO AGAINST COMPLETE DARKNESS:

EAST TEXAS, 1870s

DARKNESS

SOUNDS OF LOVEMAKING

An abrupt wedge of light as a door is opened on a darkened room, revealing man and woman in bed, making love.

Framed in the light of the doorway, a big BEARDED MAN.

ON THE BED

The light lies heavy on THE REVEREND and a WOMAN. The Reverend is a lean, hard-faced man in his mid-thirties. Woman is young and attractive. Reverend rolls off the woman, turns toward–

                BEARDED MAN
    You!

BEARDED MAN

Draws a revolver from under his coat, points it at the Reverend.

BACK TO SCENE

                            WOMAN
               No, Able!

Reverend leaps to the side of the bed, reaches for his revolver, which lies on top of a Bible on the nightstand. Woman shrieks.

Bearded Man FIRES.

Woman takes the slug meant for Reverend in the chest, melts back dead and bleeding onto the sheets.

REVEREND

hand on the .36 Navy, wheels, FIRES THREE AMAZINGLY QUICK SHOTS as Bearded Man's bullet cuts across his cheek and slams into bed's headboard.

BEARDED MAN

He's got three holes in his forehead. They aren't more than a thumb-nail apart. HOLD ON HIS AMAZED FACE, then he collapses, and we–

                                               CUT TO:

EXT. – A CHURCH – NIGHT LATER

A horse tied out front, saddled and laden with gear.

A sign that reads:

THE CHURCH OF OUR LORD'S MERCY

Reverend Jebidiah Mercer

Gladewater, Texas

Backing out of the church is the Reverend, wearing pants and boots and no shirt. His revolver is stuck in his waistband. He has a torch and a barrel of kerosene. He's pouring from the barrel as he backs away. Outside, he drops the barrel, boots it inside, tosses the torch in after it.

FLAMES POOF LOUDLY TO LIFE AND LICK OUT THE DOORWAY, lap at the Reverend, who stumbles backward, away from the heat. He finds safe distance, watches as the flames start to consume the church.

Reverend goes over to the church sign, grabs it, groans, tugs it to the earth, falls on top of it with his knees.

CLOSE ON REVEREND

As tears crawl down his face. Lifts his head to God and yells–

          REVEREND
    I'm a sinner! A sinner!

DARK CLOUDS

hint of RUMBLING THUNDER. A BURST OF LIGHTNING, and it's a strange configuration, like A READY KILOWATT SPIDER. HOLDS HOT AND WHITE for a long instant, then–

BACK TO THE REVEREND

As sudden RAIN hits his face, washes his hair in his eyes, mixes with the tears.

Slowly the Reverend rises, unties the horse, swings into the saddle, starts riding away.

                                    DISSOLVE TO:

The rain and the night, and the SOUND OF THE RAIN DIES, and the night becomes RICH DARKNESS.

HOLD THAT DARKNESS UNTIL–

SCREEN LOGO APPEARS

ONE YEAR LATER

OUT OF THE DARKNESS A LIGHT

WIDEN OUR VIEW

So we see the light is the MOON looking like a big plate with gravy stains on it.

TRACK DOWN

From the moon, and the moonlight reveals–

A NARROW, TREE-LINED TRAIL

Moonlit and shadow-marked, the trail bends to the left around a forest of tall pines, and we HEAR before we see, NOLAN.

> **NOLAN (O.S.)**
> (Gradually becomes more audible with each word.)
> You goddamned, shit-eating, wind-breaking excuses for mules. Git on, you contrary sonsabitches.

A RUMBLE, and around the bend comes a stagecoach, lanterns attached to both sides of the driver's seat. They swing left and right like huge fireflies.

DRIVER'S SEAT

Is occupied by two men. NOLAN and THE SHOTGUNNER. Nolan look like Gabby Hayes but there's something about his expression makes you think he might have a strand of barbwire up his ass. He's grizzled and wears a slouchy hat and an eye patch.

His partner is long and lean and goofy-looking. He doesn't look smart enough to outwit his dinner. If he didn't have ears, his hat would be over his face and he wouldn't notice. A double-barrel shotgun rests in a gun boot between them.

                    SHOTGUNNER
        I can't hold it much longer, Nolan. I'm gonna wet myself.

                    NOLAN
        Goddamn, you pick the worst times to piss. Whoa! Whoa!

Stage slows, stops at the side of the road.

                    NOLAN
        Hurry up, will you? We're late.

Shotgunner drops to the ground, starts into the woods.

                    NOLAN
        (shouting)
        Why you got to–

INT. – COACH

                NOLAN (O.S.) (CONT'D)
        –go so far?

LULU, a seedy dance-hall gal is inside. She's wearing too much war paint and the hat she's got on has everything on it but a fart and train schedule.

Beside her is a GAMBLER dressed up in card table duds. Oily face. Overgrown sideburns. Bowler. Black suit. Checked vest. A waxed mustache. He looks as if he'd probe a dead man's asshole for a nickel.

Across from them is a mother, FLORENCE, with a young girl, MIGNON, asleep in her lap. The mother looks nervous and innocent. The child hugs a rag doll.

We see all this in the moment we HEAR Shotgunner respond to Nolan's question.

                    SHOTGUNNER (O.S.)
        Lady present.

Lulu, feeling flattered, tries to look very proper when she hears this, and the Gambler tries to look pleasant as well, but their faces turn sour, when–

                    NOLAN (O.S.)
        You ain't askin' her to hold your pecker for
        you, you jackass.

EXT. – COACH

Gambler's head juts out the coach window and he yells at Nolan and Nolan turns to look.

                    GAMBLER
        Mind your month, Mister. You've been
        nothing but a verbal cesspool since this
        trip started. There are ladies present.

                    NOLAN
        Yeah. I keep hearing that. Let me tell you
        somethin' Mr. Tin Horn Gambler. The
        "lady" sittin' next to you, Lulu McGill,
        would suck and blow your asshole for
        four bits.

Lulu sticks her head out the opposite coach window, and Nolan responds by leaning to her side for a look.

> **LULU**
> Goddamn you, Nolan. I ain't never done
> the like for no four bits, and you know it.
> Right now I'm a lady. Hear?

> **NOLAN**
> Can't help but hear you.

Gambler, really tough now.

> **GAMBLER**
> And there's a young girl and her mother
> in here, too. Hush that mouth of yours, or
> you'll have me to deal with.

Nolan leans from the driver's seat toward the Gambler's window. He has the double-barrel shotgun. He puts the tip of it over the Gambler's nose, cocks back the hammers.

> **NOLAN**
> I know who's inside, Mr. Tin Horn. Now
> listen tight. I'd hate to blow your stupid
> head off and disturb that little girl. So git in
> there and shut up.

INT. – COACH

Gambler jerks back inside, looks embarrassed. Lulu and the mother give him a disgusted look.

> **LULU**
> Ain't you the Top Dog?

EXT. – THE WOODS – MOMENTS LATER

Shotgunner taking a leak. There are lots of shadows falling across the scene, but one of the shadows is strange. It's looped. It's right in front of Shotgunner, and he's pissing through the loop. He turns and looks toward the tree where the shadow originates, and we see a noose.

Shotgunner shakes the dew off his lily, packs it away, goes over to the rope. He takes hold of the rope, runs his hand over it, and is rewarded with a rope burn. He jerks his hand back and shoots his injured finger into his mouth to suck on it.

SHOTGUNNER
Damn hemp.

Shotgunner turns to start back toward the coach, sucking his finger, and behind him–

CLOSE ON THE ROPE

Coming down the length of it, an oddball spider with a white skull marking its back. It scurries down one side of the loop, and we go–

CLOSER

So we can see there's blood on the noose, and the spider is easing up to the blood, and it becomes obvious that it's tasting the blood, and it begins to GROW AND GROW AND GROW.

SWOLLEN SPIDER

Drops from the rope to the ground, swells as if it's being pumped full of air. Its legs twitch; the leaves rattle beneath its legs. This dude is big, and it's really got too many legs for a spider now. It's slightly nebulous. A bad dream that moves in the shadows.

SHOTGUNNER

Hears something, turns. Nothing is there. He studies the woods behind him for a moment. Empty of life. Just the trees, the leaves, and the shadows. He sighs. Turns.

And the giant spider-thing is in his face. Its legs grab Shotgunner and jerk him into its mouth and it bites, and a BRIGHT BURST OF BLOOD EXPLODES into–

A MATCH

Being struck, and the match illuminates Nolan's face, and we PULL BACK and see he is relighting one of the lanterns on the coach. Then he carefully lights the other.

                        NOLAN
        Goddamn wind. Goddamn cheap-ass lanterns.

Nolan takes out his pocketwatch and holds the match close to the watch so he can see the time. His face takes on an even more disgusted look.

                        NOLAN
        Damn idiot. Why couldn't he piss in the wind like a real man?

A SHADOW falls over Nolan and he jerks his head toward it, and we see the SPIDER'S FACE, close enough it blows its breath in Nolan's whiskers and makes them rustle.

Match goes out and Nolan yells, and the weak lantern light on either side of Nolan is extinguished as the shape of the spider takes their place, blocking our view of Nolan.

A SOUND LIKE A WALNUT CRACKING between a plier's jaws and the shape of the spider shifts to something not quite as identifiable; shifts as if it is made of India ink and mercury.

GAMBLER

Sticks his head out the window. From his angle he can see Nolan's right arm and shoulder.

                    GAMBLER
    What's all that racket? We goin' to Mud
    Creek or not?

INT. – COACH

                    LULU
                    (disdainful)
    I just love it when you take charge, Mr.
    Tin Horn.

Gambler turns his head inside to look at her, frowns. Sticks his head and arm out the window–

EXT. – COACH

As Gambler beats on the side of the stage.

                    GAMBLER
    Hey. Let's go! I'm a paying passenger here.

Action of beating on the side of the coach causes Nolan to lean farther to the right. Gambler, afraid a gun will be pulled again, flinches. Then–

NOLAN'S BODY

Falls to the side, and with his feet hung in the boot sheath, he dangles there, his face twisted toward us. There's a seriously nasty bite out of the side of the old man's jaw. No one would mistake it for acne.

                    GAMBLER
                    (almost wistfully)
    Uh oh.

A FLOWING SHAPE-SHIFTING SHADOW

Comes down on the Gambler and the women inside SCREAM, and we

                                                          CUT TO:

EXT. – MUD CREEK, MAIN STREET – DEAD OF NIGHT

TOMB SILENCE

Empty street. At the far end of the street, coming toward us, seeming to melt out of the dark, SLOW MOTION, comes the stage. Both of its lanterns are extinguished, but it is clearly visible, ghostlike. Horses are frothing. Their hoofs are pounding up dust. In the moonlight, the dust looks like snow.

A big man–from here on out we'll call him THE INDIAN–is driving the team. His face isn't visible. It's shadowed by the night and he wears a hat.

Stage continues in SLOW MOTION until it is CLOSE, then it stops before the livery, which bears this sign: BILLY JACK RHINE, BLACKSMITH AND LIVERY. Then we're–

NO LONGER IN SLOW MOTION AND DEAD SILENCE

The Indian pulls the brake. Jumps down, lithe as a cat. He seems to glide around to the back of the stage.

Out from beneath the luggage flap he pulls a long wooden crate–coffin-size. He holds the crate as lightly as a shoe box. He glides around until he stands before the livery.

The doors are closed and there's a huge padlock on them. The Indian moves his hand slightly. The padlock–without coming open–drops to the earth, à la *The Brides of Dracula*. The doors blow open with a creak.

The Indian slips inside. The doors close behind him. The padlock jumps into place.

HOLD A BEAT as we HEAR a distant rumble of THUNDER beyond the blue-black, East Texas woodlands.

DISSOLVE TO:

CREDITS AGAINST A HOT, RED SUN

Rising over the East Texas landscape, which is mostly trees, and this grass-covered rise, and riding up to it, as if riding out of the sun, is a man on a horse dark as the devil's asshole.

FRONTAL SHOT, CLOSE ON THE REVEREND

He looks better than when we saw him last, but he has a haunted look. His face looks sterner, as if it's been chipped out of flint with a dull chisel. Handsome in an almost too masculine way. Eyes the color of revolver steel. He's wearing a black hat and black suit with a white shirt and a black string tie. Visible in his waistband is an ivory-handled, converted .36 Navy pistol. A large, worn Bible juts out of one of his coat pockets. He looks tired, ready to drop. He's not a man you'd expect to smile a lot.

REVEREND'S POV

The town stretched out in the distance between huge oaks and pines. Sighing, the Reverend opens his saddlebag, takes out a whisky bottle, pulls the cork, takes a swig, and returns the bottle. He starts the horse down the rise toward the town.

THE TOWN

As the Reverend rides in, past a sign that reads: MUD CREEK. People give him looks as he comes in. He looks as much like a shootist as a preacher.

TRACK REVEREND

Taking in the town, until he stops his horse in front of–

BILLY JACK RHINE'S LIVERY

As we FINISH CREDITS. There's a boy standing out front. A Huck Finn type. His name is DAVID. He looks as if he'd rather be anywhere than where he is. He looks hot and bothered. He's cleaning his fingernails with a large jackknife. He lazily lifts his head and he and the Reverend eye each other.

                    DAVID
          Yeah. Whatcha want?

                    REVEREND
          Provided you don't think it'll tire you too
          much, I'd like my horse groomed.

                    DAVID
          Six bits. Now.

                    REVEREND
          I want him groomed, not shampooed, you
          little crook. What's your name, son? I'd like
          to know who to avoid from here on out.

                    DAVID
          David.

                    REVEREND
          At least you've got a fine biblical name,
          even if you do look like a loafer to me.

                    DAVID
          And you look like a preacher.

The Reverend studies David. He likes the boy's spunk.

                    REVEREND
          That supposed to be an insult? You say it
          as if the word is poison.

                    DAVID
            You look like a preacher, but you got
            that gun.

The Reverend dismounts, takes money from his pocket, and hands it to the boy. As he removes his saddlebags from the horse, tosses them over his shoulder, he talks.

                    REVEREND
            I AM a preacher, boy. Name is Mercer.
            Reverend Mercer to you. Perhaps you'll
            groom my horse sometime between now
            and tomorrow.

BILLY JACK RHINE enters scene.

He's a big, potbellied man with huge arm muscles and a face like a clenched fist. His bald head is pink and beaded with sweat. He's carrying a blacksmith's hammer in his hand. He looks like he could eat a bucket of tacks and shit you a toolbox. With tools inside.

                    BILLY JACK
            Boy talking you to death, Mister?

Rhine's voice strikes the boy like a blow. He immediately goes stiff, looks wary. The Reverend takes note of this. It's clear there's tension between the two.

                    REVEREND
            We were just making a deal on the groom-
            ing of my horse. You must be the owner.

                    BILLY JACK
            Billy Jack Rhine. Boy charge you two bits
            like he's supposed to?

David swallows. He looks at the Reverend.

                    REVEREND

    I'm satisfied.

David smiles, leads the Reverend's horse inside the livery. Rhine, wearing a disgusted look, watches the boy lead the horse away, turns back to the Reverend with a frown.

            RHINE
            (snide)
Boy's like his mother. A dreamer. Have to beat respect into him now and then. Damn sure wasn't born with any.

          REVEREND
Boys have their own ways. Where's the best place to stay around here?

            RHINE
Ain't but one. The Hotel Montclaire. Git a room with a window. You don't, you'll be hotter than a bitch dog in heat.

          REVEREND

    Obliged.

Reverend crosses the street heading toward the HOTEL MONTCLAIRE.

INT. – HOTEL MONTCLAIRE

A real firetrap of a building. Stairway. Ragged furniture. JACK MONTCLAIRE at the check-in desk. Montclaire is a balding fat man in a too-small shirt with his elbow on the desk and his oily, sweat-beaded head in his hand. He looks like a guy who could grow penicillin under his arms. He's snoozing, snoring like a busted accordion. Flies buzz around his head, looking for a safe place to land.

A HAND

Comes down on a desk bell in front of Montclaire, jumping him awake.

                    MONTCLAIRE
        Huh? What?

WIDER VIEW

So we see it's the Reverend who has rung the bell.

                    MONTCLAIRE
        Sorry. Jack Montclaire at your service. Caught me sleeping. It's the heat.

Reverend nods. Montciaire opens the register book. The Reverend signs in.

                    MONTCLAIRE
        Six bits a night. Clean sheets every third day. Provided you stay three days.

                    REVEREND
        I will. Meals extra?

                    MONTCLAIRE
        Would be if I served them. I don't. You want to eat, try Molly McGuires Café. Biscuits taste like dried cow shit, but the rest of what they got's all right... You ain't got no bags, do you?

Reverend pats saddlebags slung over his shoulder.

                    MONTCLAIRE
        Room Thirteen all right with you?

>   REVEREND
> Any number is fine with me, as long as it
> has a window that opens.

Reverend tosses the pen on top of the register. Montclaire turns the register around and reads it.

>   MONTCLAIRE
> Reverend Jebidiah Mercer. Ain't never
> seen no Reverend carries a gun. I mean, a
> man of the Holy Word and Peace and all.

>   REVEREND
> Who said the Lord's work was peaceable?
> Devil brings a sword, and I bring a sword
> back to him.

Montclaire pulls the room key from one of the wall boxes and hands it to the Reverend. Montclaire points toward stairs.

>   MONTCLAIRE
> I suppose that's one way to see it.

Reverend starts up the stairs.

>   REVEREND
>   (without looking at Montclaire)
> No supposing about it.

When the Reverend is out of sight and earshot:

CLOSE MONTCLAIRE

>   MONTCLAIRE
>   (soft as a falling snowflake)
> Self-righteous asshole.

INT. – HOTEL ROOM 13

Reverend unlocks the door and enters.

WIDER VIEW

It's a simple room. Curtained window across the way. The curtains are the color of dust on white and they are blowing slightly because the window is open.

The bed is sagging. On a small table to the side of the bed is a washbasin with wash materials. Chair. Mirror with a crack down the center. The wallpaper is flyspecked and dirty.

Reverend goes to the window, pushes aside the curtains, puts his head out.

REVEREND'S POV

Street. Wagon rattles by. A man on muleback rides along. A woman, ABBY PEEKNER, walks from the hotel side of the street to the opposite side. She's wearing a bright dress and bonnet. When she reaches the other side, she stops, turns to face the hotel, takes off her bonnet, and as if drawn to it, lifts her face to the Reverend's window, and we–

GO CLOSE ON ABBY

She's so goddamn beautiful she breaks your heart.

CLOSE ON THE REVEREND

He's still stern-looking, but it's clear he likes what he sees. At this moment, Jesus is not foremost on his mind.

REVEREND'S POV

As Abby disappears inside a building.

REVEREND

Pulls inside, leaves the curtains and window open. He walks to the bed, tosses the saddlebags on it, takes off his coat, hangs it on a bedpost, and tops it off with his hat. He takes the bottle of whisky out of the saddlebags, uncorks it, swigs. He lies back on the bed with his back resting against the headboard, crosses his feet, and begins to drink. He closes his eyes for a moment–

QUICK FLASH ON BEARDED MAN TAKING THREE BULLETS

ANOTHER FLASH. The Reverend on his knees in the rain. The dark sky and THE ELECTRIC-SPIDER STITCHED BY LIGHTNING.

BACK TO NOW, REVEREND WINCING

Eyes pop open. A hard breath. As Reverend tips the bottle up we go to–

REVEREND'S POV

A fat spider on the ceiling.

RETURN TO SCENE

As Reverend switches the bottle to his left hand, and then, SNAKE-STRIKE FAST, he draws the .36 Navy from his waistband and shoots the spider. The ceiling rains plaster.

LOBBY

Montclaire leaps from his chair, rushes out from behind the desk, then runs back and gets a revolver out of a drawer, starts cautiously up the stairs.

He steps into the hallway, just as the Reverend appears in the doorway of his room, the .36 Navy dangling from his hand. Other doors open down the way. A few heads peek out.

Montclaire moves toward the Reverend.

              MONTCLAIRE
              (cautious)
        You okay, Reverend?

The Reverend looks at Montclaire and nods. His face is flushed and oily.

              REVEREND
        A spider. The devil's own creature. I cannot abide them.

              MONTCLAIRE
        You shot a spider?

              REVEREND
              (wry)
        Right between the eyes.

Reverend stands aside as Montclaire looks into the room. He sees the plaster dripping down from the ceiling onto the bed. He looks up.

MONTCLAIRE'S POV

A BULLET HOLE in the ceiling, and positioned around it on the ceiling are the SPIDER'S LEGS.

BACK TO SCENE

Montclaire steps out of the room to face the Reverend.

              MONTCLAIRE
        Preacher or not. I can't have you shootin' up my place. There'd been a third floor, a gent might have caught a blue whistler in the asshole. That'd been some price to pay for a spider. This place is respectable–

The Reverend digs into his pants pocket, comes up with some money. He shoves it at Montclaire.

REVEREND
It's an outhouse and you know it. Here's a dollar for the spider. Five for the hole. That's respectable spider bounty. Take it or leave it, windbag.

Montclaire knows the truth when he hears it. He studies the money. Briefly. Then grabs it faster than a crow picking corn kernels from a pile of shit.

MONTCLAIRE
Well, all right, but–

The Reverend steps back inside the room and slams the door. Montclaire looks indignant for a moment, pockets the money, looks down the hall at the faces sticking out of doorways.

MONTCLAIRE
Go on and mind your own business.

The observers draw back inside their rooms. Montclaire starts toward the stairs.

INT. REVEREND'S ROOM

He picks the bottle off the washstand and takes a swig. He sits on the end of the bed, swigs again, and as he lowers the bottle he sees his coat hanging on the bedpost and the top of his Bible sticking out of the coat pocket.

He takes the Bible from the coat and holds it like he would a poisonous reptile.

REVEREND
Why, Lord, hast thou forsaken me?

Long pause as the Reverend seems to wait for all answer. He smiles a slow ugly smile.

REVEREND
That's what I thought you'd say.

(Lifting the bottle in toast)

Same to you.

The Reverend takes a drink, turns and TOSSES the Bible angrily toward the open window.

ON WINDOW

Bible strikes the upper part of the raised window and BREAKS THE GLASS and flies out, and suddenly there is a DARKNESS over the scene, and–

EXT – TRACKING FLIGHT OF BIBLE

As it wheels in the sudden darkness like a great bird of prey, flapping pages like wings. It JETS toward the window and SMASHES back through, BREAKING more glass–

REVEREND

Lifting his bottle, is struck in the head by the Bible, knocking the whisky bottle from his hand and causing him to fall back on the bed.

Reverend rises. The Bible is lying on the bed. Open. He is leaning over it. Where the Bible struck his head a drop of blood drips and falls on a Bible page.

INSERT BRIGHT DROP OF BLOOD AND VERSE BESIDE IT

AND BEHOLD, I COME QUICKLY; AND MY REWARD IS WITH ME. TO GIVE TO EVERY MAN ACCORDING AS HIS WORK SHALL BE.

BLESSED ARE THEY WHO DO HIS COMMANDMENTS, THAT THEY MAY HAVE RIGHT TO THE TREE OF LIFE, AND MAY ENTER IN THROUGH THE GATES OF THE CITY.

RETURN TO REVEREND

He falls down on his knees, rests his elbows on the bed, and clenches his hands in a position of prayer. With lowered head and closed eyes–

REVEREND
Thy will be done, Oh Lord. Thy will be done.

DISSOLVE TO:

INT. – MORNING – MOLLY MCGUIRE'S CAFÉ

A serious greasy spoon. Lots of hustle and bustle. Waitresses are carrying food on platters. It's mostly men eating in there, slopping down their chow like hogs at trough. The Reverend sits alone at a table, eating slowly and politely.

Sitting at a small table are SHERIFF MATT SHINER and CALEB. Matt is a Wyatt Earp, Bat Masterson type. Something for the ladies. Slick in a black suit with a waxed mustache. Caleb looks as if he could use a hosing down. He's got his hat on and the hair that sticks out from under it looks more like ass hair, unwiped, then head hair. He's got a long unkempt mustache. He makes one think of a stocky Wild Bill Hickok gone to seed. While they eat, a woman, MILLIE, in her thirties comes over, stops at the table. Matt rises, smiles at Millie. Caleb keeps his chair.

MILLIE
Anything, Matt?

Matt takes her hand and holds it. He smiles and looks at her sweetly.

MATT
Sorry, Millie. No sign of your sister or niece.

MILLIE
If Florence and Mignon weren't on the stage, then someone must have taken them.

MATT
It's possible, but don't work yourself up. They could have missed the stage. Gotten off somewhere else. It may not look like it right now, but I am checking on things, Millie. I've wired the stage line, the last stop. I just haven't heard anything yet.

MILLIE
Florence was going to stay with me for awhile, until she and Mignon could get fixed. Find some kind of work suitable for a widow.

MATT
I know. I promise, I find out anything, you'll be the first to know. I've got some ideas I'm pursuing.

Millie nods absently, goes away. Matt sits down.

CALEB
The only idea you got is how're you gonna get your dick in that.

Matt frowns.

MATT
Watch your mouth.

CALEB
Her sister and her brat turn up dead, hell, Matt, you can go out there and comfort her. There's a good side to everything.

> **MATT**
> You're gonna push once too often, Caleb.

Caleb smiles. It's not the smile of a worried man.

> **CALEB**
> Come on, Matt. You ain't got idea one about that stage, do you?

Matt frowns, shakes his head.

> **MATT**
> No. Rode out the stage trail this morning. Didn't see hide nor hair of the passengers. And I lied to Millie. Didn't want to upset her needlessly. I did get an answer to my wire. They didn't stop off anywhere. They're just plain ole gone. Could have been Indians, I guess. Or robbers.

> **CALEB**
> You're grabbin' at farts, Matt. You know well as I do ain't been no Indian trouble around here in years. 'Cept that medicine show fella and his woman, and he damn sure ain't no trouble now.

> **MATT**
> You hung him, Caleb. Not me. I wasn't there.

> **CALEB**
> Judas didn't nail up Jesus neither... You gave him to us, Matt. It's the same thing. And it ain't nothing to feel guilty about.

> **MATT**
> He was an innocent man.

CALEB
Shit, he was an Injun and his wife was a nigger. Red niggers, black niggers, Meskin niggers. They're all the same. But it don't matter now. They're both boilin' with worms. But we was talkin' about the stage. It wasn't no Indians or robbers and you know it. They wouldn't have been polite enough to bring the stage in and put on the brake. Somethin' else goin' on here, and it stinks badder'n my ass in wintertime britches.

MATT
I'd reckon nothing stinks that bad.

Reverend enters scene, tips his hat.

REVEREND
Reverend Jebidiah Mercer, Sheriff. I'm a man of God. I travel from town to town teaching and spreading the word–

CALEB
And filling your offering plates.

Reverend turns to look at Caleb, who's rolling a smoke, tobacco raining every which way.

REVEREND
Like you, sir, I must eat. But I bring something with me besides a sermon. I bring the word of our Lord and eternal salvation.

MATT
No disrespect, Reverend, but you think we could cut through the horseshit and get down to cases? What can I do for you?

REVEREND
I would like to rent a tent and, with your permission, hold a night of gospel singing, prayer, and bringing lost souls to Jesus.

CALEB
And passin' that offerin' plate.

Caleb lights his cigarette and puffs a little cloud and smiles at the Reverend. The Reverend isn't bothered.

MATT
It's all right with me. I drink on Sundays. But we got a preacher already. Reverend Calhoun. You ought to walk down and check with him. I think he's got one of them tents like you want.

REVEREND
Obliged. I shall do just that.

MATT
Main Street forks at the north end. You'll see the church there. Calhoun's most likely around.

Reverend touches his hat in thanks, heads for the door.

CLOSE ON CALEB

CALEB
(to no one in particular)
Goddamn God hounds. Sorriest bastards ever squatted to shit over a pair of boots.

EXT. – CAFÉ

Reverend steps onto the boardwalk, and there's the beautiful woman, Abby, going inside with a puffy-faced, elderly man with a shock of white hair creeping out from under his hat like dead grass rotting under a rock.

Reverend and Abby hold each other's gaze. Obvious attraction. He tips his hat. She smiles, and goes past with the old man into the café, but not before turning for a last look.

ON REVEREND

As he walks past the livery, he pauses suddenly, turns his head toward it. The doors are locked. No one's around. As he looks at the livery we–

>   CUT TO:

INT. – LIVERY

CAMERA ROAMS

And zeros in on the crate resting on the loft beneath a thin sheath of hay. The crate shifts abruptly, as if pointing toward the Reverend.

BACK TO THE REVEREND

He continues down the street, pauses, looks back at the livery, shakes as if ice has been dropped down his spine, then proceeds.

EXT. – CHURCH

CALHOUN, an old man with a long white beard, dressed in overalls, is hoeing inside a little fenced garden next to the church.

The Reverend goes to the gate in the fence and calls out to the old man.

REVEREND
Reverend Calhoun?

Calhoun lifts from his hoeing, eyes the Reverend.

                    REVEREND
        Good day, sir. I'm Reverend Mercer. I've
        come to ask you a favor. One any good
        Christian could not refuse.

Calhoun straightens his back and leans on the hoe. He's a quarrelsome-looking old man.

                    CALHOUN
        We'll see about that.

The Reverend opens the gate and comes inside the garden. Calhoun eyes him warily.

                    CALHOUN
        Mind your feet.

                    REVEREND
        Sheriff said if it's all right with you, I
        might hold a night of gospel singing and
        preaching here in Mud Creek. He also said
        you might have a tent you could rent me.
        I'm willing to pay nicely.

                    CALHOUN
        How nicely?

                    REVEREND
        You name it.

                    CALHOUN
        Six bits.

                    REVEREND
        A popular price.

CALHOUN
And I choose Saturday night for you to hold your meeting.

REVEREND
Sir, that's the worst night of the week. The saloon will he filled.

CALHOUN
Take it or leave it.

REVEREND
I reckon I'll take it.

Calhoun pauses to eye the Reverend more carefully.

CALHOUN
Sure you're a preacher? You got that pistol. That's hardly a tool of the Lord.

REVEREND
Even the Lord allowed Samson to smote the Philistines. He gave Samson the jawbone of an ass. He has given me a revolver.

Calhoun doesn't appreciate this remark. He looks even more sour, drops the hoe.

CALHOUN
Mighty high on yourself, boy. You want the tent, let's do it. I have work to do.

REVEREND
No less than I, I assure you, sir.

INT. – CHURCH

Reverend and Calhoun. They're walking down the pew-lined aisle toward the pulpit. They go around it and to the back of the church and Calhoun opens a door.

STORAGE ROOM

Calhoun and Reverend framed there. Calhoun takes a lantern from a shelf and lights it. They proceed down the stairs. Calhoun says–

> **CALHOUN**
> Watch your step.

He waves lantern at a missing stair step.

> **CALHOUN**
> Rot got that one. Got to fix it one of these days.

Down into the darkened, cobweb infested storage room. At the bottom of the stairs, stacked all around, are crates with the words COLT, WINCHESTER, and AMMUNITION written on the sides. A fistful of rifle and shotguns are strewn about. There's also the barrel of a Gatling gun poking out from under a tarp. The Reverend stops, peels back the tarp and we get a good look at the Gatling. The Reverend drops the tarp back, reaches for a loose double-barrel shotgun, feels the balance in his hands.

> **REVEREND**
> For a man who dislikes guns, you certainly have a few on hand.

> **CALHOUN**
> Don't be snide with me, Mister. When they built this church it was sort of a fortress against outlaws and Indians. We never had much of either, but the guns are still here, same as there's still bars on the windows. Come on. Tent's back here.

Reverend lays the shotgun aside, follows Calhoun to a dusty corner where a molded canvas tent lies folded in a heap.

> **REVEREND**
> Any spots on it not rotten?

> **CALHOUN**
> Take it or leave it.

Reverend sighs, pulls six bits from his pocket.

> **REVEREND**
> I'll take it. I'll send someone for it, shortly.

Calhoun takes the money and waves the Reverend up the stairs.

> **CALHOUN**
> Remember the step.

Reverend starts up the steps, pauses, turns to Calhoun.

> **REVEREND**
> One theologian to another. A question of theology?

> **CALHOUN**
> Very well.

> **REVEREND**
> Do you believe the Lord truly forgives us our sins here on earth?

Calhoun is a little taken aback.

> **CALHOUN**
> The little ones, yes. The big ones? Perhaps in heaven, but not on this earth. This is where we pay, Reverend Mercer. I'm not a believer in a merciful God.

                    REVEREND
                    (slowly)
          Nor am I.

Reverend turns, proceeds up the stairs.

INT. – HOTEL MONTCLAIRE, REVEREND'S ROOM LATE DAY

The Reverend reading his Bible. He's naked, sitting on the bed by the little table and he's got the whisky bottle nearby. He reaches for it, pulls a long drink, and there's a KNOCK at the door. The Reverend pulls on his pants and answers the door. It's David.

                    REVEREND
          Let me guess. The price of my horse has
          gone up and I supply the curry comb.

David sniffs.

                    DAVID
          Smells like a drunk's nest in here. And like
          maybe you been greasing your axle.

                    REVEREND
          I've been known to pull it from time to
          time. That's natural. A boy your age ought
          to know about that.

                    DAVID
          Yeah. But I got an excuse. I'm too young
          for women.

The Reverend leaves the door open and goes back to his position on the bed, picks up the whisky bottle and chugs it. David watches him carefully, comes inside, and closes the door.

                    DAVID (CONT'D)
          Thought you preachers don't approve of
          strong drink.

The Reverend takes another slug from the bottle.

> **REVEREND**
> I don't. But I drink it anyway. Medicinal purposes. Something I can do for you, boy, or you just come over here to give me a temperance lecture and find out if I pull my joint?

David grins.

> **DAVID**
> Sure you're a preacher?

> **REVEREND**
> Sure as I am that you're a nosy, bothersome boy. Git to it, or git out.

> **DAVID**
> You any good with that pistol?

> **REVEREND**
> I generally hit what I aim at.

> **DAVID**
> Figured you did. I want a shooting lesson. I'd pay for it.

The Reverend studies David for a moment.

> **REVEREND**
> Why you want to learn so bad?

> **DAVID**
> Papa says I ain't much at the things a man ought to know. Says I'm a dreamer.

> **REVEREND**
> My father said the same about me.

DAVID

Did he beat the hell out of you regularlike?

REVEREND

He beat hell into me, son. He didn't think I measured up.

DAVID

Shootin' is something a man ought to know. And I might even be interested in that. Papa won't teach me because he thinks I'm too stupid to shoot a gun. He thinks the thing I'm best for is shoveling horse poop.

REVEREND

And you want to show him?

David nods and the Reverend takes another long swig from the bottle.

DAVID

I wouldn't have figured you for a drunk, Reverend. You look...I don't know. Special. Like you really are the right hand of the Lord. You know?

This distresses the Reverend.

REVEREND

(snappish)

No, I don't know. Look, I'll give you a shootin' lesson. Tomorrow morning. I don't want your money. I got a sermon to do Saturday night, and I want you to get some boys, go over to the church, and get a tent I've paid for. Cut me some poles, and put the tent up on that hill just outside of town. Pass out some handbills I've had made up.

DAVID

Let me see. Get the tent, cut some poles, put the tent up, and pass out some handbills. Want me to just go on and preach your sermon for you, too?

REVEREND

Very funny. I'll pay all the boys two bits. You get a shooting lesson. Now go on, I've had about all of you I can handle.

David smiles, tips his hat, and starts out.

REVEREND

Whoa. Wait!

Reverend stands, digs money from his pants, gives it to David.

REVEREND

Hire a rig from your papa. Extra dollar is for you. We'll go out in the country and fire a few rounds.

DAVID

Thanks, Reverend.

REVEREND

Tell your pa I'm hiring you for some work. He looks like a man likes to know his son is sweating.

David grins, goes out, shuts the door. The Reverend smiles, then the smile slowly fades. He lifts the bottle, starts to drink. He sees himself in the cracked mirror, the bottle uplifted, his face split in two by the crack. One side of his face looks distorted. Perhaps it's the dust. The light. Whatever, the Reverend stares for a BEAT, doesn't like what he sees. He jerks the bottle from his lips and throws it at the mirror. Glass flies. Whisky splatters.

> REVEREND
> (distressed)
> I'm trying, Lord! I'm trying!

INT. – RHINE'S LIVERY – NEAR EVENING

LOFT

as the crate shifts subtly.

FULL VIEW

Billy Jack Rhine is pounding a horseshoe. Every once in a while he pauses. Looks around furtively. Listens. SOUND of the crate moving slightly. Hay drifts down. Rhine looks up at the loft.

> RHINE
> David?

Nothing. Rhine clenches the hammer, goes to the ladder, starts cautiously up. The higher he gets, the more frightened he looks. He starts to blow his breath, tremble slightly. He looks like a man coming down with the flu. He hurries down the ladder.

> RHINE
> David, that's you, I'll beat the hide off ya.

A BEAT. No answer. SLIGHT CREAKING SOUND.

Rhine drops the hammer, tosses a bucket of water on the forge, grabs his hat off a peg, and goes out the livery's double doors.

EXT. – LIVERY

Rhine pushes the door shut and locks it. As soon as that's done, he looks relieved.

> RHINE
> Rats. Goddamn rats.

He turns, walks briskly down the street.

EXT. – SKY – MOMENTS LATER

Clouds darken. Wind picks up. All along the street townsfolk look alarmed. They rush inside or hurry about their business. The sky continues to darken until it's as black as tar paper.

TIME DISSOLVE TO:

EXT. – LIVERY – CLOSE ON PADLOCK ON DOOR

Padlock drops off the latch and falls to the ground. The doors blow open.

INT. – LIVERY

CREAKING SOUND as we FOCUS on crate. The lid thrown back and wobbling as if it's just been lifted. Hay is twirling in the wind.

EXT. – LIVERY

A black cloud BLUSTERS out of the livery and into the street and BLOWS away with a SCREAMING noise.

Livery doors SLAM shut.

Latch closes.

Padlock jumps into place.

Wind slows. Dies.

Sky lightens. Clears.

It's NIGHT and the MOON floats HIGH and BRIGHT.

EXT. – MUD CREEK ALLEYWAY – A LITTLE LATER

NATE FOSTER, a well-dressed banker with a beard and top hat, comes out of the bank and locks the door. It's obvious he's drunk as a skunk. He's singing "Buffalo Gals" and is walking a little too carefully. He takes a metal flask from his coat pocket, opens it, and sucks at it.

TRACK NATE

Until he comes to a dark alley and goes in. He puts the flask away, uses the alley wall for support, goes down a ways, stops next to a large trash crate with this written on it: MOLLY'S TRASH ONLY. The crate is overflowing. A lot of what we see are uneaten biscuits from Molly's, the biscuits Montclaire warned the Reverend about.

Nate turns to face the wall and works with his fly. He takes a leak. When he's finished, he turns and trips over something.

            NATE
        Goddamn it!

Nate carefully lights a match, and has some difficulty doing it, due to his condition. What he sees in the match glow is a

BIG UGLY DOG

It's dead, and its throat is ripped out.

BACK TO SCENE

            NATE
        Sheeeit!

Nate wobbles to his feet. Match burns his fingers. He drops it. Sticks his finger in his mouth. He reaches into his coat pocket and gets out the metal flask. He unscrews it, dips his burned finger into the bottle, licks the finger. He takes a swig from the bottle. He points and speaks to the dog.

                              NATE
                Somethin' damn sure got your ass, Rover.

                           VOICE (O.S.)
                         (sandpaper and gravel)
            Sure did.

Nate wheels toward the voice, and it's a big dark shape of a man. We know him as the INDIAN. The Indian wears a wide-brimmed hat and a black serape. He's big and steeped in shadow. He's tall, as in REAL TALL.

                              NATE
                            (terrified)
            You! No!

Frightened, Nate scrunches up his face, bends over, pukes all over the man shape. All we can see of the Indian is a dim outline of features and his eyes glowing like two fanned coals. Indian looks down at himself, at Nate's puke. He takes Nate's head in his hands.

                             INDIAN
                   Not nice. Not nice at all.

Indian squeezes Nate's head so hard the eyeballs pop out like golf balls, the teeth jump like popcorn, and the brains leap from his skull like overboiled cauliflower; it's one big red, gray, and white blossom that SPRINKLES the scene, and we–

                                                      CUT TO:

EXT. – STAGE TRAIL – NIGHT

Moonlit. Trees stand like sentinels.

CAMERA WANDERS off the trail, into the woods. There's a cracking sound beneath the trees, then, like a Polaris missile going off, Nolan's head POPS out of the ground, tossing dirt. His eye patch is turned up, the empty eye socket is full of dirt. The wound on his face is really ugly now. It writhes with happy worms.

Hands and arms work at the dirt next to Nolan. The Gambler tears his way out of the dirt, wobbles to his feet dripping grubs. His neck is broken and his head hangs well over on his shoulder; looks like a half-filled sack of onions. His neck is elongated, like pulled taffy.

Lulu works her way free, dried leaves falling off of her. She actually looks kind of happy.

Then up comes Shotgunner. He doesn't look any dumber dead than he did alive. As he comes out of the ground and stands, a big mound of dirt and leaves on his belly sheds, and beneath it, clinging to him like a straw monkey, is the little girl, Mignon. She's holding her rag doll. Shotgunner rakes her off. She hits the ground and rolls. We get our first good look at her face. It's one nasty face. Being dead does not become her.

Now Florence is pulling out of the ground. She looks oddly sweet-faced, considering her mouth and nostrils are filled with dirt. She's missing a shoe.

Nolan and Gambler bump into each other, exchange hairy eyeballs. Nolan hauls off and hits the Gambler so hard his rubbery neck swings his head far right, then left, and back again. It comes to rest on the Gambler's opposite shoulder.

Mignon, still clutching her rag doll, tries to climb up Shotgunner's leg. He reaches down, grabs her by the leg, starts walking, carrying her so that her head hangs upside down. She accepts this, dangles in his grasp, holding her doll the way she's held.

The Dead Folk walk out of the woods, onto the stage trail, and head toward town.

INT. – SHERIFF'S OFFICE

Matt and Caleb sharing a bottle of whisky.

CALEB
Tonight reminds me of the time we hung that Injun. Great hangin' weather. Crisp and cool.

MATT
Don't start, Caleb.

Caleb reaches inside his shirt, produces a strand of rawhide from around his neck. The strand is decorated with beads and a small, human ear.

CALEB
Real pretty, don't you think? I get a gun barrel just thinkin' about it.

MATT
Jesus. Put that thing away.

CALEB
Getting squeamish in your old age, ain't you, Matt?

Matt pushes his chair back, gets up, and grabs his hat off the hat rack. As he puts it on:

MATT
Tired of seeing it is all. Why in hell I tolerate your company is beyond me. I'm gonna make my rounds.

CALEB
Do that. Me, I'm gonna sit right here and keep this bottle company. It's a hell of a lot more entertainin' than you are anyway.

EXT. SHERIFF'S OFFICE – NIGHT – MOMENTS LATER

Matt adjusts his hat, looks out at the night. His expression changes as we go–

CLOSE ON MATT

Closing his eyes, and we HOLD A BEAT.

MATT OPENS HIS EYES

And we've FALLEN BACK IN MEMORY TO–

PULL BACK WIDE

Matt is dressed differently and the street is filled by a crowd. Caleb is leading them. Rhine, Shotgunner, Nolan, Nate, town familiars are here.

Crowd is moving toward Matt who has his hand on his revolver butt. They look less than friendly.

                CALEB
    Let us by, Matt. We want that Injun and his
    nigger, and we aim to have 'em.

                MATT
    They deserve a fair trial. I can't do that.

                CALEB
    Sure you can, Matt. Can't he, boys?

Crowd crows in agreement.

                MATT
    It's for the law to decide.

DAVID WEBB

A distraught fella wearing a long billed cap, steps to the forefront.

WEBB
It was my daughter they murdered, Sheriff. What kind a trial's needed for that? Now, you step aside and let justice be done. Ain't no one gonna think less of you for doin' what you oughta.

MATT

Holds his ground, but gradually loses his resolve. He puts his revolver away, hangs his head, steps aside.

CROWD

Rushes the jail.

MATT

Lifts his head, OPENS HIS EYES, and we're–

BACK TO THE PRESENT

Face beaded with sweat, Matt shakes as if chilled, steps into the street, starts to walk. He goes by the DEAD DOG SALOON. We HEAR a tinny piano and a DRUNK WHORE SINGING.

Matt continues past storefronts, grabbing the knobs, shaking them, checking to make sure they're locked. He comes to the alley that runs alongside Molly McGuire's, not paying that much attention.

ALLEY

A SHADOW CRAWLS up the wall, swells into the shape of a large man wearing a flat-brimmed hat.

BACK TO SCENE

Matt senses something, snaps a look down the alley, sees nothing. He doesn't notice the shadow on the wall. It's too close to him, too big for him to really discern what it looks like. But we see it looming over him, leaning away from the wall, as if at any moment it will drop down on him like a bird of prey.

A NOISE like something SLITHERING.

Matt jerks his revolver.

WE SEE THE SHADOW

Change shape, appear to be a great taloned hand, and the talons reach out quickly and flow away into the greater darkness of the alley.

MATT

Jerks a look at the wall.

No shadow.

Matt is getting seriously worked up at all this rustling and movement he can't quite discern. He looks back down the alley, tries to peer into the darkness.

                MATT
          Who's there?

Out of the darkness, along the alley floor, in a RUSH, flows the shadow, a shadow like a liquid version of the man in the flat-brimmed hat. The shadow washes up close to Matt's boots.

Matt jumps back, points the revolver at–

SHAPELESS BLOB OF SHADOW at his feet.

Matt breathes a deep sigh of relief. He relaxes. He puts the revolver away.

FROM THE DARKNESS, a VOICE that sounds as if it's made of glass and asphalt–

VOICE (O.S.)
You are not forgotten.

Shadow at Matt's feet MOVES and CLUTCHES one of his boots.

Matt panics, jerks the boot loose, bolts up the street.

TRACKING MATT

Nothing is visible behind him, but the walls along the street show his RUNNING SHADOW, and the CLOSE SHAPE-SHIFTING SHADOW of his pursuer blowing along.

The shadow is like a chameleon silhouetting the inhabitants of hell. Sometimes a MAN SHAPE, sometimes a SPIDER SHAPE, sometimes a WOLF SHAPE, yet not quite any of these things.

It's in hot pursuit of Matt, who is picking up his pace. Behind him the SHADOW BECOMES a LARGE SET OF TEETH-FILLED JAWS SNAPPING at his head. A wind HOWLS behind him like a hungry wolf. Dust KICKS UP in the street as the thing gives chase.

THE CHURCH

looms before Matt at the end of the street, the cross on the steeple forms its own shadow, and it falls toward Matt.

Matt runs toward the church, losing his hat. He charges onto the church steps, turns with his back to the door, pulling his revolver.

MATT'S POV

Nothing.

Street is empty.

The moon is high and bright.

BACK TO SCENE

Matt slowly calms. He begins to smile, weakly.

                MATT
    I'm a damn fool. Jumpin' at shadows.

Matt holsters his revolver, wanders out into the street. He picks up his hat, turns it over. CROWN HAS BEEN BITTEN out of it.

                MATT
    Jesus Christ and two disciples!

WIND makes a SOUND LIKE LAUGHTER, then–

STONE DEAD SILENCE

EXT. – RHINE'S LIVERY

As a monstrous INDIAN-SHAPED SHADOW, black as the pit, flows across the screen and starts to fall apart like wet construction paper, strikes the ground, glides like oil toward the livery, and–

ON THE DOORS

Lock drops.

Doors fly open with a sigh.

Oily Shadow flows inside and joins the darkness there.

Doors close.

Lock jumps into place.

INT. – LIVERY

Flowing blackness takes shape halfway up the ladder and becomes the Indian, at least so we know it's him but not so we really get a good look at his face yet. Indian finishes off his climbing. Lid to the crate opens, and–

INSIDE THE CRATE

Is a nude, mauled, female body.

BACK TO SCENE

Indian steps into the crate, adjusts the corpse into his arms, stretches out inside, and though we're still not going to get a clear look at his entire face we go–

CLOSE ON ONE OF THE INDIAN'S EYES

A tear squeezes out. Runs down his cheek. A shadow slowly covers his face as the lid to the crate comes down, as if pulled shut by a ghostly hand.

EXT. – STAGE TRAIL – MOMENTS LATER

The Dead Folk, and they're gettin' it on. The Gambler is the best walker, and it's almost as if it's a race. He looks behind him now and then to check the position of the others. Positions noted, he picks up his pace, smiles stupidly. He's got just enough brain to be happy he's ahead.

A partial lightening in the trees. The sun is rising. The Dead Folk note this, make excited grunting noises. They start looking left and right. All except the Gambler, he's too into being first. He's really hoofing it now.

Florence stops suddenly, looks through the trees. There's a house out there. She cocks her head like a curious puppy.

FLORENCE
Sisssder...Sisssder...Millie...Millie...

Florence starts toward the house, steps in a hole, falls down. Gets up. She has a mouth full of dirt from the fall.

The sun is coming up fast now. Florence nears the house. Smoke starts to rise off of her. She begins to get agitated. She sees a root cellar and makes for it, throws open the doors and starts inside.

INT. – ROOT CELLAR

Dark and half full of brackish water. Mason jars of food float about. Water moccasins swim about. Florence comes down the steps, letting the root cellar doors fall shut behind her. She goes into the water, sinks out of sight beneath it. A huge water moccasin swims over the spot where she went down.

EXT. – STAGE TRAIL

Except for the Gambler, who is out of sight, the other Dead Folk have abandoned their walk. They're off the trail, smoking in the emerging sunlight, digging frantically in the dirt, tossing it and leaves over them.

ON DOWN THE TRAIL

Gambler is going around a bend. He's lost the others. He looks back and is as happy as if he had good sense. Smoke is starting to rise up from the top of his head. Mud Creek is visible in the distance.

INT. – REVEREND'S ROOM

He's up and washing his face in the water basin, looking at himself in a fragment of the mirror. He doesn't like what he sees. He dries off, goes to the window, looks out.

REVEREND'S POV

Sees Gambler shuffling down the street, little trails of smoke rising up from him like a half-crushed cigarette.

He watches as Gambler goes to the saloon. It's locked. Gambler grabs the doorknob and begins to pull on it. He looks frantically about. The sun is hot and yellow now.

Gambler panics. He's starting to smoke like chicken left too long on the grill. Little bursts of flames lick around his head and hands. He grabs the knob and jerks hard.

His arm comes off at the elbow with a RIP, his hand still clutching the knob.

>   **GAMBLER**
>   (gargle-spoken)
>   Dang.

Gambler uses his good hand to pry the arm loose. He sticks it in his coat pocket, elbow down. He's really cooking now. He turns, bolts into the street. He bursts into flames, starts to fall apart. He begins to look as if he is made of oatmeal and Gummy Bears. He falls flat in the street with a SPLATTING SOUND.

REVEREND

Has run out of the hotel and is in the street. He goes over to the smoking mess that was Gambler, reaches down, touches him. He recoils in horror. His hand is dripping flesh the consistency of snot.

>   **REVEREND**
>   By the saints.

A HAND

On the Reverend's shoulder–

AND WE'RE TALKING CHAIN LIGHTNING WITH A HOT COAT HANGER UP ITS ASS, as the REVEREND WHEELS, comes to a crouch with his revolver drawn, fitting it snugly over the tip of a man's nose. It's the older man who was with Abby. Hereafter known as DOC.

Standing nearby is Abby.

               DOC
Whoa! We're Good Samaritans like yourself. We saw him fall... Lord, but you're fast.

Reverend slowly replaces the .36 Navy in his waistband. His eyes go to Abby.

              REVEREND
Sorry. Guess I'm a bit jumpy.

Doc leaning over the body.

               DOC
Looks like he's been dead a week.

              REVEREND
Listen! That man was walking.

               DOC
Don't mess yourself, son. I know that. Somehow the sun did this to him. Wait here. I'll be right back.

Doc goes off, Reverend turns to look at Abby. She smiles. They look at the dead man, smoking pleasantly in the sunlight. An eyeball rolls out of the Gambler's head and swirls on the ground like a top, goes still. Reverend turns back to Abby, nods in the direction the Doc went.

              REVEREND
Your father.

               ABBY
              (nodding)
He's a doctor.

Reverend looks at the decimated Gambler, whose teeth are falling out of his head, one at a time, like hardened corn from an old cob.

> **REVEREND**
> Seems a little late to me for that.

Doc hoofs back into the scene pushing a wheelbarrow with a shovel in it.

> **DOC**
> Shovel him into the 'barrow, son, and try not to get too much dirt with him.

Reverend takes the shovel and moves toward the mess.

> **DOC**
> By the way. I didn't get your name. I'm Doc Peekner. This is my daughter, Abby.

As the Reverend scoops up the first steaming shovelful of Gambler.

> **REVEREND**
> Reverend Jebidiah Mercer. Glad to meet you, I'm sure.

INT. – DOCTOR'S OFFICE

The office is attached to living quarters. There's a table and most of the Gambler is heaped there. He's still steaming and gurgling and popping, but it's slowing down. Abby and the Reverend stand by the table watching in amazement. Doc has a trowel and he's scraping the trowel loudly along the sides of the wheelbarrow, getting what residue he can. The Gambler's clothes dangle on the side of the wheelbarrow. The Gambler's boots are beside the wheelbarrow.

Doc finishes scraping and slaps a big slab of goo off the trowel, onto the table. He drops the trowel, grabs the Gambler's boots, sets them on the edge of the table, and delicately removes the socks from inside the boots with tongs, gets the socks by the toes, upends them. Dissolving bone, flesh, and blood the consistency of cough syrup slides out of the socks onto the table.

DOC
What a mess. You two go make some coffee. I'll finish up here. I'll probably have to wring his clothes out. I want as much of him as I can find.

DOC'S KITCHEN

Abby is pouring a cup of coffee for the Reverend, who is sitting at the table. She pours herself a cup, perches on a counter. She looks very fetching there, and the Reverend can't keep his eyes off of her.

ABBY
With my father being a doctor, I've been around death all my life. Been his nurse since I was sixteen. But I've never seen anything like that.

Even as the Reverend talks, his eyes stick to Abby like flypaper.

REVEREND
Closest thing I've seen is a slug. You pour salt on a slug, it'll do like that.

ABBY
(smiling)
Do you usually look this dreamy when you talk about salting slugs, or do you have something else in mind?

The Reverend, embarrassed.

REVEREND
Sorry. You're a very attractive woman.

ABBY

I know. Every man in town has told me. At least twice, I thought perhaps you might have a fresh approach.

The Reverend, looking stupid.

REVEREND

I suppose not.

ABBY

You never did answer my question. Do you have something in mind?

REVEREND

Perhaps. But I'm not sure it's proper to mention it.

ABBY

Don't be such a stuffed shirt, Reverend.

REVEREND

Calling me Jeb ought to help.

ABBY

Jeb then.

Reverend looks as if he might actually say what's on his mind. But instead–

REVEREND

I'd better be going. I promised a boy a shooting lesson this morning. We'll be driving out of town, so I need to get started.

ABBY

Sounds wonderful. What say I invite myself along? We'll make a picnic of it.

Before Reverend can respond, Doc enters scene drying his hands on a towel.

> **DOC**
> It's not like anything I've seen or heard of. I don't think it's a disease of some kind. And I've never heard of anyone being that sensitive to the sun.

> **REVEREND**
> Then what is it?

> **DOC**
> I've got some ideas...but they're just ideas. I'll need some time to think on it. Do some research.

Doc wanders over to the stove, picks up the coffeepot, and pours himself a cup. He's obviously distracted. Abby slips off the counter and moves next to the Reverend.

> **ABBY**
> Dad, the Reverend and I were discussing going on a picnic, weren't we, Reverend?

The Reverend hesitates only a moment.

> **REVEREND**
> Yes. We thought that might be a nice idea.

> **DOC**
> Can't abide them. Damn ants and dirt. Critters gettin' in the food–

> **ABBY**
> Dad?

> **DOC**
> What?

                    ABBY
        You weren't invited.

Doc turns to see Abby taking the Reverend's arm as he rises from the chair.

                    DOC
        Oh.

EXT. – MAIN STREET – WAGON TRAVELING – LATER

Reverend is holding the reins and Abby is sitting next to him. In the back of the wagon is David, looking sullen.

                    DAVID
        You didn't say nothin' about no girl.

Reverend and Abby ignore him, smile to each other.

EXT. – STAGE TRAIL – LATER

Abby is laying out a blanket under a tree, preparing the picnic goods. Reverend is standing next to the stage trail, looking across it.

On the other side, David is finishing jabbing sticks into the ground. He runs back to the Reverend's side. In one hand he's holding more short, sharpened sticks.

When David is next to him, the Reverend removes his revolver from his waistband.

                    REVEREND
        This is a thirty-six Navy revolver; eighteen
        sixty-one model.

                    DAVID
        I don't care what it is. I just want to shoot it.

> **REVEREND**
> Always know your weapon, David. It has been converted from cap and ball to modern ammunition.

> **DAVID**
> Why don't you just get a new one?

> **REVEREND**
> This one has done well by me.

Abby has finished laying out the picnic goods. She's watching them.

> **ABBY**
> You two going to shoot or talk those sticks to death?

Reverend looks back at Abby and smiles.

> **REVEREND**
> Good point.

The Reverend wheels, and he's FAST, VERY, VERY FAST, and the Navy barks. BLAM! BLAM! BLAM! BLAM! BLAM!, and the sticks fly in half, and David, mouth wide open, looks in amazement at what's been done. The echo of gunfire is still dying as the Reverend removes the empty shell casings from the Navy, drops them in his pocket, starts to reload.

David cranks his mouth up.

> **DAVID**
> God Almighty!

> **REVEREND**
> (casual)
> Watch your language, son. The Lord is not nearly as enthused with good shooting as we are.

						DAVID

You must be as good as Wild Bill Hickok was.

						REVEREND
						(matter of factly)
Most likely better. Your turn. Go put up some more sticks.

Abby comes over.

						ABBY
You're pretty sure of yourself.

						REVEREND
Yes, I am. On the matter of shooting, anyway.

The Reverend accidentally drops a shell casing on the ground, bends to retrieve it, spies–

A SPIDER

On the ground.

BACK TO SCENE

Reverend jerks up and stomps the spider, good and hard, too enthusiastically. He's a little breathless.

						ABBY
I take it you don't like spiders.

						REVEREND
Despise them. When I was a boy, my father locked me in a closet as punishment for some childhood silliness that I forget. He was like that. A stern man. The closet was full of spiders.

Reverend picks up the casing, drops it in his pocket, finishes loading the gun.

> **ABBY**
> I'm sorry, Jeb.

> **REVEREND**
> I was bitten several times. I can't see one, or anything that looks like one, without feeling a certain...alarm. Queasiness.

David comes running back. The Reverend gets behind him, leans over a shoulder and hands him the revolver, guiding his hand with his own.

> **REVEREND**
> Don't aim. Just imagine you're lifting a finger and pointing at one of the sticks. Soft squeeze on the trigger.

VIEW FROM THE STICKS

As David fires three times in quick succession, missing wildly.

BACK TO SCENE

As the Reverend takes the revolver and takes out the spent casings and reloads with fresh shells.

> **REVEREND**
> You're trying too hard. You've got to become one with the gun.

> **DAVID**
> Can I put it in my belt and draw it?

> **REVEREND**
> Only if you want to lose your manhood.

DAVID
You mean I might shoot my pecker off?

REVEREND
Precisely.

Abby chuckles. David takes note.

DAVID
Sorry, ma'am. I forgot you were there.

ABBY
Quite all right.

The Reverend turns toward the targets.

REVEREND
You've got to kinda feel into it. Like this!

Smoke and thunder. Hot sulphur blisters on a clear, blue sky. The Reverend jerks the revolver up, fires three times, POW! POW! POW! Three sticks jump apart close to the ground.

Reverend tosses gun to his other hand. Three more shots. Three more twigs jump to pieces.

The Reverend twirls the gun, tosses it, catches it with the other hand, twirls it, sticks it in his waistband.

DAVID
Wow!

Abby strolls over, looks falsely stern.

ABBY
Show-off.

The Reverend doesn't miss a beat.

REVEREND
Vanity's a sin, Abby. I wouldn't want to teach the boy bad habits. I'm just showing him the mechanics of the gun.

ABBY
(smiling)
I think you're showing me the mechanics.

REVEREND
That, too. David, run see how I did.

David squatting over the sticks. He's counting them.

DAVID
One. Two. Three. Four. Five. Six...

David notes that one of the sticks is not a stick. It's smoking. He leans close for a look.

INSERT WHAT DAVID SEES

A dirty finger shot off at the second knuckle. Smoke drifts up from it.

DAVID
Reverend! Come quick!

BACK TO SCENE

Reverend and Abby come running. The Reverend bends down, digs around the finger, reveals a human hand. He digs some more, uncovers part of the corpse's chest, then the face. The face is full of happy, white grubs. The wound on his face is the most active part. This is in fact the ballroom of the grubs. The face begins to steam.

DAVID
It's Nolan, the missing stage driver.

> **REVEREND**
> Run back to the wagon, David. Get a blanket. Quick!

EXT. – STAGE TRAIL – THE WAGON TRAVELING

Reverend and Abby on the front seat. The body is in the back with the blanket over it. David is sitting on the open tail end of the wagon as it rumbles along.

> **DAVID**
> (to self)
> Some picnic. Some shootin' lesson.

INT. WAGON – ON BLANKET COVERED CORPSE

One hand is outside the blanket. It's smoking in the sunlight. Flesh is falling off of it in meaty, green strips. Unseen by anyone, the hand slithers beneath the blanket to safety.

EXT – MUD CREEK – LATER

Wagon with Reverend driving pulls up in front of the Doc's office. Reverend gets down off the wagon, helps Abby down. As he walks to the back of the wagon, he speaks to David.

> **REVEREND**
> Better get this rig back to your father. I'm going to haul the body in to Doc Peekner.

Reverend bundles the blanket around the corpse, pulls it out of the wagon, bends and hangs the body over his shoulder.

> **DAVID**
> What about the shooting lesson?

Reverend stepping onto the boardwalk, followed by Abby.

> **REVEREND**
> That was the first. Consider on it. Right now, you have a tent to get up, boy.

David climbs into the driver's seat, takes the reins, releases the brake. He looks a little dejected.

> **DAVID**
> I think I got the short end of this stick.

INT. – DOC'S OFFICE – LATER

Doc. Abby. Reverend. They're bending over Nolan's corpse, which is on a table. In a large tub, on ice, is the naked body of Nate Foster. Nate's head looks as if it's been in a vise. He's got dissolved patches of skin all over, as if acid has been dropped on him. Doc nods toward the tub.

> **DOC**
> They brought the banker, Nate Foster, in after y'all left. Wanted me to look him over before the undertaker got hold of him.

> **ABBY**
> What could have done that to his head?

> **DOC**
> I don't know. They found him out back of Molly's. There was a dead dog found nearby. Sheriff thought the dog did that to him. But teeth didn't crush Nate's head. It's more like he's had it in a vise. And if somehow it was the dog, how'd the dog get dead. Suicide? Ripped out its own throat? Another thing. Watch this.

Doc goes over and pulls a heavy curtain open. Sharp sunlight hits Nate in the tub and Nate starts to sizzle. Flesh drips off of him.

                    DOC
        That was startin' to happen to him in
        the alley. I got him in here, out of direct
        sunlight, it stopped. Watch Nolan now.

Doc pulls the curtain wider, so that the sunlight hits the table where Nolan lies. Nolan starts to drip flesh, like liver sliding off porcelain.

Doc drops the curtain over the window. Dissolving ceases.

                    DOC
        Sunlight's poison to their flesh.

                  REVEREND
        Same as the man this morning.

                    DOC
        Correct. Though that old boy had a
        considerably more generous dose.

Doc directs their attention to a shelf full of very large specimen jars.

TRIO'S POV

Jars have crude paper labels glued to them. The labels read, and the jars contain: HEAD FRAGMENTS. LEG FRAGMENTS. TOES. PENIS. TESTICLES. SOMETHING OR ANOTHER. BRAIN. GUTS. Etc.

BACK TO SCENE

                    DOC
        Except for the man this morning, I don't
        believe sunlight is what did them in
        though. Nate's head was crushed.
                (Nods at Nolan)
        Nolan was bitten by something. An animal
        maybe. Though it's not like any bite I've

seen. There's been a serious loss of blood... Another curious point is sunlight affects them dead or alive.

REVEREND
So you're not any closer to a solution?

DOC
Perhaps... Not sure I want to tell you this, Reverend, but you're a man who deals with immortal souls, and I think you're the one to hear it. Reverend, do you believe the dead can walk?

ABBY
What?

Doc ignores her. He keeps his eyes on the Reverend, observing his reactions.

REVEREND
I suppose so. Lazarus walked.

DOC
I'm talking about the Living Dead, not returning from the dead.

REVEREND
You mean Nosferatu? Ghouls? Zombies? I've read of such things.

DOC
God help me, Reverend. That's exactly what I mean. Do you think I'm crazy?

REVEREND
In God's universe I dismiss nothing. But I've been known to doubt.

DOC
The man who fell apart in the street... He was dead before he fell.

ABBY
Dad, that's ridiculous.

DOC
I been telling myself that all afternoon. But I examined pieces of him under the microscope, performed a couple of tests. His body was dead decaying flesh before he fell. The sun speeded up the decay, but I tell you, he was a walking dead man.

ABBY
Dad, you know better. That defies all the laws of science.

DOC
That it does. Reverend, how about curses. You believe in those?

This one hits the Reverend in a personal manner. Something moves behind his eyes.

REVEREND
I do.

Doc sits on the side of the tub containing Nate.

DOC
Both of you. Sit down.

Reverend and Abby look for a place to sit. The place is pretty well taken up with bodies and parts, but they eventually find accommodations.

                    DOC
          Mud Creek has a curse on it, Reverend.
          And I fear everyone in this town is gonna
          die like a bug-stung tomato. And the
          moment I saw you, sir, I knew you were
          part of this thing. It was like you were the
          last ingredient in the stew. You're what
          finally set it all in motion... I think maybe
          you know that.

On the Reverend, and it shows on his face that he does know.

The Doc continues talking, and as he does we–

                    TIME DISSOLVE TO FLASHBACK:

EXT. – MUD CREEK, MAIN STREET— ONE MONTH EARLIER

A medicine-show wagon. Driving is the Indian. He looks better here than the way we've seen him. Healthier. Human. Beside him is a beautiful light-skinned African-American woman, hereafter known as THE INDIAN'S WOMAN.

The wagon's sideboard reads:

Good Medicine, Fortunes, and Cures

The street is full of people and they're turning to check this unusual wagon and couple out.

                    DOC'S VOICE
          About a month ago, this wagon rolled into
          town. An Indian was driving. He was huge.
          Powerful-looking. Had a good-lookin'
          high-yeller woman with him.

JUST OUTSIDE OF TOWN BENEATH A LARGE OAK

The Indian's Woman is sitting at a table under the oak, reading an elderly woman's palm. She's talking. We can't hear what she's saying, but it's obvious the elderly woman is engrossed. Nearby, the Indian is selling bottles of medicine, lickety-split, to eager customers.

> **DOC'S VOICE**
> Bein' Indian and Colored, they might have got run out the first day they showed up, if they hadn't been such a curiosity... The Negress read palms, the Indian sold medicine, and it wasn't alcohol laced with sugar and vinegar. It was medicine that worked.

MUD CREEK, MAIN STREET

An older lady, Mrs. Jameson, is holding out her hands to a circle of surprised townsfolk. The Doc is among them.

> **DOC'S VOICE**
> Mrs. Jamieson was just one of many examples.

> **MRS. JAMESON**
> Look! Look! You've all seen 'em before. Like knotted plow lines.

She rushes to Doc Peekner, holds her hands out to him.

> **MRS. JAMESON**
> You know how they was, Doc. Wasn't nothin' you could do helped. But look at them. He gave me a salve, and it worked.

Doc takes her hands, looks at them, amazed.

> **DOC'S VOICE**
> She'd had the misery for years, and in a week's time of using the Indian's medicine, she had hands like a twenty-year-old.

INDIAN'S WAGON-NIGHT

There's a campfire. The horses are tied nearby. The Indian is leaning against the wagon, watching the Doc like a hawk. Doc, hat in hand, is talking to the Indian's Woman. She's listening intently. She has a friendly look on her face. We can't hear them, but we hear his V.O.

> **DOC'S VOICE**
> That Indian being able to do what he did sort of got my goat, I'm not ashamed to say it. After they'd been around a few days, I went out to thank them for what they'd done for the town.

Indian and Doc exchange glances. The Indian's look is one of distrust. The Doc looks nervous. Doc finishes talking to the woman, puts on his hat.

> **DOC'S VOICE**
> The Indian saw right through me. Figured I was hoping to latch onto a few of his healing secrets, which I admit I was.

Doc climbing into his buckboard, looking back at the Indian's Woman. She looks very fetching there in the firelight.

> **DOC'S VOICE**
> And the woman...I'm embarrassed to say this with Abby here, but I was attracted to her. Even at my age, I felt a stirring I didn't know I was capable of anymore. She was bewitching.

DOC IN BED

The Indian's Woman is in bed with him. It's all very surreal. Shadows jump. Sometimes Doc seems to be rolling between the woman's legs. Other moments a huge serpent with a woman's arms and head writhes about his body.

>   DOC'S VOICE
>   I had dreams about her. Not polite dreams.
>   Strange dreams.

Serpent tail wraps around his throat, starts to choke him, and–

>   DOC'S VOICE
>   They seemed remarkably real.

DOC

Sits bolt upright in bed. His face is a sweaty mess. But the scene looks different. Normal. He's the only one in bed.

Doc realizes it was a dream, sighs, swings his legs off the side of the bed and puts his head in his hands.

EXT. – MUD CREEK – ANOTHER NIGHT

It's raining hard. Puddles swell in the streets. Lightning cracks, jumps hot and white in the sky. Thunder rolls. David Webb is running across the street with a girl child in his arms.

>   DOC'S VOICE
>   Few days later, it began to rain. Folks
>   caught the summer sickness. And, of
>   course, they went to the Indian for help.

DOC'S OFFICE – MOMENTS LATER

As David Webb bursts into the office with his rain-drenched daughter in his arms.

                    WEBB
              Doc, that Indian gave her somethin', and
              she's gone limp. She's worse than she was.

Doc takes the child, puts her on a table, looks her over, touches her with a stethoscope. He lifts her eyelids for a look. He puts a mirror to her mouth. He turns to Webb, sadly shakes his head. Webb SCREAMS–

INT. – SALOON – LATER

Webb standing on the bar top. His daughter's body lies on the bar top beside him, partially covered with a blanket. Webb is yelling still, crying. Pointing at the body of his child. There's a crowd listening to him. Caleb is in the forefront, but Nate, drunk as a loon, wobbling a little, is there, too. As are Rhine, Nolan, Shotgunner, and Lulu.

                  DOC'S VOICE
              In an instant, every good thing the couple
              had done was forgotten.

                     WEBB
              That Indian and his nigger. They poisoned
              my child. Ain't no tellin' who else they'll
              poison. I trusted them with her life, and
              they mocked me. They killed her for spite,
              the goddamned heathens. Are we gonna
              stand for that?

Nolan becomes prominent.

                    NOLAN
              Hell, no.

Crowd yelling, mumbling, rushing out of the saloon, Caleb in the lead.

EXT. – JAIL

Crowd crossing the street toward the jail. Matt steps outside of the jail, ready to defend it against attack.

DOC'S VOICE
The Sheriff got wind of what was happening, brought the couple into protective custody.

INT. – JAIL

The Indian and the Indian's Woman sitting on a cot in an open cell. The noise outside causes the Indian to stand, to come to the open doorway of the cell.

EXT. – JAIL

Matt, defeated, steps aside.

DOC'S VOICE
But he didn't have enough iron in his spine.

INT. – JAIL

Crowd storms in, Lulu yelling for the men to–

LULU
Get those murderous vermin!

–And the Indian puts up a fight. A good fight. He throws men around like a kid tossing Cracker Jacks. But he is overwhelmed. Crowd pushes over his downed body and they grab the woman who tries to fight, but she's quickly overcome.

EXT. – THE WOODS NEAR STAGE TRAIL – A SHORT TIME LATER

Drunken crowd has Indian perched on top of the wagon with a rope around his neck, the other end tied to the overhanging limb of a huge oak. The horses are hooked to the wagon. The Indian has really been worked over. His shirt is torn, revealing on his chest a strange, hairy, uplifted mole in the shape of a spider with a white skull-shape on its back.

Some of the thugs, Caleb and Rhine among them, come out of the woods chuckling, carrying something bloody in a blanket. They toss the blanket on the ground and the Indian's Woman rolls out into the dust. She's nude. Mutilated.

Caleb holds up his blood-wet knife, waves it at the Indian. From Caleb's wrist dangles a rawhide thong with an ear on it. The Indian looks at what they've done to the woman. He swallows hard, but he has tremendous composure, courage.

> **CALEB**
> This here ear's gonna make me a damn
> fine necklace, Injun. I might even make me
> a backer sack out your pickle, boy.

Laughter from thugs. The Indian with a countenance of steel.

> **WEBB**
> Any last words, child killer?

INDIAN

Eyes like chipped flint.

> **INDIAN**
> We did nothing to you. My woman is dead,
> but your daughter is not dead.

> **NOLAN**
> I reckon we know dead when we see it.

> **INDIAN**
> With my death, you seal your own.

The Indian raises his head to the sky. Rain splatters on his face. Lightning moves in the heavens. A drumroll of thunder.

> **INDIAN (CONT'D)**
> I offer my soul to the dark one. Yogsith. Yuggoth...

(Trails off into unintelligible mumbles)

Rain picks up. Wind howls like a wolf with its balls in a vise.

Rhine, pushing forward out of the crowd.

> **RHINE**
> 'Nuff of this mumbo jumbo.

Caleb jumps forward, slaps the horses hooked to the wagon, and they bolt. The Indian swings, kicks once or twice, goes still.

LIGHTNING

Hot as Satan's breath, forked as his tongue, cracks out of the wet sky and strikes the Indian, and the world goes–

WHITE for a long searing instant. Then–

Our eyes adjust, and in the Indian's place is–

THE SMOKING NOOSE. EMPTY.

But then we see something scuttling up it, heading for the sanctuary of the oak. A small but odd-looking spider with a white skull-shape on its back.

> SLOW DISSOLVE TO:

EXT. – THE WOODS – LATER THAT NIGHT

Doc with a shovel, digging a grave. He has a crate by the grave and there's a lantern sitting on the crate, illuminating the scene.

                    DOC'S VOICE
        When I heard what had happened, I
        hitched up the wagon and went out and
        got the woman's body and buried it in an
        old plow crate in the woods.

Doc finishes off the hole. He places the lantern on the ground, drags the crate into the hole. Starts covering it up.

EXT. – MUD CREEK – STILL LATER

Doc driving his buckboard into town. There's a crowd in the street and David Webb is frantically loading some bags of supplies into a wagon. Caleb and the others in the crowd are mumbling to each other.

Doc stops the buckboard and stares angrily at the crowd.

                    DOC
        You folks happy with what you've done?
        You bastards. Why'd you do her that way?

Webb looks up. His face is coated with sweat and fear. His eyes are as wild as birds in flight. He stares at Doc a long instant, then picks up the last bag, tosses it in the wagon.

Next instant, out of one of the buildings comes Webb's wife, ELVIRA WEBB. She's carrying their daughter. Who is ALIVE and smiling.

The Doc is astonished.

                    DOC
        She's alive...

Elvira, frantic as a pig on slaughter day.

ELVIRA
The medicine just put her to sleep. Deep sleep. She came out of it an hour ago, fit as a fiddle. It's your fault. You said she was dead. You started the whole thing. You drove my man mad.

DOC
She was...dead.

ELVIRA
Well, she ain't.

Webb climbs onto the wagon seat, extends a hand and pulls his daughter up. Elvira climbs up. Webb turns to the Doc.

WEBB
If the medicine worked, I figure the curse he put on the town'll work. I'm gettin' out now. Spend the rest of my life makin' this up. Not that it can be made up.

(Almost as an afterthought)

Ain't your fault, Doc. I done what I done of my own free will.

Webb turns, clicks to the horses, the wagon starts to move.

ON CALEB

CALEB
Well, I ain't runnin' from a goddamned thing. Way I figure, one less nigger and Injun is one less nigger and Injun, mumbo jumbo or not, and I ain't gonna miss neither of 'em.

Caleb pulls the rawhide thong out of his shirt and out from around his neck and holds it up, displaying the bloody ear.

> **CALEB**
> They're dead. Both of 'em. One got cooked to spit by lightning, the other'n we funned to death. And that's the end of that mystery. I'm gonna get a drink.

Caleb stalks off.

INT. – DOC'S HOUSE, BEDROOM – LATER THAT NIGHT

> **DOC'S VOICE**
> That night I believe the Indian sent me a sign. Just in case I felt free of all that had happened. A little reminder, that in a way, what Caleb and Webb and the others had done was all my fault.

Doc in bed. He's tossing and turning.

Lightning FLASHES outside the window.

A PEAL of thunder. Doc rolls over.

A FLASH of lightning.

QUICK LOOK at bed and the mutilated corpse of the Indian's Woman lying, smiling, beside him.

Doc rolls with a YELL, hits the floor. Rises up slowly and looks at–

THE EMPTY BED

CLOSE ON DOC

His expression shows us he feels something nearby. He turns his head toward the window–

FLASH OF LIGHTNING–

ON THE INDIAN'S FACE

At the glass, backed by a white explosion of heavenly light.

> **INDIAN'S VOICE**
> (as if from the ether)
> Do you like the dream I sent you?

Lightning is gone. There's nothing at the window. But there is the sound of laughter. It sounds as if it's falling down a tunnel.

Then it's gone.

BACK TO THE PRESENT

Doc looks drained, frightened.

> **DOC**
> Sometimes I believe it was only my imagination.

> **ABBY**
> Dad, it was.

Doc puts his attention on the Reverend.

> **DOC**
> But what I believe now is this: I believe it's you he's been waiting for to start the ball rolling. I don't know why, but I feel it in my gut.

The Reverend listens, absorbs, and–

DISSOLVE TO:

DOC'S KITCHEN

Reverend and Abby.

> **ABBY**
> You have to forgive Dad his mumbo jumbo. I fear he's gotten fanatic about it since Mom died. He reads nothing but old books on witchcraft and demonology.

> **REVEREND**
> It might be said the Bible is full of that, and I believe it. So, why not? As for your father, I think he's a fascinating man... I find his daughter fascinating as well.

Abby likes that. She smiles.

> **ABBY**
> Perhaps this is a little undignified, Jeb. Forward. But I'd like to see you again.

> **REVEREND**
> You will. Tonight I give a sermon. Will you come?

> **ABBY**
> Of course... Jeb, what my father said about you being the last ingredient...

> **REVEREND**
> I believe your father is right. The Lord brought me here for a reason yet to be revealed. I know that. I've seen the signs. I accept it, and I wait. I had better go.

> **ABBY**
> Am I too forward now?

Abby grabs him, pulls him to her, and kisses him. He likes it. He kisses back. He forces himself to pull away from her.

The Reverend. Embarrassed. Nervous.

> **REVEREND**
> I better go.

Reverend turns to leave. Stops.

> **REVEREND**
> I'm not as righteous as I pretend, Abby. Until this town, until you, I had begun to doubt my faith. I have things in my past. The Lord is trying me. Rightfully so. I violated my calling. Even used it to manage a sin. A sin that led to another, greater sin.

> **ABBY**
> It doesn't matter. Not to me.

> **REVEREND**
> It matters to me. It matters to God. God's righteous curse on me versus the evil of this town, and the evil curse the Indian gave the town in return.
> (Wry)
> God prefers to do his own damage. No help from devils required.

> **ABBY**
> You don't believe that.

> **REVEREND**
> I do. I must go. I have a sermon to prepare.

Before the Reverend shuts the door on his way out, he pauses to look at the lovely, worried Abby. He smiles. Then he's gone.

ESTABLISH SUN SLOWLY SINKING

EXT. – HILL OVERLOOKING MUD CREEK

In the dying sunlight David, with several other boys, is putting up the Reverend's tent. They're trying to raise a central pole in the middle of the tent. They're not having an easy time of it. We can see legs scuttling like centipedes as the partially rolled tent tangles around the boys inside.

A few boys are outside, trying to pull the sides of the tent. David is ramrodding things. He's outside yelling orders.

> **DAVID**
> Come on. Were running out of daylight.
> We'll be puttin' it up around him preachin',
> rate y'all are goin'.

From inside the tent, legs only visible.

> **A BOY'S VOICE**
> Way you run your mouth, you ought to be
> preachin'.

> **ANOTHER BOY'S VOICE**
> What you ought to he doin' is using some
> of that hot air to lift this here tent up.

David, disgusted, lifts the flap, goes under the tent to help.

EXT. – STAGE TRAIL

Ground trembles, breaks open.

Fingers.

A face.

A wiggling foot.

INT. – ROOT CELLAR

Florence surfaces from the dank water. A moccasin sees her, strikes, hits her cheek, can't withdraw its fangs, flaps there like a worm on a hot griddle.

Florence, the reptile dangling from her cheek, goes up the ladder, cracks the cellar, sees red rays of the dying sun, lets the doors slam back. She looks anxious, hungry. She cocks her head. An idea has floated into her waterlogged brain.

                   FLORENCE
Millllie...Milllllie
           (Louder)
Millie...Millie...Sisssder...

EXT. – FRONT OF MILLIE'S HOUSE

Millie is out front killing a chicken to be dressed. She has it by the feet and has its head on a chopping block. She brings down a hatchet. Off goes the chicken's head. She lets go of its feet, and it runs around headless, squirting blood, then falls dead with a quiver.

She picks up the dead chicken, starts towards the house, and the sunlight plays out and the scene turns GRAY, and we HEAR–

                FLORENCE (O.S.)
Millllllie...Milllie...

Millie stops. Drops the chicken. Listens.

                      MILLIE
                  (tentative)
Florence?

As Florence continues to call, Millie sticks the ax in the stump and goes around to the back of the house.

The sound is coming from the root cellar.

                        FLORENCE (O.S.)
              Milllllieeee...Milllieeee...Milllieee...

Millie walks slowly over to the root cellar.

                              MILLIE
              Florence? Is that you, sister? You in there?

                        FLORENCE (O.S.)
                             (softly)
                    I'm tired, Millie. I'm cold. Wet.

Millie leaps toward the root cellar doors, jerks them open.

DOWN ON FLORENCE

Standing at the top of the steps. A face like death warmed over, the snake still dangling.

SHOCKED REACTION FROM MILLIE

BACK TO SCENE

As Florence shoots out an arm, grabs Millie by the throat, pulls her down as if she were made of crepe paper, simultaneously saying–

                            FLORENCE
              and hungry!

Florence, clutching the surprised Millie by the throat, walks backward down the steps, the snake flapping. Millie struggles like one of the chickens. The tops of her shoes scraping on the steps. Florence backs until she pulls Millie beneath the water.

Moonlight shines through the open cellar doors, floats on the rippled water that begins to churn and boil and turn blood-red in its center.

After a moment one of Millie's legs pokes up. Kicks. Disappears.

More blood on the water.

A large bubble that swells and pops and causes a massive ripple.

Ripple subsides.

Calm water. Spreading blood.

EXT. – STAGE TRAIL

Dead Folk shuffling along, lickety-split. These aren't the drag-your-ass-mummy-style walkers. These guys have got stiff joints, but they can truck.

Mignon wanders off the road, starts through a pasture. She steps in a cow plop. Stops. Looks at what's swelling around her foot. She lifts her foot, drags a finger through the shit, pokes it in her mouth, tastes, kind of turns her head side to side like she can't make up her mind if it's okay. Decides it isn't. Continues walking.

EXT. – A HOUSE

Standing in the fresh moonlight.

INT. – THE HOUSE

An OLD WOMAN in a rocking chair, knitting. An OLD MAN in an armchair, smoking a corncob pipe, reading the Bible.

A KNOCK at the door. Old couple stop what they're doing.

          OLD WOMAN
    Well, who could that be?

          OLD MAN
    We can sit here and guess, or open the door.

Old Woman gives Old Man a "you smartass" look. She gets up. Opens the door.

DOORWAY

Stark against the night, Mignon and her doll. She smiles. Her teeth are full of dirt and cow plop.

BACK TO SCENE

          OLD WOMAN
    I'll swan. It's a little girl.

Old man comes to the door, looks at the child. Mignon shows him her smile. It's big and wide.

          OLD MAN
    She smells like cow shit.

          OLD WOMAN
    Watch your mouth. She's a child. She's lost.

          OLD MAN
    She still smells like cow shit... Look there.
    She's got it on her shoes.

Old Woman really gives Old Man a look.

          OLD WOMAN
    It'll clean up... Come in, baby.

Mignon looks tentatively inside. Smile goes away momentarily. She steps inside.

Old Woman bends down to her, says–

          OLD WOMAN (CONT'D)
    Hungry?

The little girl nods–

AND LEAPS.

She's like a giant, starved rat. She grabs the old woman by the shoulders and starts biting her face, and the Old Woman screams, leaps, runs around the room, rolls on the floor. The kid hangs with her, tight as a cancerous mole. Blood is flying.

Old Man watches in amazement. He looks around. He grabs a fireplace tool. He goes after them.

Old Woman is lying on the floor with the little girl on top of her, tearing savagely at her with her shit-stained teeth.

OLD MAN
Let her go, you brat!

Old Man brings the tool down hard on the back of Mignon's head. It sticks there. Little girl freezes. Old Woman has quit moving. Old Man starts trying to work the tool free. As he yanks and works it back and forth, it makes a sound like someone walking while wearing tight shoes full of water.

Mignon turns slowly to look unpleasantly at the Old Man, and as she does, the tool tears free of her flesh.

Old Man swings down with the tool again.

Mignon catches it with one hand, pulls it away from him.

And BAM! Mignon hits him on the foot with it, drops it, leaps on him, leaving the bleeding, barely moving Old Woman lying there, a pool of blood forming around her.

Old Man runs around the room with Mignon holding on to him. She climbs him, clings to his back. Old Man runs into a wall and goes down, and the little girl finishes him with a–

CLOSE FLASH OF NASTY KID TEETH AND A SPRAY OF RED—

And we're gone to MUD CREEK where we—

ESTABLISH BLACKIE MERTZ FUNERAL PARLOR AND COFFIN MAKER SHOP – THIS SAME NIGHT AND TIME, and we—

DISSOLVE TO:

INT. – FUNERAL PARLOR

Naked bodies of Nate Foster and Nolan are in cheap, open, pine coffins perched on sawhorses. The mortician, BLACKIE MERTZ, a skinny, hook-nosed man, who has been drinking, carries clothes over to Nolan's box. He puts the clothes on the side of the coffin, lifts Nolan up, starts to put the shirt, which is split down the back for convenience, on him. It's a bitch of a job anyway.

>   **BLACKIE**
> Hope you boys 'preciate all I've done
> for you.
>   (Pauses)
> Course, who the hell's gonna see you?

Blackie suddenly drops Nolan back in the box with a THUD.

>   **BLACKIE**
> And that being the case, and since nothin's
> gonna make you pretty, why in hell am I
> wastin' my time?

Blackie tosses the clothes into the box on top of Nolan.

>   **BLACKIE**
> Keep 'em. You done stunk up the shirt.

Blackie goes around to Nate's coffin. There are dress clothes hung on the side of the box. Boots on the floor. Blackie looks inside the coffin.

                    BLACKIE
          You'll do just fine way you are, too. Ain't
          like anybody's comin' to the funeral. 'Cept
          worms and flies. So you can go back the
          way you come in. With your bare ass
          hangin' out.

Blackie chuckles to himself. He looks down at the boots.

                    BLACKIE
          I might even be able to see your boots get
          proper wear.

Blackie picks up a boot and measures it against his own foot. Looks as if it might fit.

A NOISE BEHIND BLACKIE.

Blackie doesn't like this.

He turns slowly, still holding the boot.

NOLAN

Is sitting up in his coffin, struggling frantically to get the shirt on.

                    BLACKIE
          No. You're dead as hell.

Nolan still struggling with the shirt. He's getting frantic.

                    NOLAN
          Don't fit.

Nolan struggles to get the shirt on, overturns the coffin. Nolan rolls out. He gets up and stands in front of Blackie. He seems more concerned with the shirt that's hanging off of him.

                        BLACKIE
        But you're dead!

                        NOLAN
        Still don't fit.

HANDS

From behind Blackie. They belong to–

FOSTER

Who grabs Blackie by the neck.

                        FOSTER
        My boots!

A RED MOMENT

As Nolan grabs Blackie from the front and teeth begin to SNAP AND RIP.

INT. – DOC PEEKNER'S OFFICE

Doc sitting at his desk. He's reading a book. It is bound in leather. The title of it is *The Necronomicon*. On the desk beside him, spine out, we glimpse *De Vermis Mysteriis, Cabal of Saboth, Book of Doches.*

CAMERA MOVES PAST DOC, TOWARD LAB DOOR

                                                DISSOLVES TO:

INT. – LABORATORY

PAN LABORATORY

Shelves containing Gambler's body parts in jars.

Jars rattle.

Flesh and goodies inside jars crawl.

Lids on the jars turn from the inside as blobs of flesh try to unscrew them.

DOC'S OFFICE

As there is a CRASH from the lab.

Doc lifts his head, turns slowly in his chair. Listens.

ANOTHER CRASH.

SEVERAL OTHERS.

SOUNDS OF CRUNCHING BONE, SLURPING.

Doc opens his desk drawer, removes a big horse pistol, gets up, moves toward the lab.

He stops at the door.

Puts his ear to it. Listens.

CRACKLING AND SLURPING NOISES.

LABORATORY

As the door opens and we see Doc framed by his office light. He steps inside, into the shadows. He shoves the pistol into his belt, picks up a lantern and lights it.

Lantern throws a–

BEAM OF LIGHT ON SHELVES

Shelves are empty. Except for one jar containing skeletal hands. The hands are pushing at the jar from the inside. It rocks. Falls.

We HEAR the jar BURST behind a table and supplies.

BACK TO SCENE

Doc pulls the pistol with his free hand, moves cautiously around the table. As he gets to one end of it, starts to peer around–

ON SKELETAL HANDS

As they SCUTTLE away, sneaking around to the other side of the table.

Doc HEARS the SCUTTLE but sees nothing except broken glass. He turns and looks around on the other side of the table. Quickly.

NOTHING. But we hear the bony fingers scuttling. They've dodged him again.

Doc, scared, sets the lantern on the table, turns it up, eases around the table with the gun–

AND HANDS JUMP OUT OF THE SHADOWS AND GRAB

His pants leg and start scrambling up his body until they grab at his throat and try to choke him.

Doc SCREAMS, drops the pistol, jerks at the hands. They come free. He tosses them across the room.

ON HANDS

As they hit the floor and slide into a mess of something writhing.

DOC'S POV

As he snatches up the lantern for a look. And is shocked to see that the hands have slid into a heap of maggot infested flesh that wobbles like meat on a fat man's ass.

The skull is reassembling itself like a puzzle being snapped together.

Eyeballs roll into the skull's mouth, poke through the skull eye sockets, adjust themselves like roulette balls coming to a stop.

Flesh leaps to the bone and the bone clicks together with a sound like dice in a Yahtzee cup.

Hair pokes out of the head.

A tongue crawls into the mouth, turns, finds its place. Flaps a few times as if tasting the air.

AND THIS MESS

Starts to rise to its feet, one of which is on backward.

The monstrosity is on the major homely side. I mean, we're talking a seriously ugly patchwork dude here, known hereafter as PATCHES. Hair is poking out of the face. The skull has bare bone sections. The flesh is haphazard, and there's a nose under his chin. A few teeth stick out of his face, but there are enough in place for Patches's jaws to click together like castanets.

Patches takes in Doc with his wet, roll-around-marble eyes. He hunches a little, smiles with what he's got to smile with, and waddles toward Doc. Teeth chatter. He drags the foot that's on backward.

DOC AND PATCHES

Doc grabs up the pistol. He starts to back way. He fires off a round, and the round hits Patches in the chest, and the back of Patches's body bursts open with a leap of flesh, and the–

FLESH

Hits the wall, and worms fall out of it, and the flesh slides slowly down the wall like a tossed pizza.

PATCHES

Pokes a finger in the hole in his chest, and isn't happy. He's not hurt. He's pissed.

Once again, Patches starts walking.

DOC AND PATCHES

DOC gets behind the table. Patches lunges for him over the table, surprises us by how far he can reach. He clamps those bony, hair-spotted hands on the Doc's shoulders, and digs his fingers in.

Doc lets out a yell as Patches's face comes forward to bite him. Doc pokes his revolver forward, quicklike, and–

WE'RE ON PATCHES'S MOUTH

As the revolver slips right in and Patches clamps down on the gun, hard. Teeth fly out of Patches's rotten head like hot popcorn, and the barrel slides down his throat like a Deep Throat trick, and–

BLAM!

DOC AND PATCHES

As the revolver bucks and a chunk of skull leaps away, and Patches hits the floor faster than a second-rate boxer with a mob connection.

Doc leaps back, slams himself into the shelf. Shelf wobbles.

On the table edge we see Patches's ugly hands appear, grabbing, pulling himself upright.

And now he's up. Half his skull is gone, and there are some brains wobbling in the cup of his head, like oatmeal mixed with moldy Jell-O, and the brains drip out in plops and glops, and Patches, he's got one eye left, and it is on strands of tendons that dangle down around his chin.

Patches puts both skeletal palms on the table and leans forward and HISSESSSSS.

Doc grabs the lantern, tosses it. Patches ducks. Lantern hits the far wall explodes into flames on the floor.

Patches glares at Doc, opens his mouth in a confident smile, sticks out that ugly tongue and flaps it like a curtain blowing in a breeze.

Doc leaps to the side, by the shelf, grabs it, pushes it forward, and down it comes–

PATCHES

As his one remaining eyeball lifts on its tendons for a look. His nasty bottom jaw drops like a steam shovel opening up. He tries to step away from the table, but he's too slow, and–

                  PATCHES
                  (resigned)
     Shit.

Shelf comes down hard, hits Patches in what is left of his head, drives it down to the edge of the table, clips it off clean as the guillotine that gave Robespierre the trim.

HOLD ON the table and Patches a BEAT. Patches's brains start to ooze out from between the shelf and table and drip onto the floor.

ANOTHER ANGLE ON SCENE

Doc goes around for a look. He pulls the shelf back. It's ugly under there.

DEAD IN THE WEST

He runs over and stomps out the fire made by the lantern, grabs another lantern, fires it up, hangs it on a peg.

By lantern light, he drags the corpse over to the large tub that had contained Nate Foster. He throws the body inside, grabs a bucket and trowel, scoops up Patches's brains and skull fragments on and beneath the table, dumps them in the bucket, hurries them to the tub, pours them inside.

ABBY

Enters the scene carrying a candle as Doc is pouring lantern fuel in the tub. She gives the room a once over.

                ABBY
     Dad, what in the name of heaven...

Doc takes the candle from her.

                DOC
     Heaven had nothing to do with it.

Doc drops the candle in the tub. Flames jump. The mutilated corpse burns. Abby looks at the tubs contents with surprise.

                ABBY
     My God!

CLOSE ON THE TUB

And the black smoke, and gradually we realize we are no longer looking at black smoke, but instead a–

DARK COTTONY CLOUD

And the cloud rolls away and reveals the moon.

PAN DOWN TO

THE HILL

Moonlight in the wind-blown trees. The tent writhing like a living thing.

BENEATH THE TENT

Where all the boys are struggling to raise it. They're having a bad time of it, and the wind isn't helping. The tent flaps and heaves. David is trying to encourage everyone to lift at the same time, pushing up on a tent pole. Then, out of the corner of his eye–

DAVID'S POV

Glimpse of someone's legs outside of the tent.

ANOTHER ANGLE ON SCENE

As David waits for the wind to flap the tent up again.

The wind comes. The tent flap moves.

There's nothing out there.

Down goes the flap.

Wind again. Flap goes up.

Someone's out there. Slightly different spot. Shotgunner and Lulu. They don't look good.

Down goes the flap.

                        DAVID
          Someone's here already.

                    ONE OF THE BOYS
    Maybe he could just preach under a tree.

DEAD IN THE WEST

David fights the wind-blown canvas, struggles from beneath the tent.

EXT. – THE HILL

No one's there.

David glances to his left. Sees the bottom of Lulu's shoe as it pulls beneath the tent.

A SCREAM

A SERIES OF SCREAMS and VICIOUS NOISES

Tent shakes, starts to fall. The wind blows hard, catches the tent, fills it with air, carries it away and down the hill and out of sight.

Lulu and Shotgunner are revealed. They've got a boy apiece, and the boys are obviously dead, their necks twisted like coat-hanger wire. Lulu and Shotgunner are biting big chunks out of them.

The other boys are in a terrified heap. Now, free of the tent, they bolt down the hill like frightened mice.

David, startled, turns to follow them. Runs like the wind.

LULU AND SHOTGUNNER

Enjoying their meal.

EXT. – STAGE TRAIL

Mignon and Old Man and Old Woman stumbling along. Ahead of them we see Mud Creek.

CLOSER ON MUD CREEK

And farther down the trail. Florence and Millie, dripping water, shoes slurping like sucking wounds. Florence still has that water moccasin on her face. It's flapping, trying to get out of her face. It finally grows tired and just dangles.

EXT. – MUD CREEK, MAIN STREET

Dead Folk are starting to show up in town. There's Nolan and Foster and new folks, too. Nolan has the burial shirt on now, and nothing else. And he's right about the shirt. It doesn't fit. Nate is naked except for a pair of boots.

Blackie Mertz has joined their ranks. He doesn't have a hook to his nose now. In fact, he doesn't have a nose.

And stumbling down the street in his long handles is David's father, Billy Jack Rhine. The trap door is open and his naked butt moons us.

The dead clutch up in the middle of the street. Some are coming out of buildings, dragging living victims. Like the boys who were with David. Other townsfolk.

When fresh meat arrives, the crowd gets down on them like ducks on June bugs.

FEEDING FRENZY

Flash of hands and teeth. Red gleams. Meat between teeth. One ghoul, Rhine, crunches an eyeball like a grape.

Crowd backs off, moves down the street. The recently mauled lie there. Some of the bodies are little more than raggedy skeletons.

SHOT OF THE MOON

Rolling happily in the heavens.

PAN DOWN TO MAIN STREET

A bony corpse twitches. Opens its eyes. Well, one eye. The other got sucked out of its head. Corpse stands. It's sort of like a cheap erector set being pulled upright by strings.

The other corpses twitch. They struggle to stand. They seem stunned. Amazed. They start to wander down the street in search of meat. They rattle doors.

EXT. – SHERIFF'S OFFICE

Caleb running up to the door. He grabs the knob, pulls–

Locked.

He turns, looks behind him.

Dead Folk are coming toward him, and they look happy to see him.

> **CALEB**
> Matt! Open the door! Matt! Open the goddamned door!

> **MATT (O.S.)**
> Go the hell away. I got a headache.

Caleb glancing behind. The dead are close now. He turns back to the door, tugs.

> **CALEB**
> Matt! You goddamned sonofabitch. Quit pullin' your dick. Let me in! They're after me.

Caleb takes another look, draws his revolver, leans his back against the door.

> **CALEB**
> All right, then. Come and get me, you stinky-ass sonsabitches!

Door opens. Light. Caleb falls back and inside, just as hands snatch the air.

INT. – SHERIFF'S OFFICE

Matt stares amazed at the dead faces in the doorway as Caleb stumbles back, regains his balance, kicks one of the Dead Folk in the chest and knocks them back, upsetting some of the others like bowling pins.

                CALEB
      Out of the way, goddamnit!

Caleb pushes Matt aside, slams the door, bolts it.

Matt is stunned.

                MATT
      What in the world?

Pounding on the door.

                CALEB
      Well, it damned sure ain't the welcome wagon. Those bastards wanted to eat my ass. They're eatin' sonsabitches all over town. And they ain't cookin 'em.

Caleb grabs one of the Winchesters out of the rack, goes over to the barred window for a look.

CALEB'S POV

Quite a crowd. It looks like a cemetery occupant convention. They're milling, moaning, watching.

                CALEB
      Jesus Christ with a wooden dick.

BACK TO SCENE

As Matt joins Caleb for a look.

          MATT
    My God, they're dead.

Caleb gives Matt a special look.

          CALEB
    Reckon that's why you're sheriff. You're so goddamned observant.

          MATT
    Wha... How?

          CALEB
    That goddamned Indian, I reckon. That curse. Webb was right.

          MATT
    What are they waiting on? What do they want?

          CALEB
    They want supper. And we're it. As for what they're waitin' on, I ain't got a figure. Maybe one of 'em went to get the salt.

ON THE DEAD FOLK

Waiting. Milling. Drooling.

INT. – DOC'S LABORATORY

Doc and Abby are stirring what's left of Patches with a stick. There's nothing in the tub but ashes.

DOC
Only way I could stop him was destroyin' his brain. Whatever controls them, makes them walk, it comes from there, way it would if they was livin'.

ABBY
But how can they live at all?

DOC
They don't live. They're undead. Ghouls. It's the Indian, like I thought. I've been researching his curse. From what I can tell it comes out of the cult of Chtuhulu. The Indian may in fact call it something else, but it's the same thing. He has been given powers by the Old Ones to manage his revenge, and he, in turn, will give them his soul. And the souls of others. These dark gods of his are eaters of souls.

A CRASH FROM DOC'S OFFICE

Doc grabs the horse pistol and rushes in there. Abby follows.

DOC'S OFFICE WINDOW

It's broken and a hand is reaching in from the outside, waving around, trying grab anything. It grabs the curtains. Pulls them down.

At the window. Nate Foster.

Doc fires a perfect shot, hits Foster dead center of the forehead. Like a board, Nate falls back.

Doc leaps to his desk, grabs a box of shells.

DOC
Get the Winchester, Abby.

INT. – REVEREND'S ROOM

He's sitting on the bed reading the Bible. He pauses, looks at his watch. He rises, casually pulls on his coat, straightens it.

NOISE at the door. The doorknob BATTLES. BANGING on the door.

The Reverend goes over and opens the door and David rushes in, almost knocking him down. Reverend grabs him by the shoulders.

>   **REVEREND**
> Whoa! Whoa, boy.

>   **DAVID**
> Reverend! There's a problem.

>   **REVEREND**
> You got the tent up?

>   **DAVID**
> Hell with the tent. There ain't gonna be no preachin' tonight.

>   **REVEREND**
> What are you saying, boy? Your father out to whip you?

David, frightened, trying to hold it together.

>   **DAVID**
> Worse. He wants to eat me. They all want to eat me. And Daddy's in his underwear.

Reverend gives David a quizzical look.

>   **REVEREND**
> You been nipping your old man's shine?

Reverend grabs David's chin, bends close to his face, and sniffs his breath.

Frustrated, David grabs the Reverend's arm and pulls him to the window.

DAVID
Look!

Reverend looks. Street is full of people, in all manner of dress and undress. They're in the process of tearing a man apart, feasting on him.

A gnawed leg flashes in the moonlight.

An arm.

A boy bursts from the frenzied huddle, runs off on all fours with a head in his mouth, his teeth clamped around an ear.

REVEREND
What in God's name?

DAVID
They're back from the dead, Reverend. And they wanta eat. They ain't a bit sociable neither.

REVEREND AND DAVID'S POV

From the side of Doc's office comes a HEYAH noise. Someone yelling to horses. From around the building's side, charging like steeds from hell, two horses appear pulling a buckboard. Doc's driving. Abby's in the back. She has a rifle and she's wearing bandoleers across her chest. Dead Folk are jumping onto the buckboard. She's firing damn near point-blank, blowing skulls to hell. She kicks one in the head, knocks him loose of the buckboard as the buckboard makes a corner practically on two wheels, rights itself, smashes a Dead Folk beneath a wheel rim, squirting his head in all directions.

Buckboard darts down Main Street. Dead Folk make a wall in front of the horses, foam over the buggy. Abby's still popping these suckers, one hand cocking the Winchester.

Dead woman leaps onto a horse, starts biting at its neck. Blood flies. Horse wobbles.

BACK TO SCENE

                REVEREND
   Abby!

Reverend grabs his .36 Navy off the washbasin, charges for the door.

                DAVID
   No, Reverend. No! They'll eat you.

But the Reverend's gone.

David stands where he is a moment, glances out the window.

DAVID'S POV

Horses down, kicking, screaming, their guts are being ripped and dragged out of their bodies like coils of steaming wet rope. Abby and Doc being surrounded by enthusiastic and hungry Dead Folk.

BACK TO SCENE

                DAVID
   Oh, hell.

David turns, rushes out of the room

EXT. STREET – AND WE'RE GONNA HOT WIRE THIS BABY FROM HERE ON OUT

Dead Folk have the stranded buckboard enveloped. It's as if Abby and Doc are becalmed amid a sea of boat-climbing sharks.

Doc has his horse pistol, and he's firing it close range. Dead Folk's heads explode like overripe cantaloupes.

Abby is down to swinging the Winchester. She cracks heads. Some Dead Folk go down. Others just take the blow and keep climbing.

CLOSE ON DOC AND ABBY

back to back as the Dead Folk's hands reach for them. Dead Folk's faces circle Doc and Abby as if they are planets and the Dead Folk are orbital craft being pulled groundward by their gravity.

SUDDENLY, Dead Folk fly backward. The wall of Dead Folk starts to collapse. An opening is made, and it shows us–

THE REVEREND

He's snatching them by the hair, collars, necks, slinging them back. He kicks them and throws them. He shuns the Navy against heads.

FULL SCENE

Doc, slams his horse pistol down on a Woman's head so hard it creases it almost to the nose.

DOC
You got to destroy their brains.

Reverend shoots one of the Dead Folk through the head, and the Dead Folk does a little pirouette, goes down for a big finish.

A DEAD MAN IN OVERALLS about to grab the Reverend, who's preoccupied kicking a ravenous child away from his feet. As the child soars like a football, Dead Man in Overalls grabs the Reverend's shoulders–

ANGLE ON DEAD MAN IN OVERALLS

As an arm goes around his neck from behind, and legs wrap around his hips and a knife flashes and stabs Dead Man in Overalls in the eye.

This doesn't bother Dead Man in Overalls in the least, but it saves the Reverend, because Dead Man in Overalls lets go of him and becomes preoccupied with his rider.

Dead Man in Overalls is spinning, trying to shake what's on his back, and what's on his back is David. As they whirl around, the Reverend reaches out and snatches David free of the Dead Man in Overalls and puts a .36 Navy slug through the dead man's head, dropping him.

Our defenders have a little gap now, and they make for it, except David. He's frozen.

In front of him is

BILLY JACK RHINE

His father, his long handle flap hanging open, his butt gathering moonlight. And he's smiling, and he's turning his head from side to side as if he's trying to recognize the boy.

BEAT.

Rhine shows recognition. He takes off his belt, comes for David. Past experience holds David sure as a vise.

      DAVID
     (soft and sad)
 No, Daddy.

      RHINE
 Hit. Then eat. Like your mama.

      DAVID
 Mama. No!

CLOSE ON RHINE

Then his head flies apart and he falls forward, revealing–

THE REVEREND

Looking over his smoking pistol.

FULL SCENE

Reverend grabs David, drags him back, and we–

TRACK

As our team makes like track stars up the street–

>   DOC
>   (yelling)
>   Run for the church! It's holy ground.

Dead Folk coming. They're not Olympic material, but they're not slow either. You wouldn't want to stop and tie your shoe, in other words.

David cuts in front of Reverend. They collide, go down, Reverend flies into Doc who flies into Abby. Bowling pin reaction. They're all in the dirt.

Dead Folk let out a gasp of excitement. Things look good. Lunch is down. They start really hoofing.

Reverend rises to a knee, picks off a couple of leaders. Bullets through the brains.

Abby, Doc, and David scramble to their feet and run.

Reverend backing, reloading, firing at a few more, hitting dead center of their heads, covering his comrades' exit.

Abby and others on the church porch. Doc frantically trying to open the door, which is locked.

Abby is reloading her Winchester. David runs around to a window, beats on it–

> **DAVID**
> (yelling)
> Reverend Calhoun! Let us in, Reverend!

Doc, winded, yells to David–

> **DOC**
> Try around back, where he lives.

David darts away, around the side of the church.

Abby's loaded up. She makes a one-hand swing, cocking the Winchester lever. She fires.

POW. A Dead Folk down.

Abby, three times in succession SWING COCKS THE WINCHESTER AND DELIVERS FAST FIRE.

BLAM! BLAM! BLAM! Three Dead Folk eat dirt.

Reverend on the church steps now, reloading.

> **REVEREND**
> (to Abby)
> I thought you said I was a show-off.

> **ABBY**
> (laconically)
> Takes one to know one.

Dead Folk gathering like locusts for the last grains of wheat. Doc looks out over the closing multitude of Dead Folk. They're happy and slobbery.

>   **DOC**
> Looks like it's die dog or eat the hatchet.

Reverend, Abby, Doc pressed against the door.

>   **REVEREND**
> I hope David keeps goin'.

A Dead Folk puts a boot on the porch–

AND BURSTS INTO BLUE AND RED AND YELLOW FLAMES.

>   **DOC**
> Holy ground!

>   **REVEREND**
> The power of God Almighty.

Door behind them opens. David and Calhoun in the light. Calhoun looks a little like a rabbit in the headlights. He can't believe what's lurking below his front porch.

Our team rushes in, closes the door, throws the heavy wooden bar.

>   **CALHOUN**
> I'm sorry. I heard you. I thought it was
> them. They been here once already. I
> heard them outside, calling. I saw them
> take down poor Mrs. O'Fee. Oh, Jesus,
> they tore her apart. They tossed her head
> through a window.

Calhoun gestures. Mrs. O'Fee's head lies beneath a window of shattered glass.

CALHOUN
I saw what they were doin'. I wanted to help. There was nothing I could do. I wanted to help.

REVEREND
You did right. There was nothing you could do.

ABBY
(to her dad)
Are we safe here, on holy ground?

Doc finds a pew, sits, puts his head between his hands.

DOC
For a time. Until their master comes.

CALHOUN
Master?

DOC
That Indian. That's what it's about, Calhoun. That curse he put on the town for what was done.

CALHOUN
But I didn't do anything. I didn't touch either of them.

DOC
It's as much for what we didn't do as what we did. As far as the Indian's concerned, we're all guilty. The whole damn town... And I'm not sure he's wrong.

REVEREND

What do you mean, we're safe until their master comes? God stands against the power of the devil. Whether it's the devil's lacky or the devil himself.

Doc looks up, wears a wan smile.

DOC

You seem to think there's only one god involved here, my friend.

REVEREND

I'll not listen to blasphemy.

Doc stands, angrily points to the door.

DOC

The blasphemy is outside that door, Reverend. And it's got teeth. Now, do you want to hear the truth, or do you want to talk about God's good grace?

REVEREND

Very well.

DOC

As it nears morning, the Indian loses strength. But he's stronger than these folks he's made his own. When he comes he will give it all he has. Our trappings of religion will only hold him so long. You may not believe this, but his powers of darkness are equal to God's powers of light.

REVEREND

Even the devil bows to God.

DOC
The things that give the Indian his powers owe nothing to the devil. Pardon me, Reverend, but the Indian's demons would make your devil piss blood. You don't get it, do you, Reverend? Your God. Your devil. They're but one of many gods and devils fighting for dominance in this world. And they don't never get together to have no tea party.

What this town did. Who you are. Who you represent–the Christian God. It's all been ordained. The forces of your God against the forces of his. It's as much a chess game between deities as anything else. With our lives as the stakes.

We're pawns, Reverend. Rooks and bishops and knights. You're the white king. The Indian the dark king.

The Reverend doesn't like hearing this. But he forces himself to ask.

REVEREND
Can we stop the Indian? It? Can God stop it?

DOC
The only thing that will truly contain him is the sunlight. God's greatest power. But now, in the dark, the Indian is nearly all powerful. The best we can do is hold him until the Lord's powers are at their peak.

Doc pops open his pocket watch, stares at the face of it.

                    DOC (cont'd)
              And until daylight... Well, we have quite a
              ways to go.

MEANWHILE...

EXT. – SHERIFF'S OFFICE

Dead Folk all over, looking through the barred windows, pushing at the door.

INT. – SHERIFF'S OFFICE

Matt and Caleb, armed, watching hands and faces at the barred windows.

                    MATT
              What are we gonna do?

                    CALEB
              Unless you can chew a hole through the
              floor with your asshole big enough for us
              to crawl down, we're gonna fight.

A SOUND from outside. The hive sighing of the Dead Folk. Hands and faces move away from the window.

                    CALEB
              What in hell?

                    MATT
              Maybe they're givin' up.

Caleb moves to the window, followed by Matt.

THEIR POV

As the crowd of Dead Folk parts like the Red Sea. And there, visible through the rift of Dead Folk, is a thick cloud of insects.

Fat, black flies. In their midst is the crate, supported by and surrounded by flies.

THE FLIES

Consolidate to form the shape of a man, then they become solid. Abruptly, they are the Indian, walking effortlessly, carrying the big crate on his shoulder as easily as a baseball bat.

MATT AND CALEB

>**CALEB**
>I been to a shitload of rodeos, but I ain't never seen nothing like that.

>**MATT**
>Can't be.

>**CALEB**
>Better start dealing with what is, boy, 'stead of what you think can't be. We're about to step off in some deep shit, and you goddamn better be well ready to swim and eat turd at the same time.

EXT. – ON INDIAN

He sets the crate on the ground, long side up. He waves a hand. The lid of the crate POPS off.

INSIDE THE CRATE

The Indian's Woman. What a mess.

BACK TO SCENE

The Indian just stands there. Dead Folk crowd around him. Grovel at his feet. Touch him.

INT. – SHERIFF'S OFFICE

                    MATT
        What's he doin'?

                    CALEB
        Showin' us what got us in trouble in the
        first place. That gal of his.

                    MATT
        But I tried to stop you. I tried to stop all
        of you.

                    CALEB
        Take it up with him.

Caleb grabs the window bars, yells angrily–

                    CALEB
        You red nigger! Git on back to hell!

ON INDIAN

Suddenly gliding across the ground, Dead Folk scrambling.

Indian reaches the Sheriff's Office door, draws back his fist.

INT. – SHERIFF'S OFFICE

As the fist STRIKES, and INDIAN'S FIST slams through the wood, jerks side to side, splintering lumber. Hand grabs the wooden cross bar, flips it away.

Matt grabs a double-barrel shotgun from the rack, a fistful of shells. He and Caleb back toward the jail cells as Dead Folk peer around the Indian like shy kids looking around a parent.

Matt's got the shotgun loaded. He's backing up, holding it, waiting for the right moment.

Caleb switches the Winchester to his left hand, draws his revolver, and calmly FIRES SIX TIMES in rapid succession at the Indian as his hands move VERY FAST, plucking the bullets from the air.

Indian smiles. Opens his clenched fists.

INSERT: FISTS

He's got all of Caleb's bullets.

Closes his hands.

Opens them again.

Six plump bluebottle flies buzz up from his palms and fly away.

BACK TO SCENE

Matt cuts loose with both barrels of the shotgun.

Blasts hit the Indian. Chunks fly out of him, splatter all over the Dead Folk behind him.

CLOSE ON INDIAN

As the gaping wounds reseal themselves. His clothes rethread.

BACK TO CALEB AND MATT

Caleb tosses down his revolver and pumps Winchester shots at the Indian with no effect. He grabs the Winchester by the barrel.

Caleb rushes the Indian and swings the Winchester. Indian's hand goes up like a fat dove taking flight, grabs the barrel of the Winchester, jerks it away from Caleb, and tosses it.

Caleb slugs the Indian. Indian isn't bothered.

Caleb swings again. Indian grabs Caleb's arm, twists, snaps it off at the shoulder. Caleb SCREAMING. BLOOD FLYING.

Indian begins to beat Caleb with the arm. He goes savage. Caleb goes down. The Indian pulls the ear necklace from Caleb's neck, pushes it lovingly into his shirt pocket.

The Dead Folk, like dogs given the signal, leap forward and start ripping, biting and tearing at Caleb, jerking his chest apart, exposing his ribs and his still-beating heart.

INDIAN

Stabs his hand between Caleb's rib cage, jerks out the heart. He bites a plug from the heart and tosses it at–

MATT

whom it strikes right in the mouth.

Matt turns to run into the cell row. He finds an open cage and goes inside and slams the door. He backs up until he's on one of the bunks.

ANOTHER ANGLE ON SCENE

Indian at the bars. The dead gather behind him, chewing on parts of Caleb. Matt empties the shotgun again. Same lack of effect.

Indian smiles.

And smiles.

And smiles.

His mouth is WAY TOO WIDE, and goddamn Grandma, what great big teeth you have!

And then the Indian grabs the bars and starts to bend them apart as if they're made of chewing gum.

MATT
Jumpin' dog shit.

Matt drops the empty shotgun. Draws his pistol. He puts the gun to his head, starts to fire–

BUT THEN THE INDIAN'S THERE. Faster than you can say "Uh oh" he's on Matt like a wart. Grabs the gun, stops Matt from taking his own life. Indian squeezes the gun to a buttery pulp. He grabs Matt by both ears, jerks him forward, and opening his mouth to the size of a bear trap, bites away Matt's face.

Indian grabs Matt up, tosses him toward the bars where they have not been stretched. Tosses him so hard Matt hits them and goes through like cheese through a grater. Dead Folk are knocked over. They spring up and scramble for Matt's remains.

ON INDIAN

Shaking his head like a dog worrying a bone as his TOO MANY GODDAMN TEETH chew up Matt's face, sucking down the eyeballs as if they're olives.

He lifts his head to the ceiling and his lips stretch into a snout like a wolf and his teeth drip goo, and he lets out with a triumphant HOWL, and as the HOWL CONTINUES, we–

CUT TO:

A HAND

Snatching the tarp off the Gatling gun.

PULLBACK

INT. – CHURCH, BASEMENT

It's the Reverend's hand. He's in the basement with Doc and Calhoun, who have their arms full of shotguns and ammunition. They are frozen as the HOWL goes on and on. Then stops.

CALHOUN
I don't suppose that was a dog?

DISSOLVE TO:

A VIEW THROUGH A NARROW SLIT

Where WE SEE the Dead Folk outside the church, standing still and silent, as if waiting for a train.

A BOARD COMES INTO VIEW, FILLS OUR VISION

PULLBACK

And we see Abby pushing the board into place so Doc can nail it up. We were looking through a gap in the boards being nailed over the church window.

FULL VIEW, INT. – CHURCH

Front door is blockaded with several pews. Abby and David are at the windows, holding boards utilized from pews while Doc and Calhoun nail them up. All of their belts bristle with revolvers and against the wall lean shotguns and rifles.

Reverend is finishing up mounting the Gatling gun on its support. (This is one of the later versions with ten barrels, developed after the Civil War. It can fire 400 rounds a minute. It is fired by rotating the barrels with a crank so that bullets are fed into the gun by a tall clip.)

There is a stockpile of weapons in two pews that have been pulled up close to the Gatling. Other pews have been heaped three feet high in front of the Gatling as a barrier. They are pulled around in a semi-circle till they reach the wall. Behind all this is the open door to the basement.

Reverend cranks the Gatling to see how it rotates. Then he pushes a clip into place. Pauses suddenly as we again HEAR THE HOWL. It sounds both sad and triumphant.

Doc and others are finishing the nailing. They pause to listen as the HOWL COMES AGAIN. They find places to look through the boards to the outside.

                DOC
      The bastard has us treed.

AS HOWL ENDS, Reverend grabs a double-barrel shotgun from one of the pews, hustles over the barricade to the window. He looks out through a split in the boards.

REVEREND'S POV

The dead start to move aside, forming an alley. But there's nothing in the alley but darkness.

Then stepping out of the darkness, as if from a crack between our world and another, is the Indian with the crate, lidded. We glimpse something in that moment, something in the crack. Something dark and evil and writhing, but it's just a glimpse, then it's gone. The crack is closed.

BACK TO SCENE

                DAVID
      What was that?

                DOC
      I don't know. And I'd rather not know.

OUR GANG'S POV

The Indian sets the crate down on one end, throws off the lid. The Indian's Woman doesn't look any better than when we saw her last.

BACK TO SCENE

                DOC
He's making it clear what this is all about.

              CALHOUN
How come she's not like one of...them?

              REVEREND
Simple. He's the one in control, and he doesn't want her to be like one of them.

              ABBY
He loved her. He really loved her. Even in death.

              DAVID
Yeah, but he don't love us none.

              CALHOUN
What do we do?

              REVEREND
Our best. This is our first line of defense. The church doesn't hold them–

              DOC
It won't. Not for long.

              REVEREND
–then we back toward the Gatling. We make a stand back there behind it. They get through us there, we make one last-ditch effort. The basement. Comments?

              DOC
Shoot for the head. You can tear them apart with that Gatling, but it doesn't matter, you don't destroy their brains.

That's what stops them. That's where the
Indian's power lies. If one of them gets to
you, bites you, save a bullet for yourself.

Our defenders pause on that cheery note. Abby goes to the Reverend. They kiss. For along time.

DAVID
Sorry, Reverend. Abby. But you'll have to
break it up. We got company.

Reverend goes to the window, stands by David, looks through a crack in the boards.

DEFENDERS' POV

Dead Folk are coming. Their feet are smoking as they come up the church steps, get closer to the church itself. But they keep coming. The Indian is directing them as if he's a conductor. Waving his hands, gesturing.

Flames wrap around the feet of the Dead Folk. They try to fade back. The Indian gestures wildly, lets out a HISSSSSSS of displeasure that makes your ears hurt. He grabs up one of the flaming Dead Folk, and throws him like a spear at the door.

INT. – CHURCH DOOR

As DEAD MAN'S HEAD slams through it. Dead Man looks as surprised as the defenders. His teeth start to snap at midair.

Doc lifts his shotgun, blows the Dead Man's head to shards of flesh and bone. Messy brains drip down the door.

EXT. – CHURCH

As the Dead Folk HOWL and CHARGE the church!

INT. – CHURCH

As bodies slam against the structure, vibrating the boards at the windows, shaking the door.

DAVID
Nice knowin' you, Reverend.

REVEREND
Don't count yourself out till it's over. You got to hang in there to your last fiber. Trust in God and your weapons.

DEFENDER'S SIGHTS AND SOUNDS:

BATTERING AT THE DOOR.

BATTERING AT THE WINDOWS, FRONT AND SIDE.

SHATTERING GLASS.

CRACKING BOARDS.

FACES AT THE WINDOWS. HANDS ON THE BARS AT THE WINDOWS, PULLING, TUGGING, BITING. BODIES SQUIRMING THROUGH GAPS. ALMOST INSIDE.

REVEREND
I love you, boy.

David hugs the Reverend.

DAVID
I love you, too. I'm scared.

Abby reaches out and touches David, gently.

REVEREND
We're all scared, but we can't let it take us. Courage is not absence of fear. It's control of fear. Using it to your advantage.

Reverend lets go, smiles at David.

> **REVEREND**
> Hallowed be the name of the Lord, and shotgun do your stuff.

David smiles. Smile melts as–

–Dem ole debil Dead Folk, they be a smokin' as that holy ground lights them up, and they're HITTING the windows and PULLING at the bars and BANGING at the door, and TEARING at the gap the tossed Dead Folk's head made in the door, and we see in glimpses through the windows, the Indian, outside, walking around SNATCHING at the bars in the windows, removing them as easy as jerking pesky nose hairs–

AND THE DEAD ARE COMING THROUGH, and they done got them that smorgasbord smile.

DEFENDERS' GUNS

Rock with a one-two rhythm, and the Dead are ceasing to smoke. They're coming through gaps, pushing through windows. They're strong now. They look happy and powerful.

> **DOC**
> (yelling)
> Holy ground ain't shit to 'em no more.

> **REVEREND**
> Back up.

LAST STAND

Defenders are pumping shotgun loads, and Dead Folk are banging apart, and when their heads remain intact, their flesh tries to come back to them, crawling up their legs, looking for home.

Some Dead Folk's guts fall out like huge strands of spaghetti, drag behind them to be stepped on and pulled free by others. Guts coil and writhe like snakes, seek their owners, try to rejoin by writhing up their legs, heading for body cavities.

Defenders don't have time to reload as they back up and the dead do that We Sho Is Hungry Shuffle, and Defenders are drawing their revolvers, and the revolvers are barking like angry dogs, and the Dead Folk take loads in the heads and go down, but right behind them, MORE OF THE SAME.

Defenders make the semi-circle of pews just ahead of Dead Folk, grab shotguns or Winchesters and the ROCKING RHYTHM returns. Now, dear hearts, it's ALAMO TIME, and the Dead Folk are boiling over those pews like ants on gingerbread, and it's seriously elbows and assholes as Defenders kick Dead Folk back and swing rifles and shotgun stocks, popping Dead Folk's heads open like they're cracking rotten walnuts.

Reverend on the Gatling, and he starts to crank that baby and the Dead be a poppin' and hoppin' to the gunsmoke tune. And he swings that ole Gatling, and chunks of Dead Folk meat flys every which way, and ole Caleb, little more than a head and rib cage mounted on legs, gets cut off at the waist, and he's pulling himself across the floor, trying to drag himself over the pews–

Calhoun reloading, and Caleb grabs him by the sleeve, pulls him down, and Caleb reaches up with his other hand and grabs Calhoun by the hair and yanks his partial body up, and it's bite city.

Abby throws down an empty shotgun, draws a revolver, sees Calhoun in shock as Caleb nibbles, and she takes Caleb out with a revolver shot to the head.

Calhoun turns, looks at her, happy. Then his face changes as his hand darts to his cheek and the wounds Caleb made. Then a horde of Dead Folk rise and GRAB HIM, bite him, pull him back.

Abby mercifully shoots Calhoun right between the eyes. Moment of regret, then she pulls another revolver from her belt. Two-gun Abby. .44s bark and bite.

Swarm of Dead Folk on the Gatling, and Reverend has to relinquish. Grabs up an empty shotgun and starts swinging the stock, trying for home runs.

REVEREND
Move back to the storage room. Now!

Doc has a Winchester and he's COCKING AND FIRING faster than a rabbit can mate, and–

David pokes a pistol forward and shoots Florence. Down she goes.

Montclaire, looking really nasty, reaches out and grabs David's pistol, and David pulls back, and Montclaire really pulls, dragging David over the pews, and–

WE'RE CLOSE ON THIS DISASTER IN THE MAKING

And it looks like that's all she wrote for young David, when–

A SHOTGUN STOCK

Comes down on Montclaire's head BAM! BAM AGAIN. Brains ooze out of his ears like creek mud between clutched fingers.

FULL VIEW

Reverend snatches David from Montclaire's hands, even as Montclaire collapses, and the Dead Folk all start over the pews, and our team is crabbing for that open storage room door.

UGLY FAT DEAD SUMBITCH

Grabs Abby by the waist from behind, picks her up, and she twists around and shoots him in the head, and down they both go, tumbling over the pews into the Dead Folk, Ugly Fat Dead Sumbitch on top, spurting brains, writhing like a snake without a head.

Abby's pistol flies from her hand, and she's trapped beneath this "horizontally impaired" Dead Fella, and now there are shadows as a crowd of Dead Folk come down on her.

ABBY

Jerks out from under Ugly Fat Dead Sumbitch just in time to dive for her pistol, but the Dead, they done got her. They drop down on her faster than two-dollar whores at the Mardi Gras, and bite her all over.

Abby yells in pain, raises her head–

SEES THE REVEREND

And his mouth falls open because he knows she's doomed, and she yells–

ABBY
I love you.

–Grits her teeth, sticks the revolver in her mouth. BAM!!!!! She checks out.

DOC

Loses it, jumps over the pews–

DOC
(yelling)
Abby! Abby!

Then he's just yelling cause THEY GOT HIM.

HORDE OF DEAD FOLK

On Doc, grabbing and biting. All that's visible amid the spider web of their arms is his shocked face.

REVEREND

Jerks up the .36 Navy, fires and we FLASH TO–

DOC

As he takes the bullet twixt the peepers, then we JUMP TO–

REVEREND AND DAVID

Armed with a pistol apiece, easing back into the–

STORAGE ROOM

Reverend slams the door, pinching off a Dead Folk's fingers, He throws the wooden bar in place as Dead Folk SLAM against it. Reverend grows weak, he leans against the door.

              REVEREND
    Oh God. Abby.

David touches his arm.

              DAVID
    Wasn't nothin' you could do, Reverend.

              REVEREND
    Seems like there never is.

WHAM! WHAP! SMACK! The door is taking some licks.

               DAVID
    Single-minded sumbitches, ain't they?

Reverend takes the lantern off the shelf and lights it. He and David hustle down the stairway, and the Reverend restrains David long enough to hold the lantern over the missing step.

They step over it, hurry down into the storeroom proper. They start reloading their revolvers. Their hands shake. David drops a bullet on the floor, scuttles after it, loads.

REVEREND'S POV

A window. A curtain held by a strand of rope is over it. Reverend grabs a nail keg, climbs on it, pulls back the curtain, and we got–

Bars.

          REVEREND
  Damn!

REVEREND'S POV THROUGH BARS

The sky is lightening.

          REVEREND
  It's near morning.

BACK TO SCENE

          DAVID
  Almost don't count for nothin'.

TOP OF STAIRS

Door heaves like a chest pulling in air. Wooden bar stretches, cracks.

REVEREND AND DAVID

Reverend jumps down from the keg. He and David watch the bar expand and crack.

> **REVEREND**
> This is our last stand, boy. Be sure you got one in that gun for yourself things get final.

> **DAVID**
> I don't know I can.

> **REVEREND**
> Think about if you don't.
> (Softer)
> Just put it dead center of your forehead and pull the trigger, quick. Don't think. Just do it. You'll leap on over to the other side, and you'll be there with Jesus.

> **DAVID**
> I'll be dead is what I'll be.

SOUND OF DOOR CRACKING.

TOP OF STAIRS

EXPLOSION OF THE WOODEN BAR.

The Indian framed in the light at the top of the stairs. On his shoulder, like a parrot, sits Mignon. She smiles, and she's got a major set of teeth here. These babies would make a crocodile proud.

> **MIGNON**
> (not a little girl's voice)
> *Boo,* Preacher Man.

REVEREND AND DAVID

Flinch. Then they look disgusted with themselves.

MIGNON

Cackles, bites a chunk out of her doll's rag head, she's so frenzied.

DEAD FOLK

Try to push around the Indian, they're so anxious to eat.

CLOSE ON INDIAN

He HISSES, speaks. And it is the VOICE OF DOOM.

                    INDIAN
Back! They're mine!

TRACKING INDIAN

He comes down the stairs, and he's about to reach the missing step–

REACTION SHOT, REVEREND AND DAVID

Hopeful.

INDIAN

Steps where the step ought to be, and–

Nothing.

He steps on MIDAIR and keeps right on keepin' on.

REVEREND AND DAVID

Disappointed.

                    REVEREND
     Figures.

MIGNON

She cackles. Waves her chewed doll.

> MIGNON
> You've had it now, Preacher Boy.

FULL SCENE

Reverend pissed, jerks up his revolver and shoots Mignon's eye out. Her head goes back, then she falls forward, her doll leaving her hand. The doll bumps down the stairs, and Mignon bumps after it, lands in a similar heap.

Indian becomes the Shadow Spider with a semi-human head and face, and he Fast Flows the rest of the way down and he comes at the Reverend in a rush, and the–

Reverend, freezes momentarily, and he's got that ole spider bugaboo on his mind, and you can see it on his face, but he YELLS in defiance, jerks up the revolver, FIRES, hits Indian in the forehead, dead center–

–And the Indian isn't fazed, comes on jetlike, grabs the Reverend by the throat with one of his prehensile legs, smiles, sticks his face close to the Reverend's so that we're–

CLOSE ENOUGH ON INDIAN TO COUNT TEETH

> INDIAN
> That shit don't work on me, God's underling. I'm gonna swallow you like a snake swallows an egg.

Spider Image melts away. Demonic-reptile look. Yellow eyes with black slits. A flash of lizard tail. Clawed hands. Indian's mouth opens and unhinges, and he pulls the Reverend forward for a spit bath, pauses–

> INDIAN
> But it's the spider you fear, isn't it, Reverend?

Transformation to the spider-thing. But God, Almighty, it's never looked this nasty.

DAVID

Limps forward, kicks the Indian. Indian flicks him across the room with a spider limb. David's revolver slides away from him, out of sight under junk.

INDIAN AND REVEREND

INDIAN
I'm gonna chew your soul, Mister Preacher.

WIDEN VIEW

To include David as he jerks the jackknife out of his pocket, runs at the Indian SCREAMING. The Indian has just put his spider mouth over the Reverend's head, saliva dripping like snot.

But David's yelling causes him to pause. He pulls the Reverend's dripping head from his mouth. Turns to stare at David.

David, almost on the Indian, dives low, drives the jackknife through one of the Indian's spider legs, pins it to the floor.

Indian looks down at his leg, looks at David. He can't believe how stupid the kid is. He smiles. And with that mouth, it is a SMILE. WET AND RED AND SHARP.

REVEREND

Dangling. Choking. His wind is going. He roves an eye to his right.

REVEREND'S POV

The curtained window. A red ray of sunlight.

BACK TO SCENE

Reverend lifts his Navy, FIRES. He hits the windowsill. FIRES AGAIN as–

–Indian's knife-trapped spider leg comes free and he spreads his spider-demon jaws WIDE to finish Reverend–

–And Reverend's shot hits the rope holding the curtain, and the curtain swings down, and a–

RAY OF SUNLIGHT

Slices into the room and cuts through the Indian's arm smooth as a laser beam. The arm falls off, and the Reverend is dropped to the floor.

REVEREND

Rolls, snatches the dead hand, for it is now a hand, away from his throat.

INDIAN

Staggers, starts to disintegrate.

He's lost the spider transformation.

He tries to transform into a wolf. No luck. Just a glimpse of that.

Reptilian form. Nope. That won't get it either. Forked tail thrashes, disappears.

Various transformations flap by, but they don't hold. Nothing's working here.

Indian in human form starts to crawl up the stairway, his back smoking.

THE LIGHT

From sunrise is expanding. It fills the storage room, falls on the INDIAN who bursts into flames. He rolls down the stairs, tries to get beneath them, out of the light.

REVEREND

Grabs a keg, charges the stairs, bangs some of the plank steps to pieces. No shade for the Indian.

LIGHT

Falls on the Indian full force again. He bursts into brighter flames, and the flames lick up through the steps, and–

DEAD FOLK

At the top of the stairs cringe as the light expands to include them, and we–

FOLLOW DEAD FOLK

Wheeling from storage room, running throughout the church. Sunrise is coming through the windows and the breaks in the door and walls, and it's lighting them up like Christians at the Coliseum on the emperor's birthday.

BACK TO STORAGE ROOM

David looks at the gap in the steps. Flames are leaping up and licking the steps and catching them on fire, and it looks bad. They're trapped.

Reverend grabs David by the collar and the seat of the pants.

DAVID
Hey!

Reverend tosses David toward the higher steps, through the flames.

David grabs hold.

Flames lick at him.

He YELLS, scrambles up the steps, away from the flames. Almost to the top.

He turns, looks down at the Reverend through the smoke and flames.

                 DAVID
        Reverend!

                REVEREND
        Go, boy! Go!

                 DAVID
        Not without you.

Steps sag. Flames lick up amid around David's feet.

Reverend sees he means it. He grabs an ammo box, puts it on the one surviving lower step. He backs up, jumps his foot onto the box, springs.

Charred step crumbles under the weight, but–

–The Reverend makes it, grabs the step high above him.

Flames bite him.

He YELLS.

David grabs him.

Reverend, with David's aid, pulls himself up with a gasp. His clothes are on fire. David helps him beat out the flames.

Fire washes up from below, and with a surge, the flame expands and takes on the form of THE INDIAN'S HAND, which then takes the form of a huge tarantula, and the Tarantula/Hand GRABS the Reverend's foot.

Reverend jerks free, and the Tarantula/Hand falls back into flames, and the flames take the stairs.

Reverend and David race up to the church. Behind them, the steps are dissolved by fire.

INDIAN

He looks like a humanoid-hunk of green shit on fire.

HOWLLLLLLLLLLLL OF PAIN AND DISAPPOINTMENT.

AMMO BOX

Explodes and blows the flaming Indian into several sticky, burning pieces.

CHURCH

Smoking. Burning. Dead Folk running together. Falling down.

The Reverend grabs up a shattered piece of pew planking, and with David behind him, he swings it, batting aside the Dead Folk who are only interested in trying to find shade. Some of them are crawling under pews, dropping to their knees, pushing their heads to the floor and trying to protect themselves with their hands. They're burning anyway, bursting into flames as they are poisoned by the sunlight.

TRACK REVEREND AND DAVID

As they battle their way to–

EXT. – CHURCH

Sunlight. Hot and yellow. Reverend and David practically tumble out of the church, flames at their backs.

A couple of Dead Folk fall out behind them, but they're not dangerous now. Food is the least of their worries. They drop down near the crate containing the Indian's Woman and blaze into charred ruins. It's all over for the Dead Folk.

David collapses to the ground, breathing hard. The Reverend stands, watching the church.

> **REVEREND**
> Abby. Abby...

ON THE CHURCH

A ROAR OF COLORFUL FLAME licks out of all the windows. Then there's a sound like THE GODDAMNEST SCREAM IN CREATION, and the FLAMES LICK HIGH, HIGH, HIGH, and they have the GENERAL SHAPE OF THE INDIAN, and they FLICKER in that position momentarily, then FALL TO EARTH with a BANG and the church goes in all directions, and–

SILENCE

The church is black smoking rubble.

REVEREND

Looks at the body in the crate. He lowers the crate back so that it lies on the ground like an open coffin. He removes his jacket and takes out the Bible. He lifts the woman's head gently. He places the jacket under her.

He pulls a burning brand out of the debris of the church. He places the Bible on the dead woman's body. He sets the torch to the jacket. It takes a couple of tries before the jacket catches and her head is enveloped, followed by her body.

REVEREND
God take and rest your soul.

DAVID
Is it over, Reverend?

Holding the torch, the Reverend turns to David.

REVEREND
As much as it's ever over. Come, son. No rest for the wicked, and the good don't need any.

(He looks at the burning torch)

We have some cleansing to do.

EXT. THE HILL – LONG VIEW LATER

The hill and the hot yellow sun rising above it.

Then the Reverend and David appear, riding double on horseback. They ride slowly up the hill. At its peak they stop, and we go–

CLOSE ON REVEREND AND DAVID

As they look back at the town.

THEIR POV – THE ENTIRE TOWN

Is on fire.

BACK TO SCENE

David watches silently as the Reverend lifts his head to the heavens, asks loudly–

REVEREND
Am I redeemed?

LONG PAUSE.

NOTHING.

Reverend smiles sadly,

REVEREND
Thy will be done.

Reverend touches his heels to the horse, and they ride down the hill, and disappear from sight and into history.

HOLD FOR A MOMENT ON

The empty hill. The hot yellow sun.

SLOW DISSOLVE TO:

BURNING TOWN

A quick camera tour. This place is most definitely scourged.

DOLLY SLOWLY DOWN MAIN STREET

As the flames lick this way and that. Arrive at the remains of the church and go–

CLOSE ON CHURCH RUBBLE

A spider, the exact shape of the hairy mole on the Indian's chest, skull design and all, wobbles over the debris. The spider smokes as if on fire. It weakly scuttles toward a small dark hole near where the church steps still stand. The spider tumbles into the hole. A wisp of white smoke boils out of the hole to mark its passing.

PULL BACK FOR THE COMPLETE VIEW

The smoking hole.

The town blazing.

The sun, high and bright. And we–

                                                    FADE OUT

DISCARD

8/12

East Baton Rouge Parish Library
MAIN LIBRARY

DEMCO